FOOLS AND OTHER STORIES

M

Fiction

FOOLS
And Other Stories

Njabulo Ndebele

1475

readers international

ANN ARBOR, MICH. PUBLIC LIBRARY   OCT 1 7 1986

First published by Ravan Press (Pty) Ltd, Johannesburg, South Africa.
Copyright © Njabulo S Ndebele 1983

This edition of *Fools and Other Stories* is published in the UK by
arrangement with Longman Group Limited, London.

Published in 1986 by Readers International Inc., New York and London,
whose editorial branch is at 8 Strathray Gardens, London NW3 4NY,
England. US/Canadian inquiries to Subscriber Service Department,
P.O. Box 959, Columbia, LA 71418 USA.

Design by Jan Brychta

Printed and bound in Great Britain by Richard Clay
(The Chaucer Press), Bungay, Suffolk

ISBN 0-930523-19-9 Hardcover
ISBN 0-930523-20-2 Paperback

To the memory of my mother,
Makhosazana,
and to my father,
Nimrod.

CONTENTS

The Test

As he felt the first drops of rain on his bare arms, Thoba wondered if he should run home quickly before there was a downpour. He shivered briefly, and his teeth chattered for a moment as a cold breeze blew and then stopped. How cold it had become, he thought. He watched the other boys who seemed completely absorbed in the game. They felt no rain, and no cold. He watched. The boys of Mayaba Street had divided themselves into two soccer teams. That was how they spent most days of their school vacations: playing soccer in the street. No, decided Thoba, he would play on. Besides, his team was winning. He looked up at the sky and sniffed, remembering that some grown-ups would say one can tell if it is going to rain by sniffing at the sky the way dogs do. He was not sure if he could smell anything other than the dust raised by the soccer players around him. He could tell, though, that the sky, having been overcast for some time, had grown darker.

Should I? he thought. Should I go home? But the ball decided for him when it came his way accidentally, and he was suddenly swept into the action as he dribbled his way past one fellow. But the next fellow

took the ball away from him, and Thoba gave it up
without a struggle. It had been a quick thrill. He had
felt no rain, no cold. The trick is to keep playing and
be involved, he thought. But he stopped, and looked
at the swarm of boys chasing after the tennis ball in a
swift chaotic movement away from him, like a whirl-
wind. They were all oblivious of the early warnings of
rain. He did not follow them, feeling no inclination to
do so. He felt uncertain whether he was tired or
whether it was the fear of rain and cold that had
taken his interest away from the game. He looked
down at his arms. There they were: tiny drops of
rain, some sitting on goose pimples, others between
them. Fly's spit, he thought.

Soon there was a loud yell. Some boys were jumping
into the air, others shaking their fists, others dancing
in all sorts of ways. Some, with a determined look on
their faces, trotted back to the centre, their small
thumbs raised, to wait for the ball to be thrown in
again. Someone had scored for Thoba's team. The
scorer was raised into the air. It was Vusi. But Vusi's
triumph was short-lived for it was just at that moment
that the full might of the rain came. Vusi disappeared
from the sky like a mole reversing into its hole. The
boys of Mayaba Street scattered home, abandoning
their match. The goal posts on either side disappeared
when the owners of the shoes repossessed them.
Thoba began to run home, hesitated, and changed
direction to follow a little group of boys towards the
shelter of the walled veranda of Simangele's home.

Thoba found only Simangele, Vusi, Mpiyakhe, and
Nana on the veranda. He was disappointed. In the
rush, it had seemed as if more boys had gone there.
Perhaps he really should have run home, he thought.
Too late, though. He was there now, at the veranda of

Simangele's home, breathing hard like the others from the short impulsive sprint away from the rain. They were all trying to get the rain water off them: kicking it off their legs, or pushing it down their arms with their fingers, the way windscreen wipers do. Simangele wiped so hard that it looked as if he was rubbing the water into his skin. Only Vusi, who had scored the last goal, was not wiping off the water on him. There was an angry scowl on his face as he slowly massaged his buttocks, all the while cursing:

'The bastards,' he said. 'The bastards! They just dropped me. They let go of me like a bag of potatoes. I'll get them for that. One by one. I'll get them one by one.'

'What if you *are* a bag of potatoes?' said Simangele laughing. 'What do you think, fellows?' He was jumping up and down like a grown-up soccer player warming up just before the beginning of a game. He shadow-boxed briefly then jumped up and down again.

Simangele got no response from the others. It would have been risky for them to take sides. Thoba rubbed his arms vigorously, making it too obvious that he was shamming a preoccupation with keeping warm in order to avoid answering Simangele's question. But Vusi did not fear Simangele.

'This is no laughing matter,' he said.

'Then don't make me laugh,' replied Simangele, shadow-boxing with slow easy sweeps of his arms.

Vusi uttered a click of annoyance and looked away from Simangele. He continued to massage his buttocks.

Simangele looked at Vusi for a while, and then turned away to look at Nana.

'Are you warm?' he asked, suddenly looking gentle.

Nana, who was noticeably shivering, sniffed back mucus and nodded.

'Perhaps you should sit there at the corner.' said Simangele.

Thoba looked at Nana and felt vaguely jealous that Nana should receive such special attention from Simangele. But then Nana always received special attention. This thought made Thoba yearn for the security of his home. He began to feel anxious and guilty that he had not run home. Not only did he feel he did not matter to Simangele and Vusi, he also feared the possibility of a fight between these two. Quarrels made him uneasy. Always. What would his mother say if he was injured in a fight? Rather, wouldn't she be pleased to hear that he had run home as soon as the rain started? The rain. Yes, the rain. He looked at it, and it seemed ominous with its steady strength, as if it would go on raining for ever, making it impossible for him to get home before his mother. And how cold it was now! Should he? Should he run home? No. There was too much rain out there. Somewhat anxiously, he looked at the others, and tried to control his shivering.

The other three boys were looking at Nana huddling himself at the corner where the house and the veranda walls met. He looked frailer than ever, as if there were a disease eating at him all the time. Thoba wished he had a coat to put over Nana. But Nana seemed warm, for he had embraced his legs and buried his head between his raised knees. The only sound that came from him was a continuous sniff as he drew back watery mucus, occasionally swallowing it. Thoba wondered if Nana's grandmother was home. Or did the rain catch her far in the open fields away from the township, where it was said she dug all over for roots and herbs? She was always away looking for roots to heal people with. And when she was away,

Nana was cared for by everyone in Mayaba Street. Thoba looked at Nana and wished that he himself was as lucky.

Just then, Mpiyakhe turned round like a dog wanting to sit, and sat down about a foot from Nana. He began to put his shoes on. Mpiyakhe's shoes had been one of the two pairs that had been used as goal posts. Thoba looked at Mpiyakhe's feet as Mpiyakhe slipped them into socks first, and noticed how smooth those feet were compared to Nana's which were deeply cracked. Then he looked at Vusi's and Simangele's feet. Theirs too were cracked. His were not. They were as smooth as Mpiyakhe's. Thoba remembered that he had three pairs of shoes, and his mother had always told him to count his blessings because most boys had only one pair, if any shoes at all, for both school and special occasions like going to church. Yet Thoba yearned to have cracked feet too. So whenever his mother and father were away from home, he would go out and play without his shoes. But Mpiyakhe never failed to wear his shoes. Perhaps that was why Mpiyakhe's shoes were always being used as goal posts. They were always available.

Soon, Thoba, Mpiyakhe, Vusi, and Simangele stood in a row along the low wall of the veranda, looking at the rain, and talking and laughing. The anxiety over a possible fight had disappeared, and Thoba felt contented as he nestled himself into the company of these daring ones who had not run home when the rain started. And it no longer mattered to him that his mother has always said to him: 'Always run home as soon as it begins to rain. I will not nurse a child who has said to illness "Come on, friend, let's hold hands and dance." Never!' And Thoba would always wonder how a boy could hold hands with a disease.

He must ask his uncle next time he came to visit.

For the moment, Thoba was glad that there was nobody at home. His mother was on day duty at the Dunnotar Hospital, and, although it was the December vacation, his father still went to school saying there was too much preparation to be done.

'You ought to take a rest, Father,' Thoba's mother had said on the last Sunday of the school term. The two had been relaxing in the living room, reading the Sunday papers.

'Never!' Thoba's father had replied with offended conviction. 'Moulding these little ones requires much energy and self-sacrifice. I will not ever say "wait a minute" to duty. Don't you know me yet?'

'Oh, you teachers!' Thoba's mother had said with a sigh.

'Thoba!' called his father.

'*Baba!*' responded Thoba who had been in his bedroom memorising Psalm 23. He had to be ready for the scripture oral examination the following morning.

'Show yourself,' said his father. Thoba appeared timidly at the door and leaned against it.

'What,' his father asked, 'is the square root of three hundred and twenty-five?' Thoba looked up at the ceiling. After some silence his father looked up from his newspaper and cast a knowing glance at his wife.

'You see,' he said. 'It takes time.'

Thoba's mother rose from her chair, dropped her paper and walked towards Thoba, her arms stretched out before her in order to embrace him. Thoba allowed himself to be embraced, all the while wishing his mother had not done that. It made him too helpless.

'Only yesterday,' his father drove the point home, 'we were working on square roots, and he has already forgotten. What kind of exams he is going to write this coming week is anybody's guess. Son, there has got to be a difference between the son of a teacher and other boys. But never mind. Einstein, if you care to know . . . . Do you know him? Do you know Einstein?'

Thoba shook his head, brushing his forehead against his mother's breasts.

'Well, well,' his father said, 'you will know him in time. But that great mathematics genius was once your age; and then, he did not know his square roots.'

That was three weeks ago. And now, as Thoba looked at the other boys with him on the veranda, he felt glad that his father had gone to work, or else the man would certainly have turned the day into a tortuous tutorial. Instead, there was Thoba with Simangele and Vusi and Mpiyakhe, all by themselves, looking at the rain from the shelter of the famed veranda of Mayaba Street.

The veranda of Simangele's home was very popular with the boys of Mayaba Street. Simangele's parents had done all they could to chase the boys away. But then, it was the only veranda in the neighbourhood that was walled round. To most boys, its low front wall came up to their shoulders, so that anyone looking at them from the street would see many little heads just appearing above the wall. The boys loved to climb on that wall, run on it, chasing one another. There had been many broken teeth, broken arms, and slashed tongues. Yet the boys, with the memory of chickens, would be back not long after each accident.

Once, Simangele's parents decided to lock the gate leading into the yard. But the boys of Mayaba Street, led by none other than Simangele himself, simply scaled the fence. Then it became a game to race over it: either from the street into the yard, or from the yard into the street. The fence gave in. By the time

it was decided to unlock the gate, it was too late.
People either walked in through the gate, or walked
over the flattened fence. Simangele's father then
tried to surprise the boys by sneaking up on them
with a whip. But it did not take long for them to enjoy
being surprised and then chased down the street. He
gave up.

Thoba, who was never allowed to play too long in
the street, always felt honoured to be on that veranda.
He was feeling exactly this way when, as he looked at
the rain, he gave way to an inner glow of exultation.

'Oh!' he exclaimed, 'it's so nice during the holidays.
We just play soccer all day.' He spoke to no one in
particular. And nobody answered him. The others,
with the exception of Mpiyakhe, really did not share
Thoba's enthusiasm. They were always free, always
playing in the street. Just whenever they wanted.
Thoba envied these boys. They seemed not to have
demanding mothers who issued endless orders, in-
spected chores given and done, and sent their children
on endless errands. Thoba smiled, savouring the thrill
of being with them, and the joy of having followed
the moment's inclination to join them on the veranda.

'How many goals did we score?' asked Mpiyakhe.

'Seven,' replied Vusi.

'Naw!' protested Simangele. 'It was six.'

'Seven!' insisted Vusi.

'Six!' shouted Simangele.

The two boys glared at each other for the second
time. Thoba noticed that Nana had raised his head
and was looking fixedly at the brewing conflict.

The rain poured gently now; it registered without
much intrusion in the boys' minds as a distant background to the brief but charged silence.

'It doesn't matter, anyway,' said Vusi with some

finality. We beat you.'

'Naw!' retorted Simangele. 'You haven't beaten us yet. The game was stopped by the rain. We are carrying on after the rain.'

'Who said we'll want to play after the rain?' asked Vusi.

'That's how you are,' said Simangele. 'I've long seen what kind you are. You never want to lose.'

'Of course! Who likes to lose, anyway,' said Vusi triumphantly.

There followed a tense silence, longer this time. All the boys looked at the rain, and as it faded back into their consciousness, the tension seemed to dissolve away into its sound. They crossed their arms over their chests, clutching at their shoulders firmly against the cold. They seemed lost in thought as they listened to the sound of the rain on the corrugated roofs of the township houses. It was loudest on the roof of the A.M.E. church which stood some fifty yards away, at the corner of Mayaba and Thelejane Streets. The sound on this roof was a sustained, heavy patter which reverberated with the emptiness of a building that was made entirely of corrugated iron. Even when the rain was a light shower, the roar it made on the church roof gave the impression of hail. Occasionally, there would be a great gust of wind, and the noise of the rain on the roofs would increase, and a gust of sound would flow away in ripples from house to house in the direction of the wind, leaving behind the quiet, regular patter.

'If there was a service in there,' said Thoba breaking the silence, and pointing towards the church with his head, 'would the people hear the sermon?'

'Reverend Mkhabela has a big voice,' said Mpiyakhe, demonstrating the size of the voice with his hands and his blown up cheeks.

'No voice can be bigger than thunder,' said Vusi matter-of-factly.

'Who talked about thunder?' asked Simangele, and then declared emphatically, 'There's no thunder out there. It's only rain out there.'

'Well,' said Vusi who probably had not meant his observation to be scrutinised, 'it seems like thunder.'

'Either there is thunder, or there is no thunder,' declared Simangele.

'Exactly what do you want from me?' asked Vusi desperately. 'I wasn't even talking to you.'

'It's everybody's discussion,' said Simangele. 'So you don't have to be talking to me. But if I talk about what you have said, I will talk to you directly. So, I'm saying it again: either there is thunder there, or there is no thunder out there. And right now there is no thunder out there.'

Vusi stepped away from the wall and faced Simangele, who also stepped away from the wall, faced Vusi, and waited. There was only Thoba between them. A fight seemed inevitable, and Thoba trembled, out of fear, and then also from the cold, which he could now feel even more, because it again reasserted both itself and the rain as the reasons he should have gone home in order to avoid a silly fight. He should have gone home. His mother was right. Now, he could be caught in the middle. He felt responsible for the coming danger, because he had said something that had now gone out of control.

Mpiyakhe moved away from the wall and squatted next to Nana, who was also looking at the conflict. But a fight did not occur. Vusi stepped towards the wall, rested his hands on it, and looked out at the rain. Simangele made a click of annoyance and then turned towards the wall. Mpiyakhe sprang to his feet, and everybody looked at the rain once more. Thoba desperately tried to think of something pleasant to say; something harmless.

Then he saw two horses that were nibbling at the grass that loved to grow along the fence that surrounded the church. Horses loved to nibble at that grass, thought Thoba. And when they were not nibbling at the grass, they would be rubbing themselves against the fence. They loved that too. Horses were strange creatures. They just stood in the rain, eating grass as if there was no rain at all.

'Does a horse ever catch cold?' asked Thoba, again to no one in particular. It had been just an articulated thought. But Vusi took it up with some enthusiasm.

'Ho, boy! A horse?' exclaimed Vusi. 'A horse? It's got an iron skin. Hard. Tough.' He demonstrated with two black bony fists. 'They just don't get to coughing like people.'

'Now you want to tell us that a horse can cough,' said Simangele.

Nobody took that one up. The others looked at the two horses. Thoba considered Vusi's explanation, while at the same time frantically trying to find something to say before Simangele pressed his antagonism any further. An iron skin? thought Thoba, and then spoke again.

'What sound does the rain make when it falls on the back of a horse?' But Vusi ignored the question and made another contentious statement.

'Me,' said Vusi, 'I don't just catch cold. Not me!' he declared.

'Now you are telling us a lie,' said Simangele. 'And you know that very well.'

'Now, don't ever say I tell lies,' shouted Vusi.

'There's no person in this world who never gets ill,' insisted Simangele.

'I never said "never",' Vusi defended himself. 'I said, "don't just".'

Simangele did not pursue the matter. He had made his point. He was a year or two older than the other boys, and by far the tallest. The wall of the veranda came up to his chest. He had a lean but strong body. It was said he was like that because he was from the farms, and on the farms people are always running around and working hard all day, and they have no chance to get fat. So they become lean and strong. And when they get to the towns they become stubborn and arrogant because they don't understand things, and people laugh at them; and when people laugh at them they start fighting back. Then people say 'beware of those from the farms, they will stab with a broad smile on their faces.'

Simangele had lived in the township for two years now, but he was still known as the boy from the farms. And he could be deadly. Whenever there were street fights between the boys of Mayaba Street and those of Thipe Street, Simangele would be out there in front, leading the boys of Mayaba Street and throwing stones at the enemy with legendary accuracy. Sometimes Simangele would retreat during a fight, and then watch the boys of Mayaba Street being forced to retreat. Then he would run to the front again, and the enemy would retreat. And everybody would have seen the difference. Few boys ever took any chances with Simangele.

Vusi, on the other hand, was one of those boys who were good at many things. He was very inventive. He made the best bird traps, the best slings, the best wire cars; and four-three, and six-one, and five-two, always came his way in a game of dice. But it was in soccer that he was most famous. He was known to all the boys in the township, and everybody wanted to be on his side. He was nicknamed after Sandlane, Charterston Rovers' great dribbling wizard, who had a deformed right hand that was perpetually bent at the wrist, with the fingers stretched out firmly. And Vusi would always bend his wrist whenever the ball was in his possession. And his team mates would cheer 'Sandla-a-a-ne-e-e-!' And they would be looking at his deformed hand and its outstretched fingers, dry and dusty on the outside like the foot of a hen when it has raised its leg. And Vusi would go into a frenzy of dribbling, scoring goals with that sudden, unexpected shot.

Vusi was the only boy in Mayaba Street who could stand up to Simangele. The two had never actually fought, but they had been on the brink of fighting many times. The general speculation was that Simangele really did not want to take a chance; for who knew what would happen? Vusi was known to have outbraved many boys, even those acknowledged to be stronger than he. The problem with Vusi was that he fought to the death. All the boys knew he was a dangerous person to fight with, because you would be hitting and hitting him, but Vusi would keep coming and coming at you, and you would begin to lose hope. And then he might defeat you not because he was stronger, but because he kept coming at you, and you lost all hope. That is why it was thought Simangele never wanted to go all the way. In any case, there was really nothing awesome about Simangele's bravery. He had to be brave: he was older. But Vusi? He was a wonder.

It was for this reason that Thoba was busy considering Vusi's claim that he never got ill. It sounded

familiar. Vusi was like Thoba's father. He was just
that kind of person. Thoba's father was not the sick
type; and Thoba's mother had always told visitors
that her husband was a very strong man. And since
Thoba felt instinctively on Vusi's side, he felt a pressing
need to bear witness, if only to establish the truthfulness of Vusi's claim.

'My own father doesn't just get ill,' he declared.
There was a brief silence after this and then the others
began to laugh. And Thoba felt how terrible it was to
be young and have no power. Whatever you said was
laughed at. It was a deeply indulgent laugh that helped
to blow away all the tension that had existed just
before. They just laughed. It was always the case
when you are not very strong, and you have to say
something.

'What is he telling us, this one?' said Mpiyakhe in
the middle of a guffaw. 'Your family gets knocked
down with all kinds of diseases. Everybody knows
that. Softies, all of you. You're too higher-up. That's
your problem. Instead of eating *papa* and beans, you
have too many sandwiches.'

'Now, that is a lot of shit you are saying,' said
Thoba trying to work up anger to counter the laughter.

'Don't ever say that about what I'm saying,' threatened Mpiyakhe.

'And what if I say it?' retorted Thoba.

'Take him on, boy, take him on,' said Simangele
nudging Mpiyakhe in the stomach with an elbow.

Thoba began to feel uneasy. It was strange how the
conflict had suddenly shifted down to him and
Mpiyakhe who were at the lower end of the pecking
order among the boys of Mayaba Street. He had
fought Mpiyakhe a few times, and it was never clear
who was stronger. Today he would win, tomorrow he

would lose. That was how it was among the weak; a
constant, unresolved struggle. Why should a simple
truth about one's father lead to ridicule and then to a
fight? Thoba looked at Mpiyakhe and had the impulse
to rush him. Should he? What would be the result of
it? But the uncertainty of the outcome made Thoba
look away towards the rain. He squeezed his shoulders,
and felt deeply ashamed that he could not prove his
worth before Vusi and Simangele. He had to find a
way to deal with his rival.

Mpiyakhe's father was a prosperous man who ran a
flourishing taxi service. His house, a famous landmark,
was one of the biggest in the township. If a stranger
was looking for some house in that neighbourhood,
he was told: 'Go right down Mayaba Street until you
see a big, green house. That will be Nzima's house.
Once there, ask again . . . .'

Screwed on to the front gate of the big, green house
was a wooden board on which was painted 'Love
Your Wife' in white paint. And whenever a man got
into Mpiyakhe's father's taxi, he was always asked:
'Do you love your wife?' Thus, Mpiyakhe's father was
known throughout the township as 'Love Your Wife'.
As a result, Mpiyakhe was always teased about his
father by the boys of Mayaba Street. And whenever
that happened, he would let out steam on Thoba,
trying to transfer the ridicule. After all, both their
families were 'higher-ups' and if one family was a
laughing stock the same should be applied to the other.

Thoba and Mpiyakhe were prevented from fighting
by Nana, who suddenly began to cough violently.
They all turned towards him. The cough was a long
one, and it shook his frail body until he seemed to be
having convulsions. Thoba wondered if Nana was
going to die. And what would Nana's grandmother do

to them if Nana died in their presence? If she healed
people, surely she could also kill them. Nana continued
to cough. And the boys could see his head go up and
down. They looked at each other anxiously as if
wondering what to do. But the cough finally ceased;
and when Nana looked up, there were tears in his
eyes and much mucus flowing down in two lines over
his lips. He swept his lower arm over his lips and nose
and then rubbed it against the side of his shirt.

'You should go home,' said Vusi to Nana.

'How can he go home in this rain?' said Simangele,
taking advantage of Nana's refusal. Vusi turned away
indignantly. Thoba wondered if he should take off his
shirt and give it to Nana. But he quickly decided
against it. He himself could die. He turned away to
look at the rain. He saw that Vusi was looking at the
horses eating grass in the rain. He saw the concentration
on Vusi's face. He watched as a sudden gleam came to
Vusi's eye, and Vusi slowly turned his face away from
the rain to fix an ominously excited gaze on Simangele.
He looked at the rain again, and then his look took
on a determined intensity. He turned to Simangele
again.

'Simangele,' called Vusi. 'How would you like to
be a horse in the rain?'

'A horse in the rain?' said Simangele tentatively.
He looked at Thoba and Mpiyakhe, and seemed
embarrassed, as if there was something he could not
understand.

'Yes, a horse in the rain,' said Vusi. There was a
look of triumph in his face. 'Look at the horses. They
are in the rain. Yet they have nothing on them. I bet
you can never go into the rain without your shirt.'

Simangele laughed. 'That is foolishness,' he said.

'No,' said Vusi. 'It is not foolishness.' And as he

spoke, Vusi was slowly pulling out his shirt without loosening the belt that held it tightly round the waist where it was tucked into the trousers. All the while he was looking steadily at Simangele.

Simangele stopped laughing and began to look uneasy. Once more he looked at Vusi and Mpiyakhe. And then he looked at Nana on the floor. Their eyes met, and Simangele looked away quickly. Meanwhile, his jaws tightened, Vusi was unbuttoning his shirt from the rumpled bottom upwards. Then he took off his shirt slowly, exposing a thin, shining, black body, taut with strength. Thoba felt a tremor of iciness through his body as if it was his body that had been exposed. Vusi had thrust his chest out and arched his arms back so that his shirt dangled from his right hand. Soon his body was looking like a plucked chicken.

'I'm a horse now,' said Vusi. 'Let's see if you too can be a horse.' He did not wait for an answer. Dropping his shirt with a flourish, Vusi flung himself into the rain. He braced his head against the rain and ran up Thelejane Street, which was directly opposite Simangele's home and formed a T-junction with Mayaba Street. Thelejane Street went right up and disappeared in the distance. Vusi ran so fast, he seemed to have grown shorter. Soon he was a tiny black speck in the rain; and the far distance of the street seemed to swallow him up. Not once did he look back.

It had all happened so suddenly, Thoba thought. Just like the day a formation of military jets had suddenly come from nowhere and flown low round the township a number of times, deafening the place with noise. And then they were gone, leaving behind a petrifying, stunned silence which totally blocked thinking until many minutes later.

Simangele looked like someone who thought he

had enough time, but when he got to the station found that the train was already pulling out, and that he had to suffer the indignity of running after it. He looked at Thoba and Mpiyakhe. They looked back. Then a wave of anger and frustration crossed his face.

'What are you doing here on my veranda?' he yelled at the two boys. They moved towards a corner away from him. There was silence. Then Simangele looked at Nana.

'I didn't mean you,' he said with a faint plea in his voice. Then he looked at the small figure in the rain. It was so far now that it did not even seem to be moving. He looked at the sky. It was grey, and the rain was grey. He looked at the two boys, again. Thoba cringed, and looked well into Simangele's eyes. And then suddenly Thoba did not feel afraid any more. As he looked into Simangele's eyes, he felt a strange sense of power over Simangele. Simangele did not want to go into the rain, but he would go, because Thoba was looking at him. Mpiyakhe was looking at him. Nana was looking at him with those large eyes. And they had all been there when Simangele was challenged. He would have to go.

Slowly, and seemingly with much pain, Simangele fingered the buttons of his shirt. He unbuttoned only the three upper buttons and pulled the shirt over his head. Just then, a gust of wind swept the rain, making it sound harder on the roofs of houses. Simangele shuddered. He threw his shirt on the floor and then stretched his leg out into the rain and watched his gray, dry skin turn brown and wet. Then he eased himself into the rain. He shivered, and that made him seem to decide he had better run. He was out there now, running in the street, following Vusi. But his strides were much less confident than Vusi's mag-

nanimous strides. Simangele jumped over puddles
where his challenger had just waded in and out of
them like a galloping horse. Thoba and Mpiyakhe
watched him in silence until he vanished into the
distance.

Thoba and Mpiyakhe moved out of the corner at
the same time, and went to stand before the low wall.
They stood there looking out at the streets in silence.
Thoba became aware that he was stealing glances at
Mpiyakhe. Of course he was not afraid of him. Yes,
indeed, Mpiyakhe was stealing glances at him too. But
now that there were only the two of them, there really
seemed no reason to quarrel. There was nobody else
to entertain at the expense of each other. Nana?
Thoba looked at him. Their eyes met. He looked
away. Wouldn't questions be asked later? What did
Thoba and Mpiyakhe do after Vusi and Simangele
had run into the rain to settle scores? Weren't Thoba
and Mpiyakhe known rivals? And then there was
Nana to tell the story. There was the rain. There were
the empty streets. It was cold out there. But there
could be glory out there for a shirtless boy.

Thoba wondered if he should issue a challenge.
That was certainly attractive. But less attractive was
the ordeal of running in the rain. But there was no
thunder. Only water. That's all. No lightning to fear.
Only water falling from sky. What was water? Only
water. And the cold? Once he was out there he would
forget about it, because he would be involved in the
running. That's the trick. The horses went on eating
wet grass. They were involved. How was the sound of
the rain on the back of a horse? What sound would
the rain make on a boy's body?

Thoba and Mpiyakhe looked at each other again,
only to look away once more. Clearly there was some-

thing they could not confront. When Thoba stole a
glance at Mpiyakhe through the corner of his eye, he
noticed that Mpiyakhe was looking at him. When
Mpiyakhe finally spoke, it was slowly and tentatively.

'Do you . . .' he asked, 'do you want to go into the
rain?'

Thoba pretended he had not heard, and continued
to look at the rain. But then he broke into a smile,
and turned his face to look at Mpiyakhe. Mpiyakhe
had not issued a challenge. He had not. He had
merely asked a question. Here was an uneasy boy
who was trying to persuade him into an intimate
truce. Here was a boy who assumed there were
mutual fears; who did not know for sure. Here was a
boy asking his way into a compromise. This boy did
not deserve an answer.

Slowly and deliberately, and with a gleam in his
eye, Thoba unbuttoned his shirt, and as he pulled it
over his head, he felt the warmth of his breath on his
chest. And that gave him a momentary impression of
dreaming, for he had a clear image of Vusi taking off
his shirt. But the image did not last; it was shattered
by the re-emergence of his head into the cold. He
shivered as goose pimples literally sprang out on his
skin before his eyes. But he would have to be reckless.
That was bravery. Bravery meant forgetting about
one's mother.

Thoba threw his shirt on to the floor where it joined
Vusi's and Simangele's. And the last thing he did
before he burst into the rain was look at Nana, as if
pleading for approval. Their eyes met. Those were the
eyes he would carry in his mind into the rain, as if the
whole township was looking at him. Mpiyakhe? He
did not even deserve a glance.

When the cold water of the rain hit him, Thoba

had the impulse to run back on to the veranda. But when he got into the street, he felt nothing but exhilaration. There was something freeing in the tickling pressure of the soft needles of rain on his skin. And then he ran in spurts: running fast and slowing down, playing with the pressure of the rain on him. It was a pleasant sensation; a soft, pattering sensation. And the rain purred so delicately against his ears. And when he waded in and out of puddles, savouring the recklessness, it was so enchanting to split the water, creating his own little thunder from the numerous splashes. He was alone in the street with the rain. He was shirtless in the rain. How many people were watching him from the protective safety of their houses? How many? They were sitting round their kitchen stoves, taking no challenges. Mpiyakhe? Was he watching him? Of course. Mpiyakhe, the vanquished. Everybody would know. Vusi and Simangele would know that he, Thoba, had bravely followed them into the cold rain.

He passed the A.M.E. church and crossed Thipe street. Where were the boys of that street? They would not come out to fight on such a day. Weaklings, the lot of them. Up he went, crossing Ndimande Street. Where were the boys of that street? Weaklings too. They were not in the rain.

He ran up towards the crèche now. He had been there as a child, when he was younger than he was now. Would he be recognised from the windows as the man who had been there as a child? Would the matron see him? Would she say, 'There is my little man?' Should he slow down and be seen? No. The man broke into a sprint. Wouldn't it be better for them to say, 'Doesn't that look like Thoba?' They wouldn't be sure. That way they would think about

him a little longer, trying to be sure. He wished he
were a blur. The wind and the water! He could not
feel them anymore, for they had dissipated into the
sustained alacrity of speed.

Beyond the crèche was the Dutch Reformed Church,
and beyond that, far out of the township, were the
rugged, rocky hills where men and women always
went in pairs, on Sunday afternoons. Thoba slowed
down somewhat. If he ran further up the street, he
would get nearer those hills, and one could never be
sure about those hills. It was said there was a beast
there which swallowed up little children, especially
in bad weather. He wondered if Vusi and Simangele
had gone further up. No, he would not go towards
the hills. Thoba passed the church, but instead of
going up, he turned left into Twala Street. Even
though he could outrun the beast, it would be foolish
to go nearer it first.

As he turned into Twala Street, he tried to increase
his speed once more, but noted with faint anxiety
that he was unable to. He was slowing down now, and
that was not good. He was very far from home now.
Did he reach the limits of his endurance so soon? And
yet the surge of exhilaration was definitely beginning
to fade away. But he would have to keep up the pace
at least until the crèche was well out of sight. Why
did people tire? Did Vusi tire, or did he run all the
way? There was no sign of him. Maybe it was the
Dutch Reformed Church; he shouldn't have looked at
it. He should have closed his eyes when he passed it,
for that was the church of ill luck. Everybody said so.
But he would have to run, all the same. At least until
the crèche was well out of sight. And as soon as he
made that commitment, Thoba suddenly felt as he
had the day his mother had beaten him with a wet

dishcloth for cracking open an egg that had a half-formed chick in it.

Thoba had vowed that he would cry until his father came back home to deal with his mother. His father did not come. So long after the tears and the anger had gone, Thoba had continued to cry with his voice only. It had been painful in his throat and somewhere in his chest. And now, as he continued to run, Thoba realised that the fire was going out of him. There was left only the pain of tiring legs. Yet, he was too far from home to tire. He looked back briefly. The crèche was out of sight; and just then, the tiredness assailed him. He could feel the ache in his calves. He slowed down to an easy trot. If only he could reach Nala Street; that would take him back home.

Then he became conscious of the sound of water rushing down in two streams on the sides of the street, towards the Dutch Reformed Church. His eyes followed the direction of the water until he saw the church in the distance back there. He turned away quickly. What would happen if the water went into the church and flooded it? Would it float like Noah's ark?

When he turned left at Mosotwana Street, he saw Nala Street some five houses away. And only then did he realise why he had heard the sound of the rushing streams so clearly. It had stopped raining. There was a heavy stillness around him, for the roofs of houses had gone silent. And the sound of rushing water made the streams sound bigger than they actually were. He began to feel exposed. He broke his trot and walked, arms akimbo. He was tired, and the rain was as embarrassingly tired, for it was now falling in tiny droplets as weak as the sprays at the edge of a waterfall. There was no one else in the street, not even a stray dog. And then he began to feel cold.

He was about three houses from Nala Street when
a familiar taxi turned into Mosotwana Street, forcing
him to run towards the nearest fence away from
danger. He wondered if Mpiyakhe's father had seen
him. Thoba stopped, rested his arms on the fence, so
that those in the taxi could see only his back. He
enjoyed the wonderful sensation of stillness. But that
was not to last very long. The taxi stopped only
about ten yards away from Thoba. A man got off and
ran into the next house as if he thought it was still
raining. Thoba heard Mpiyakhe's father shout after
the man: 'Love your wife!' In a few seconds, the taxi
started up, but it did not go forward; instead it
reversed and stopped about two yards from Thoba.
Thoba froze. So the man had recognised him.

'Hey, boy!' shouted Mpiyakhe's father. 'Are you
not teacher Mbele's son?'

Thoba turned his head and nodded. The passengers
in the taxi were all looking at him. Why did Mpiyakhe's
father not leave him alone?

'Yes, I thought so,' said Mpiyakhe's father. 'Do
your parents know you are here?'

Thoba looked away and did not answer.

'Boy, I'm talking to you.'

Thoba looked at the man again. His head was sticking out of the driver's open window. What would
happen if another car came and the head was still
sticking out? Surely that head would be sliced off.

'Boy, I'm talking to you.'

First it was Mpiyakhe; now it was his father.

'Now get into this car, and let me take you home.'

It could not be. To be taken home like a drenched
chicken! To be taken home in his enemy's car! It could
not be. His own feet would carry him home.

'Come on. Get into the car.'

Thoba began to walk away.

'Boy, I will not let your parents accuse me of killing you!'

Thoba continued to trudge away.

'Boy, get into this car!'

Nothing would stop him.

'You all saw him defy me, didn't you!'

When Thoba heard the engine of the car revving up, he tried to run. But he needn't have: the car went on its way in the opposite direction. Thoba ran for only a few yards before he reached Nala Street.

When he looked down Nala Street in the far distance, Thoba saw something which discouraged him further. Two buses were lugging up slowly towards the township. They were the first afternoon buses bringing workers who knocked off early. If only he could reach the bus stop and pass it before the buses got there. If not it would be embarrassing. All those people! What would they say? What was a shirtless boy doing in the cold rain? But the pain in the calves. The pain in the thighs. He just wanted to stand still. Then he began to shiver violently. It always got colder after the rain. He must move on. But try as he might, he could not run. He knew then that he would never beat the buses to the bus stop. And by the time they got there, and the passengers were streaming out of them like ants, Thoba was still very far from the bus stop, and would surely meet the workers coming up.

And he saw them: the bulk of them. Women. They knocked off too early. That was their problem. They were coming up: a disordered column of women with shopping bags balanced on their heads. He would meet them somewhere in the middle of the street. If only he could run so fast that when he passed them, they would be a blur to him; and he would be a blur

to them. He knew he wouldn't make it. He felt so
exposed: shirtless; shoeless; a wet body in a dripping
pair of pants that clung tightly and coldly to him.
They would surely see the outline of his buttocks.
And his penis? Would they see it too? That would be
worse.

Indeed, there was mother Mofokeng, one of Thoba's
mother's many friends. Everybody knew his mother.
Mother Mofokeng would certainly recognise him.
Then he stepped on to a pointed stone. At first the
pain was dull, but once it cut through his almost iced
foot, it tore up to his chest. He jerked to a stop,
grimacing with pain, as he raised the hurt foot ever
so slightly as if he wanted to keep it on the ground at
all costs. He felt like a sleeping horse when it lifts one
hoof a fraction from the ground. He was far from
home. And he felt tears forming in his eyes. But he
fought them back by blinking repeatedly.

'Wonder of wonders!' exclaimed mother Mofokeng.
'What am I seeing? God in heaven what am I seeing?
Curse me if this isn't the nurse's child!'

'Which nurse?' asked another mother.

'Staff nurse Mbele's son,' said mother Mofokeng.

'Is this the nurse's child? He looks so much like her!'

'Son,' inquired mother Mofokeng, 'what are you
doing here in the cold?'

Thoba looked at her, and then looked at the batter-
ed leather shopping bag balanced on her head. It was
bulging with vegetables. Some spinach and carrots
were peeping from a hole on the side.

'Here's a child who will die of cold,' said a mother
who had just joined the crowd.

'And you'd think his mother would know better,'
said another.

'Where's your shirt, son?' asked mother Mofokeng.

'This is what I've always maintained about school holidays,' said another. 'You are busy working your heart out at the white man's, and your children are busy running wild. I don't know why they have these holidays.'

'And in this weather of all weathers in the world,' said another.

'Woman!' exclaimed another. 'I'm telling you, what else can you do with children?'

How could Thoba explain? Should he walk away or continue to listen? The questions were piling up; being as many as there were women returning from work. He would wait. Surely it would be disrespectful to walk away from elders. Yet the questions came; and the piercing cold; and the stinging pain of muscles. His teeth began to chatter.

'Whose child is this?'

'Shame! What happened to him?'

'Where's his shirt? Did anybody take your shirt, son?'

'Who has done this sin?'

'Leave the child alone! Run home, son!'

'It's so easy to die!'

'Exposure!'

'Sponge wet. Look how the trousers cling to him.'

'Women of the township! Why don't you leave this child alone?'

Thoba had crossed his arms across his chest as if that way he could create some heat. Better the rain than the cold which follows it. He was far from home, and the women had created a cordon of humiliation around him. Then he felt two thin lines of heat flowing down his cheeks. His tears had betrayed him. And the eyes grew painful. Instead of the speed he had desired, it was now his tears that had turned the women into a

blur. He could not see them now. That was the time
to leave.

'Here's my jersey, son,' said mother Mofokeng.
'Bring it back tomorrow.'

Thoba felt the warm wool settle on his shoulders.
But he had begun to move. And he saw the forms
before him part; and then came a grey emptiness. He
limped away, wounded with sympathy. A few feet
away from the women, he impulsively began to run.
He did not see where he was going; as he picked up
speed, the jersey slipped from his shoulders. And he
heard the countless voices of women shouting: 'It has
slipped! It has fallen! Pick it up! The jersey has fallen!
Pick it up, son! Stop him! Stop him!' Thoba broke
into a sprint. It was the most satisfying sprint, for it
was so difficult, so painful. It had led him out of
humiliation.

When he finally cleared his eyes with the back of
his hand, Thoba realised that he was at the junction
where Nala, Moshoeshoe, and Ndimande Streets met.
Just across the street was the Police station. More
buses were coming up. More women were coming.
Thoba definitely felt no pain now. He flew past the
Police station, the bus stop, Thipe Street . . . . Mayaba
Street was the next. Where were the boys of Mayaba
Street? Would they be waiting for his return? As he
took the corner into Mayaba Street, Thoba increased
his speed; and, spreading his arms out like the wings
of an aeroplane, he banked into Mayaba Street.

The street was as empty as he had left it at the
other end. No Vusi, no Simangele, no Mpiyakhe, no
Nana. No boys had come out yet to race little twigs
on the streamlets in the street. Was anybody looking
through the window? Was Mpiyakhe, the vanquished,
still on the veranda? Or had his father rescued him?

Thoba wondered if he should run on to the veranda to collect his shirt. No. Let it lie there on the floor of the veranda of Simangele's home. It would be tomorrow's testimony.

There was no one at home yet when Thoba arrived. He would have to make the fire before his mother came. But the stillness inside his home suddenly made him feel lonely, and all the pain came back again. No, he would not make the fire. Let his mother do whatever she liked with him. He would not make the fire. He passed on from the kitchen into his bedroom. There, he took off his trousers, and left them in a wet little heap on the floor close to his bed. He felt dry, but cold, as he slipped into the blankets. He felt warm, deep inside him. And as he turned over in bed, looking for the most comfortable position, he felt all the pain. But, strangely enough, he wished he could turn around as many times as possible. There was suddenly something deeply satisfying and pleasurable about the pain. And as he slid into a deep sleep, he smiled, feeling so much alive.

The Prophetess

The boy knocked timidly on the door, while a big
fluffy dog sniffed at his ankles. That dog made him
uneasy; he was afraid of strange dogs and this fear
made him anxious to go into the house as soon as
possible. But there was no answer to his knock. Should
he simply turn the doorknob and get in? What would
the prophetess say? Would she curse him? He was not
sure now which he feared more: the prophetess or the
dog. If he stood longer there at the door, the dog
might soon decide that he was up to some mischief
after all. If he left, the dog might decide he was running
away. And the prophetess! What would she say when
she eventually opened the door to find no one there?
She might decide someone had been fooling, and
would surely send lightning after the boy. But then,
leaving would also bring the boy another problem: he
would have to leave without the holy water for which
his sick mother had sent him to the prophetess.

There was something strangely intriguing about the
prophetess and holy water. All that one was to do,
the boy had so many times heard in the streets of the
township, was fill a bottle with water and take it to
the prophetess. She would then lay her hands on the

bottle and pray. And the water would be holy. And the water would have curing powers. That's what his mother had said too.

The boy knocked again, this time with more urgency. But he had to be careful not to annoy the prophetess. It was getting darker and the dog continued to sniff at his ankles. The boy tightened his grip round the neck of the bottle he had just filled with water from the street tap on the other side of the street, just opposite the prophetess's house. He would hit the dog with this bottle. What's more, if the bottle broke he would stab the dog with the sharp glass. But what would the prophetess say? She would probably curse him. The boy knocked again, but this time he heard the faint voice of a woman.

'*Kena!*' the voice said.

The boy quickly turned the knob and pushed. The door did not yield. And the dog growled. The boy turned the knob again and pushed. This time the dog gave a sharp bark, and the boy knocked frantically. Then he heard the bolt shoot back, and saw the door open to reveal darkness. Half the door seemed to have disappeared into the dark. The boy felt fur brush past his leg as the dog scurried into the house.

'*Voetsek!*' the woman cursed suddenly.

The boy wondered whether the woman was the prophetess. But as he was wondering, the dog brushed past him again, slowly this time. In spite of himself, the boy felt a pleasant, tickling sensation and a slight warmth where the fur of the dog had touched him. The warmth did not last, but the tickling sensation lingered, going up to the back of his neck and seeming to caress it. Then he shivered and the sensation disappeared, shaken off in the brief involuntary tremor.

'Dogs stay out!' shouted the woman, adding, 'This

is not at the white man's.'

The boy heard a slow shuffle of soft leather shoes receding into the dark room. The woman must be moving away from the door, the boy thought. He followed into the house.

'Close the door,' ordered the woman who was still moving somewhere in the dark. But the boy had already done so.

Although it was getting dark outside, the room was much darker and the fading day threw some of its waning light into the room through the windows. The curtains had not yet been drawn. Was it an effort to save candles, the boy wondered. His mother had scolded him many times for lighting up before it was completely dark.

The boy looked instinctively towards the dull light coming in through the window. He was anxious, though, about where the woman was now, in the dark. Would she think he was afraid when she caught him looking out to the light? But the thick, dark green leaves of vine outside, lapping lazily against the window, attracted and held him like a spell. There was no comfort in that light; it merely reminded the boy of his fear, only a few minutes ago, when he walked under that dark tunnel of vine which arched over the path from the gate to the door. He had dared not touch that vine and its countless velvety, black, and juicy grapes that hung temptingly within reach, or rested lusciously on forked branches. Silhouetted against the darkening summer sky, the bunches of grapes had each looked like a cluster of small cones narrowing down to a point.

'Don't touch that vine!' was the warning almost everyone in Charterston township knew. It was said that the vine was all coated with thick, invisible glue.

And that was how the prophetess caught all those who stole out in the night to steal her grapes. They would be glued there to the vine, and would be moaning for forgiveness throughout the cold night, until the morning, when the prophetess would come out of the house with the first rays of the sun, raise her arms into the sky, and say: 'Away, away, sinful man; go and sin no more!' Suddenly, the thief would be free, and would walk away feeling a great release that turned him into a new man. That vine; it was on the lips of everyone in the township every summer.

One day when the boy had played truant with three of his friends, and they were coming back from town by bus, some grown-ups in the bus were arguing about the prophetess's vine. The bus was so full that it was hard for anyone to move. The three truant friends, having given their seats to grown-ups, pressed against each other in a line in the middle of the bus and could see most of the passengers.

'Not even a cow can tear away from that glue,' said a tall, dark man who had high cheek-bones. His bala-clava was a careless heap on his head. His moustache, which had been finely rolled into two semi-circular horns, made him look fierce. And when he gesticulat-ed with his tin lunch box, he looked fiercer still.

'My question is only one,' said a big woman whose big arms rested thickly on a bundle of washing on her lap. 'Have you ever seen a person caught there? Just answer that one question.' She spoke with finality, and threw her defiant scepticism outside at the receding scene of men cycling home from work in single file. The bus moved so close to them that the boy had feared the men might get hit.

'I have heard of one silly chap that got caught!' declared a young man. He was sitting with others on the long seat at the rear of the bus. They had all along been laughing and exchanging ribald jokes. The young man had thick lips and red eyes. As he spoke he applied the final touches of saliva with his tongue to brown paper rolled up with tobacco.

'When?' asked the big woman. 'Exactly when, I say? Who was that person?'

'These things really happen!' said a general chorus of women.

'That's what I know,' endorsed the man with the balaclava, and then added, 'You see, the problem with some women is that they will not listen; they have to oppose a man. They just have to.'

'What is that man saying now?' asked another woman. 'This matter started off very well, but this road you are now taking will get us lost.'

'That's what I'm saying too,' said the big woman, adjusting her bundle of washing somewhat unnecessarily. She continued: 'A person shouldn't look this way or that, or take a corner here or there. Just face me straight: I asked a question.'

'These things really happen,' said the chorus again.

'That's it, good ladies, make your point; push very strongly,' shouted the young man at the back. 'Love is having women like you,' he added, much to the enjoyment of his friends. He was now smoking, and his rolled up cigarette looked small between his thick fingers.

'Although you have no respect,' said the big woman, 'I will let you know that this matter is no joke.'

'Of course this is not a joke!' shouted a new contributor. He spoke firmly and in English. His eyes seemed to burn with anger. He was young and immaculately dressed, his white shirt collar resting neatly on the collar of his jacket. A young nurse in a white uniform sat next to him. 'The mother there,' he continued, 'asks you very clearly whether you have ever seen a person caught by the supposed prophetess's supposed trap. Have you?'

'She didn't say that, man,' said the young man at the back, passing the roll to one of his friends. 'She only asked when this person was caught and who it was.' The boys at the back laughed. There was a lot of smoke now at the back of the bus.

'My question was,' said the big woman turning her head to glare at the young man, 'have you ever seen a person caught there? That's all.' Then she looked outside. She seemed angry now.

'Don't be angry, mother,' said the young man at the back. There was more laughter. 'I was only trying to understand,' he added.

'And that's our problem,' said the immaculately dressed man, addressing the bus. His voice was sure and strong. 'We laugh at everything; just stopping short of seriousness. Is it any wonder that the white man is still sitting on us? The mother there asked a very straightforward question, but she is answered vaguely about things happening. Then there is disrespectful laughter at the back there. The truth is you have no proof. None of you. Have you ever seen anybody caught by this prophetess? Never. It's all superstition. And so much about this prophetess also. Some of us are tired of her stories.'

There was a stunned silence in the bus. Only the heavy drone of an engine struggling with an overloaded bus could be heard. It was the man with the balaclava who broke the silence.

'Young man,' he said, 'by the look of things you must be a clever, educated person, but you just note one thing. The prophetess might just be hearing all this, so don't be surprised when a bolt of lightning strikes you on a hot sunny day. And we shall be there at your funeral, young man, to say how you brought misfortune upon your head.'

Thus had the discussion ended. But the boy had remembered how, every summer, bottles of all sizes filled with liquids of all kinds of colours would dangle from vines and peach and apricot trees in many yards in the township. No one dared steal fruit from those trees. Who wanted to be glued in shame to a fruit tree? Strangely, though, only the prophetess's trees had no bottles hanging from their branches.

The boy turned his eyes away from the window and focused into the dark room. His eyes had adjusted slowly to the darkness, and he saw the dark form of the woman shuffling away from him. She probably wore those slippers that had a fluff on top. Old women seem to love them. Then a white receding object came into focus. The woman wore a white *doek* on her head. The boy's eyes followed the *doek*. It took a right-angled turn — probably round the table. And then the dark form of the table came into focus. The *doek* stopped, and the boy heard the screech of a chair being pulled; and the *doek* descended somewhat and was still. There was silence in the room. The boy wondered what to do. Should he grope for a chair? Or should he squat on the floor respectfully? Should he greet or wait to be greeted? One never knew with the prophetess. Why did his mother have to send him to this place? The fascinating stories about the prophetess, to which the boy would add graphic details as if he had also met her, were one thing; but being in her actual presence was another. The boy then became conscious of the smell of camphor. His mother always used camphor whenever she complained of pains in her joints. Was the prophetess ill then? Did she pray for her own water? Suddenly, the boy felt at ease, as if the discovery that a prophetess could also feel pain somehow made her explainable.

'*Lumela 'me,*' he greeted. Then he cleared his throat.

'*Eea ngoanaka,*' she responded. After a little while she asked: 'Is there something you want, little man?' It was a very thin voice. It would have been completely detached had it not been for a hint of tiredness in it. She breathed somewhat heavily. Then she coughed, cleared her throat, and coughed again. A mixture of rough discordant sounds filled the dark room as if everything was coming out of her insides, for she seemed to breathe out her cough from deep within her. And the boy wondered: if she coughed too long, what would happen? Would something come out? A lung? The boy saw the form of the woman clearly now: she had bent forward somewhat. Did anything come out of her on to the floor? The cough subsided. The woman sat up and her hands fumbled with something around her breasts. A white cloth emerged. She leaned forward again, cupped her hands and spat into the cloth. Then she stood up and shuffled away into further darkness away from the boy. A door creaked, and the white *doek* disappeared. The boy wondered what to do because the prophetess had disappeared before he could say what he had come for. He waited.

More objects came into focus. Three white spots on the table emerged. They were placed diagonally across the table. Table mats. There was a small round

black patch on the middle one. Because the prophetess
was not in the room, the boy was bold enough to
move near the table and touch the mats. They were
crocheted mats. The boy remembered the huge lacing
that his mother had crocheted for the church altar.
ALL SAINTS CHURCH was crocheted all over the
lacing. There were a number of designs of chalices
that carried the Blood of Our Lord.

Then the boy heard the sound of a match being
struck. There were many attempts before the match
finally caught fire. Soon, the dull, orange light of a
candle came into the living room where the boy was,
through a half closed door. More light flushed the
living room as the woman came in carrying a candle.
She looked round as if she was wondering where to
put the candle. Then she saw the ash tray on the
middle mat, pulled it towards her, sat down and turned
the candle over into the ash tray. Hot wax dropped
on to the ash tray. Then the prophetess turned the
candle upright and pressed its bottom on to the
wax. The candle held.

The prophetess now peered through the light of
the candle at the boy. Her thick lips protruded, pulling
the wrinkled skin and caving in the cheeks to form a
kind of lip circle. She seemed always ready to kiss.
There was a line tattooed from the forehead to the
ridge of a nose that separated small eyes that were
half closed by large, drooping eyelids. The white *doek*
on her head was so huge that it made her face look
small. She wore a green dress and a starched green
cape that had many white crosses embroidered on it.
Behind her, leaning against the wall, was a long
bamboo cross.

The prophetess stood up again, and shuffled towards
the window which was behind the boy. She closed

the curtains and walked back to her chair. The boy saw another big cross embroidered on the back of her cape. Before she sat down she picked up the bamboo cross and held it in front of her.

'What did you say you wanted, little man?' she asked slowly.

'My mother sent me to ask for water,' said the boy putting the bottle of water on the table.

'To ask for water?' she asked with mild exclamation, looking up at the bamboo cross. 'That is very strange. You came all the way from home to ask for water?'

'I mean,' said the boy, 'holy water.'

'Ahh!' exclaimed the prophetess, 'you did not say what you meant, little man.' She coughed, just once. 'Sit down, little man,' she said, and continued, 'You see, you should learn to say what you mean. Words, little man, are a gift from the Almighty, the Eternal Wisdom. He gave us all a little pinch of his mind and called on us to think. That is why it is folly to misuse words or not to know how to use them well. Now, who is your mother?'

'My mother?' asked the boy, confused by the sudden transition. 'My mother is staff nurse Masemola.'

'Ao!' exclaimed the prophetess, 'you are the son of the nurse? Does she have such a big man now?' She smiled a little and the lip circle opened. She smiled like a pretty woman who did not want to expose her cavities.

The boy relaxed somewhat, vaguely feeling safe because the prophetess knew his mother. This made him look away from the prophetess for a while, and he saw that there was a huge mask on the wall just opposite her. It was shining and black. It grinned all the time showing two canine teeth pointing upwards. About ten feet away at the other side of the wall was a picture of Jesus in which His chest was open, revealing His heart which had many shafts of light radiating from it.

'Your mother has a heart of gold, my son,' continued the prophetess. 'You are very fortunate, indeed, to have such a parent. Remember, when she says, "My boy, take this message to that house," go. When she says, "My boy, let me send you to the shop," go. And when she says, "My boy, pick up a book and read," pick up a book and read. In all this she is actually saying to you, learn and serve. Those two things, little man, are the greatest inheritance.'

Then the prophetess looked up at the bamboo cross as if she saw something in it that the boy could not see. She seemed to lose her breath for a while. She coughed deeply again, after which she went silent, her cheeks moving as if she was chewing.

'Bring the bottle nearer,' she said finally. She put one hand on the bottle while with the other she held the bamboo cross. Her eyes closed, she turned her face towards the ceiling. The boy saw that her face seemed to have contracted into an intense concentration in such a way that the wrinkles seemed to have become deep gorges. Then she began to speak.

'You will not know this hymn, boy, so listen. Always listen to new things. Then try to create too. Just as I have learnt never to page through the dead leaves of hymn books.' And she began to sing.

> *If the fish in a river*
> *boiled by the midday sun*
> *can wait for the coming of evening,*
> *we too can wait*
> *in this wind-frosted land,*
> *the spring will come,*

the spring will come.
If the reeds in winter
can dry up and seem dead
and then rise
in the spring,
we too will survive the fire that is coming
the fire that is coming,
we too will survive the fire that is coming.

It was a long, slow song. Slowly, the prophetess began to pray.

'God, the All Powerful! When called upon, You always listen. We direct our hearts and thoughts to You. How else could it be? There is so much evil in the world; so much emptiness in our hearts; so much debasement of the mind. But You, God of all power, are the wind that sweeps away evil and fills our hearts and minds with renewed strength and hope. Remember Samson? Of course You do, O Lord. You created him, You, maker of all things. You brought him out of a barren woman's womb, and since then, we have known that out of the desert things will grow, and that what grows out of the barren wastes has a strength that can never be destroyed.'

Suddenly, the candle flame went down. The light seemed to have gone into retreat as the darkness loomed out, seemingly out of the very light itself, and bore down upon it, until there was a tiny blue flame on the table looking so vulnerable and so strong at the same time. The boy shuddered and felt the coldness of the floor going up his bare feet.

Then out of the dark, came the prophetess's laugh. It began as a giggle, the kind the girls would make when the boy and his friends chased them down the street for a little kiss. The giggle broke into the kind

of laughter that produced tears when one was very
happy. There was a kind of strange pleasurable rhythm
to it that gave the boy a momentary enjoyment of
the dark, but the laugh gave way to a long shriek. The
boy wanted to rush out of the house. But something
strong, yet intangible, held him fast to where he was.
It was probably the shriek itself that had filled the
dark room and now seemed to come out of the mask
on the wall. The boy felt like throwing himself on the
floor to wriggle and roll like a snake until he became
tired and fell into a long sleep at the end of which
would be the kind of bliss the boy would feel when
he was happy and his mother was happy and she
embraced him, so closely.

But the giggle, the laugh, the shriek, all ended as
abruptly as they had started as the darkness swiftly
receded from the candle like the way ripples run
away from where a stone has been thrown in the
water. And there was light. On the wall, the mask
smiled silently, and the heart of Jesus sent out yellow
light.

'Lord, Lord, Lord,' said the prophetess slowly in a
quiet, surprisingly full voice which carried the same
kind of contentment that had been in the voice of the
boy's mother when one day he had come home from
playing in the street, and she was seated on the chair
close to the kitchen door, just opposite the warm
stove. And as soon as she saw him come in, she
embraced him all the while saying: 'I've been so ill;
for so long, but I've got you. You're my son. You're
my son. You're my son.'

And the boy had smelled the faint smell of camphor
on her, and he too embraced her, holding her firmly
although his arms could not go beyond his mother's
armpits. He remembered how warm his hands had

become in her armpits.

'Lord, Lord, Lord,' continued the prophetess, 'have mercy on the desert in our hearts and in our thoughts. Have mercy. Bless this water; fill it with your power; and may it bring rebirth. Let her and all others who will drink of it feel the flower of newness spring alive in them; let those who drink it, break the chains of despair, and may they realise that the desert wastes are really not barren, but that the vast sands that stretch into the horizon are the measure of the seed in us.'

As the prophetess stopped speaking, she slowly lowered the bamboo cross until it rested on the floor. The boy wondered if it was all over now. Should he stand up and get the blessed water and leave? But the prophetess soon gave him direction.

'Come here, my son,' she said, 'and kneel before me here.' The boy stood up and walked slowly towards the prophetess. He knelt on the floor, his hands hanging at his sides. The prophetess placed her hands on his head. They were warm, and the warmth seemed to go through his hair, penetrating deep through his scalp into the very centre of his head. Perhaps, he thought, that was the soul of the prophetess going into him. Wasn't it said that when the prophetess placed her hands on a person's head, she was seeing with her soul deep into that person; that, as a result, the prophetess could never be deceived? And the boy wondered how his lungs looked to her. Did she see the water that he had drunk from the tap just across the street? Where was the water now? In the stomach? In the kidneys?

Then the hands of the prophetess moved all over the boy's head, seeming to feel for something. They went down the neck. They seemed cooler now, and the coolness seemed to tickle the boy for his neck was colder than those hands. Now they covered his face, and he saw, just before he closed his eyes, the skin folds on the hands so close to his eyes that they looked like many mountains. Those hands smelled of blue soap and candle wax. But there was no smell of snuff. The boy wondered. Perhaps the prophetess did not use snuff after all. But the boy's grandmother did, and her hands always smelled of snuff. Then the prophetess spoke.

'My son,' she said, 'we are made of all that is in the world. Go. Go and heal your mother.' When she removed her hands from the boy's face, he felt his face grow cold, and there was a slight sensation of his skin shrinking. He rose from the floor, lifted the bottle with its snout, and backed away from the prophetess. He then turned and walked towards the door. As he closed it, he saw the prophetess shuffling away to the bedroom carrying the candle with her. He wondered when she would return the ashtray to the table. When he finally closed the door, the living room was dark, and there was light in the bedroom.

It was night outside. The boy stood on the veranda for a while, wanting his eyes to adjust to the darkness. He wondered also about the dog. But it did not seem to be around. And there was that vine archway with its forbidden fruit and the multicoloured worms that always crawled all over the vine. As the boy walked under the tunnel of vine, he tensed his neck, lowering his head as people do when walking in the rain. He was anticipating the reflex action of shaking off a falling worm. Those worms were disgustingly huge, he thought. And there was also something terrifying about their bright colours.

In the middle of the tunnel, the boy broke into a run and was out of the gate: free. He thought of his

mother waiting for the holy water; and he broke into
a sprint, running west up Thipe Street towards home.
As he got to the end of the street, he heard the hum
of the noise that came from the ever-crowded barber
shops and the huge beer hall just behind those shops.
After the brief retreat in the house of the prophetess,
the noise, the people, the shops, the street lights, the
buses and the taxis all seemed new. Yet, somehow, he
wanted to avoid any contact with all this activity. If
he turned left at the corner, he would have to go
past the shops into the lit Moshoeshoe Street and its
Friday night crowds. If he went right, he would have
to go past the now dark, ghostly Bantu-Batho post
office, and then down through the huge gum trees
behind the Charterston Clinic, and then past the quiet
golf course. The latter way would be faster, but too
dark and dangerous for a mere boy, even with the
spirit of the prophetess in him. And were not dead
bodies found there sometimes? The boy turned left.

At the shops, the boy slowed down to manoeuvre
through the crowds. He lifted the bottle to his chest
and supported it from below with the other hand. He
must hold on to that bottle. He was going to heal his
mother. He tightened the bottle cap. Not a drop was
to be lost. The boy passed the shops.

Under a street lamp just a few feet from the gate
into the beer hall was a gang of boys standing in a
tight circle. The boy slowed down to an anxious stroll.
Who were they, he wondered. He would have to run
past them quickly. No, there would be no need. He
recognised Timi and Bubu. They were with the rest of
the gang from the boy's neighbourhood. Those were
the bigger boys who were either in Standard Six or
were already in secondary school or were now working
in town.

Timi recognised the boy.

'Ja, sonny boy,' greeted Timi. 'What's a picaninny like you doing alone in the streets at night?'

'*Heit,* bra Timi,' said the boy, returning the greeting. 'Just from the shops, bra Timi,' he lied, not wanting to reveal his real mission. Somehow that would not have been appropriate.

'Come on, you!' yelled another member of the gang, glaring at Timi. It was Biza. Most of the times when the boy had seen Biza, the latter was stopping a girl and talking to her. Sometimes the girl would laugh. Sometimes Biza would twist her arm until she 'agreed'. In broad daylight!

'You don't believe me,' continued Biza to Timi, 'and when I try to show you some proof you turn away to greet an ant.'

'Okay then,' said another, 'what proof do you have? Everybody knows that Sonto is a hard girl to get.'

'Come closer then,' said Biza, 'and I'll show you.' The boy was closed out of the circle as the gang closed in towards Biza, who was at the centre. The boy became curious and got closer. The wall was impenetrable. But he could clearly hear Biza.

'You see? You can all see. I've just come from that girl. Look! See? The liquid? See? When I touch it with my finger and then leave it, it follows like a spider's web.'

'Well, my man,' said someone, 'you can't deceive anybody with that. It's the usual trick. A fellow just blows his nose and then applies the mucus there, and then emerges out of the dark saying he has just had a girl.'

'Let's look again closely,' said another, 'before we decide one way or the other.' And the gang pressed close again.

'You see? You see?' Biza kept saying.

'I think Biza has had that girl,' said someone.

'It's mucus man, and nothing else,' said another.

'But you know Biza's record in these matters, gents.'

'Another thing, how do we know it's Sonto and not some other girl. Where is it written on Biza's cigar that he has just had Sonto? Show me where it's written "Sonto" there.'

'You're jealous, you guys, that's your problem,' said Biza. The circle went loose and there was just enough time for the boy to see Biza's penis disappear into his trousers. A thick little thing, thought the boy. It looked sad. It had first been squeezed in retreat against the fly like a concertina, before it finally disappeared. Then Biza, with a twitch of alarm across his face, saw the boy.

'What did you see, you?' screamed Biza. 'Fuck off!'

The boy took to his heels wondering what Biza could have been doing with his penis under the street lamp. It was funny, whatever it was. It was silly too. Sinful. The boy was glad that he had got the holy water away from those boys and that none of them had touched the bottle.

And the teachers were right, thought the boy. Silliness was all those boys knew. And then they would go to school and fail test after test. Silliness and school did not go together.

The boy felt strangely superior. He had the power of the prophetess in him. And he was going to pass that power to his mother, and heal her. Those boys were not healing their mothers. They just left their mothers alone at home. The boy increased his speed. He had to get home quickly. He turned right at the charge office and sped towards the clinic. He crossed the road that went to town and entered Mayaba Street.

Mayaba Street was dark and the boy could not see.
But he did not lower his speed. Home was near now,
instinct would take him there. His eyes would adjust
to the darkness as he raced along. He lowered the
bottle from his chest and let it hang at his side, like a
pendulum that was not moving. He looked up at the
sky as if light would come from the stars high up to
lead him home. But when he lowered his face, he saw
something suddenly loom before him, and, almost
simultaneously, felt a dull yet painful impact against
his thigh. Then there was a grating of metal seeming
to scoop up sand from the street. The boy did not
remember how he fell but, on the ground, he lay
clutching at his painful thigh. A few feet away, a
man groaned and cursed.

'Blasted child!' he shouted. 'Shouldn't I kick you?
Just running in the street as if you owned it. Shit of a
child, you don't even pay tax. Fuck off home before
I do more damage to you!' The man lifted his bicycle,
and the boy saw him straightening the handles. And
the man rode away.

The boy raised himself from the ground and began
to limp home, conscious of nothing but the pain in
his thigh. But it was not long before he felt a jab of
pain at the centre of his chest and his heart beating
faster. He was thinking of the broken bottle and the
spilt holy water and his mother waiting for him and
the water that would help to cure her. What would
his mother say? If only he had not stopped to see
those silly boys he might not have been run over by a
bicycle. Should he go back to the prophetess? No.
There was the dog, there was the vine, there were the
worms. There was the prophetess herself. She would
not let anyone who wasted her prayers get away without punishment. Would it be lightning? Would it be

the fire of hell? What would it be? The boy limped
home to face his mother. He would walk in to his
doom. He would walk into his mother's bedroom,
carrying no cure, and face the pain in her sad eyes.

But as the boy entered the yard of his home, he
heard the sound of bottles coming from where his
dog had its kennel. Rex had jumped over the bottles,
knocking some stones against them in his rush to
meet the boy. And the boy remembered the pile of
bottles next to the kennel. He felt grateful as he
embraced the dog. He selected a bottle from the
heap. Calmly, as if he had known all the time what he
would do in such a situation, the boy walked out of
the yard again, towards the street tap on Mayaba
Street. And there, almost mechanically, he cleaned
the bottle, shaking it many times with clean water.
Finally, he filled it with water and wiped its outside
clean against his trousers. He tightened the cap, and
limped home.

As soon as he opened the door, he heard his mother's
voice in the bedroom. It seemed some visitors had
come while he was away.

'I'm telling you, *Sisi,*' his mother was saying, 'and
take it from me, a trained nurse. Pills, medicines, and
all those injections, are not enough. I take herbs too,
and then think of the wonders of the universe as our
people have always done. Son, is that you?'

'Yes, Ma,' said the boy who had just closed the door
with a deliberate bang.

'And did you bring the water?'

'Yes, Ma.'

'Good. I knew you would. Bring the water and
three cups. MaShange and MaMokoena are here.'

The boy's eyes misted with tears. His mother's
trust in him: would he repay it with such dishonesty?

He would have to be calm. He wiped his eyes with the back of his hand, and then put the bottle and three cups on a tray. He would have to walk straight. He would have to hide the pain in his thigh. He would have to smile at his mother. He would have to smile at the visitors. He picked up the tray; but just before he entered the passage leading to the bedroom, he stopped, trying to muster courage. The voices of the women in the bedroom reached him clearly.

'I hear you very well, Nurse,' said one of the women. 'It is that kind of sense I was trying to spread before the minds of these people. You see, the two children are first cousins. The same blood runs through them.'

'That close!' exclaimed the boy's mother.

'Yes, that close. MaMokoena here can bear me out; I told them in her presence. Tell the nurse, you were there.'

'I have never seen such people in all my life,' affirmed MaMokoena.

'So I say to them, my voice reaching up to the ceiling, "Hey, you people, I have seen many years. If these two children really want to marry each other, then a a beast *has* to be slaughtered to cancel the ties of blood . . . ." '

'And do you want to hear what they said?' interrupted MaMokoena.

'I'm listening with both ears,' said the boy's mother.

'Tell her, child of Shange,' said MaMokoena.

'They said that was old, crusted foolishness. So I said to myself, "Daughter of Shange, shut your mouth, sit back, open your eyes, and watch." And that's what I did.'

'Two weeks before the marriage, the ancestors struck. Just as I had thought. The girl had to be rushed to hospital, her legs swollen like trousers full of air on the washing line. Then I got my chance, and opened my mouth, pointing my finger at them, and said, "Did you ask the ancestors' permission for this unacceptable marriage?" You should have seen their necks becoming as flexible as a goose's. They looked this way, and looked that way, but never at me. But my words had sunk. And before the sun went down, we were eating the insides of a goat. A week later, the children walked up to the altar. And the priest said to them, "You are such beautiful children!" '

'Isn't it terrible that some people just let misfortune fall upon them?' remarked the boy's mother.

'Only those who ignore the words of the world speaking to them,' said MaShange.

'Where is this boy now?' said the boy's mother. 'Son! Is the water coming?'

Instinctively the boy looked down at his legs. Would the pain in his thigh lead to the swelling of his legs? Or would it be because of his deception? A tremor of fear went through him; but he had to control it, and be steady, or the bottle of water would topple over. He stepped forward into the passage. There was his mother! Her bed faced the passage, and he had seen her as soon as he turned into the passage. She had propped herself up with many pillows. Their eyes met, and she smiled, showing the gap in her upper front teeth that she liked to poke her tongue into. She wore a fawn chiffon *doek* which had slanted into a careless heap on one side of her head. This exposed her undone hair on the other side of her head.

As the boy entered the bedroom, he smelled camphor. He greeted the two visitors and noticed that, although it was warm in the bedroom, MaShange, whom he knew, wore her huge, heavy, black, and shining overcoat. MaMokoena had a blanket over her shoulders. Their *doeks* were more orderly than the boy's mother's. The boy placed the tray on the dressing chest close to his mother's bed. He stepped back and watched his mother, not sure whether he should go back to the kitchen, or wait to meet his doom.

'I don't know what I would do without this boy,' said the mother as she leaned on an elbow, lifted the bottle with the other hand, and turned the cap rather laboriously with the hand on whose elbow she was resting. The boy wanted to help, but he felt he couldn't move. The mother poured water into one cup, drank from it briefly, turned her face towards the ceiling, and closed her eyes. 'Such cool water!' she sighed deeply, and added, 'Now I can pour for you,' as she poured water into the other two cups.

There was such a glow of warmth in the boy as he watched his mother, so much gladness in him that he forgave himself. What had the prophetess seen in him? Did she still feel him in her hands? Did she know what he had just done? Did holy water taste any differently from ordinary water? His mother didn't seem to find any difference. Would she be healed?

'As we drink the prophetess's water,' said MaShange, 'we want to say how grateful we are that we came to see for ourselves how you are.'

'I think I feel better already. This water, and you .... I can feel a soothing coolness deep down.'

As the boy slowly went out of the bedroom, he felt the pain in his leg, and felt grateful. He had healed his mother. He would heal her tomorrow, and always with all the water in the world. He had healed her.

Uncle

After school, Monday. A hot November afternoon. Doksi, Wanda and I are walking home. We are kicking things as we walk along. We always do that. But today, just as we were walking out of the school yard, we entered into a pact. I had linked my index finger with Doksi's, then with Wanda's; and they in turn had also linked their index fingers. It was a pact. Each of us would kick something all the way home. Each to his home. And whatever we were going to kick was to stay on the traffic island in the middle of Letsapa Street. Because I am wearing shoes, I kick a little stone. Wanda has found an empty Nestlé's condensed milk tin along the school fence. He is kicking that. His big toe, which is peeping through a hole at the front of his sandal, cringes whenever he is about to kick. The tin makes a noise as it rolls down the traffic island. Doksi, who wears no shoes (no one has ever seen shoes on Doksi), is kicking a ball of wool he has forcibly taken from Mapula, a tiny girl in our class whom Doksi wants to marry. Sometimes the wool gets hooked to Doksi's furrowed feet and dangles to and fro when he tries to kick it away. The wool just sticks to his foot, refusing to be kicked away. Wanda and I laugh whenever that happens. 'Here's a fellow with furrowed feet!' we say. 'Here's a fellow whose feet have become shoes!' Sometimes the children in class tease Doksi and say his father once said to him, 'Son, I can't afford shoes for you, so you're going to have to learn to make yourself some. Just walk bare-footed through hot and cold and soon there'll be some thick skin on those feet. What more will you need?'

This business of shoes. Doksi had said when one day I visited him: 'It's because I have no uncle.' We were sitting under the huge apricot tree in the yard at Doksi's home, and we had an old hat full of apricots between us. 'An uncle gets you anything you need,' he said looking very sad. 'An uncle looks after you.'

'Well,' I said, 'at least you have an apricot tree in your yard. We have no apricot trees in our yard. And the other children too, they have no apricot trees in their yards. Just a lot of peach trees. Peach trees are common.'

Doksi was quiet for a while. Maybe he was considering what I had just said. I couldn't say for sure. But his face seemed to say so. Maybe he was thinking I was right in what I said.

Then he said: 'Please don't laugh with them when they laugh at me. Sometimes when you laugh too, I think you are not my friend, and I feel lonely.'

'I promise,' I said. But sometimes one cannot help laughing. You laugh knowing that you shouldn't. But I promised.

Then Doksi gave me an apricot out of his father's old hat when I could have taken one myself. And we leaned back against the tree. And we were silent. The only sound we made was when we spat out apricot pips. There were so many around us, like small stones still wet with rain.

We are kicking. There are many other children around us who are also going home. Some of them are also kicking things. They have their own pacts.

It is hot. I am wondering if all the other children feel the heat as much as I do. It is as if there is a breeze of heat blowing out of my pores. Then sometimes there is a breeze of heat in the sky. But this outside breeze is stronger, and makes my shirt cling to me. And I feel like taking off the shirt and leaving it standing there in the street without me. But I go on kicking. All three of us are kicking.

'Boys,' I say after a while. 'Doesn't the day look sort of yellow?'

'Yellow?' asks Doksi, rolling the ball of wool under his feet as we do when we soften an orange. He looks puzzled. 'Maybe,' he says looking at the sky. 'To me it looks red. Maybe orange, sort of.'

'It depends,' says Wanda, following his tin with his eyes like a golfer follows his putt. 'It depends. It depends what you're looking at. If you look at the soil, the day looks brown. If you look at red roofs, the day looks red. If you look at the grass, the day looks green. If you look at the puddles around a tap, the day kind of shines. And if you look at all these things, then the day takes all their colours, sort of mixing them.'

'Well,' I say, 'I was only talking about the heat. The sun makes everything look yellow.'

'That's what I'm saying,' says Wanda. 'The heat. The colours rise up with the heat, and there is a mixture in the air. Not yellow, not black, not brown or this or that colour, but all of them fighting back. That's what my uncle says.'

Now I did not mean to be so complicated. I was only making a comment about the heat. I guess that's what happens when you ask people. They always answer according to what they think, not seeing what you meant. Wanda is like that, he always asks questions when you thought you were just joking. Then there is no joke any more. And then he swears by his uncle. Doksi has said many times that next time Wanda says 'That's what my uncle says,' we should seize him and put him under the tap and open it into his mouth so that all the words 'uncle' inside him would be washed out. And then we would all breathe a little more.

We are kicking. I, the stone. Wanda, the tin. Doksi, the soundless ball of wool.

Wanda's tin! Wanda's tin! It's rolling away from the traffic island onto the left side of the divided street. There are two stones along the edge of the traffic island that are too far apart, and the tin just found a way through the gap. It is rolling away on the tarred street and is making a lot of noise. Empty tins make the most noise. Wanda is going to have to buy sweets and offer them to our girlfriends. That's the penalty. And we have a pact. He would have to give a sweet to Gwendoline, who is mine, and another sweet to Mapula, who is Doksi's. Doksi and I are full of joy. Wanda smiles. But he is not really smiling, he is sad. He will have to pay the penalty.

It is just as well that Wanda's tin has rolled away from the traffic island for we are very close to the T-junction where Letsapa Street meets Moshoeshoe Street. That is where the island ends. There is a huge rockery at its end. We have to leave the traffic island now, so we link our index fingers again to cancel the pact. I kick my stone across the left side of the street. Doksi does the same to his wool ball, but it stops in the middle of the street and he picks it up and crosses the street with it.

There is a big cottonwood tree on the corner, and Doksi suggests that we rest under it for a while. Wanda and I agree. But I am a bit uneasy for there is a circle of big brothers under the tree and they are playing dice. They are gambling. Terrible thing. They always end up fighting. I want to say so, but I cannot. I have just seen Doksi's brother there in the circle. It is easy to see him because he is the one throwing. He breaks away from the circle, crouching, rattling the dice. And then he throws the dice saying: 'Ahh, two-two!' He then follows them to rejoin the circle momentarily, then picks up the dice again. He comes out once more and says: 'Ahh, two-two!' He comes out once more and says: 'Ahh, two-two! TWO-TWO-OO-OO!' And then he squats and is collecting money. Then he says: 'I do! I do! I do!' The others are throwing money into the centre of the circle, and Doksi's brother says: 'More! More!' More money is thrown in. Then he says: 'No more!' Then he picks up the dice and steps back once more and says: 'Ahh, pop!' I look at the other brothers squatting there. Next to Doksi's brother is Nzule. This makes me scared. Nzule? I give Doksi a nudge. But when he looks at me it is not to him I talk. It is to Wanda.

'Look! It's Nzule.'

'I have seen him already,' he says. 'A fire is going to blaze here soon, my boy. You will see.'

'What makes you think so?' I ask, knowing the answer very well.

'Well,' he says, 'whenever there's a fighting man in a group of people, there's bound to be war. That's what my uncle says.'

'Boy, I want to see this fire,' says Doksi.

I look at Doksi with surprise. How can he want to see a fire in which his own brother might burn? I want to ask him this, but I don't. People trust their brothers. Even when their brothers come back home with stab wounds in their backs. They trust their brothers. Doksi likes to tell us that his brother has four stab wounds in his back. But there is one stab wound that he never talks about. It is the one in his brother's left buttock. The injection stab. Doksi's brother was once given the injection stab with a big knife, and he left the township because he could not sit and people laughed at him. Rumours went that even where he disappeared to in Daveyton, people also laughed. When you have the injection stab it is not easy to show off the bandages because they are on the wrong place.

There are many schoolchildren now under the tree. We are all resting in the shade and looking at the game of dice from a safe distance. One of the brothers turns his face away from the circle to spit. I had seen him gathering the spit with his moving cheeks. The spit lands on the ground, collects soil and rolls for a while. Then it stops, looking like a big dirty brown marble with some green in it. Before he turns back to the game he looks at us. He is brother Malunda. His fingers are thick. His nails are yellow. His eyes are yellow. His lips are puffed, and his cheeks are kind of swollen.

'What are you children doing there?' Brother Malunda glares at us. We begin to move away rather uncertainly.

'Leave the children alone,' says another brother. 'Why do you chase away your luck?' But he is the only one who thinks that children are luck. The others also turn round to shout at us.

'Go home, you!' Doksi's brother growls at him.

'Fuck off! *Voetsek!*' shout the others. Nzule even stands up and makes as if to take off his leather belt. We scatter away.

Just as we are running away we see a police van coming fast towards us. There are two Boer policemen in it laughing as they drive through the scattering children towards the circle of gamblers. Wanda trips and falls and his tin drops out of his hand and rolls towards the van and is crushed. The circle of gamblers has broken up. The driver slams his brakes short of the big cottonwood tree. All the big brothers are running for their lives. Even Nzule. Which is funny because there are many stories in the township about how Nzule always fights white policemen to the death. But he is running now. Maybe he is going to fetch his weapons. Then I see Wanda running back. He picks up the crushed tin and hurls it at the police van. We hear it land. The van backs off. We all run away fast. But when we hear the van speeding as we run, it is in the opposite direction towards the running brothers. But we run until we reach Mayaba Street, from the corner of which we can see my home. And all along as we run Wanda is saying: 'Did you see? Did you see what I did? Did you see? Did you see what I did? Did you see? Did you see what I did?'

And when we stop at the corner to rest because the policemen are not following us, Wanda is still saying: 'Did you see? Did you see what I did?' We are all laughing but no one is paying attention to Wanda. But suddenly I stop laughing. I want Wanda to stop asking his questions because I can hear something else.

'Quiet!' I shout.

'Did you see? Did you see what I did?'

'Just listen, man!'

'Did you see? Did you see what I did?'

'Okay, Wanda, I saw what you did. You hit the police van with your crushed tin. Doksi, did you see what he did?'

'Yes,' says Doksi. 'He was very brave.'

'When you see a chance, use it. That's what my uncle says.'

'Okay, now,' I say. 'Let's listen to something.' We listen.

'It's a trumpet,' I say. 'And it's coming from a house nearby.' We listen. We look. We are searching. And I look at my home. And I can see that when people pass my home, they slow down and look at my home. There are some schoolchildren leaning against the fence of my home. I look at Doksi. He is looking at me. I look at Wanda. He too is looking at me. Then Wanda and Doksi look at each other. And we break into a run all at once.

As we get closer to my home, the sound of the trumpet gets louder. There is no doubt now, it is coming from my home. It is coming from nowhere else. It is coming from the house where I stay. Number 1310. We rush into the yard and cluster at the door. I hold the doorknob. This is home and I need not knock. But I just hold the doorknob, not opening the door.

'Open!' Doksi shouts.

'Yes,' says Wanda. 'Open!'

They are excited, they cannot wait. I am looking at them. And I look beyond them at the children who are standing at the fence. They cannot come in. But my friends and I can, and will. They can only stand at the fence and listen, wishing they could see. Who is playing a trumpet in my home? I wish to know. I turn the knob, and we rush in like paper being blown in by the wind. It's certainly here in the house. The sound is clear now and it is coming from the living room. I open the living room door, my friends behind me.

It is my uncle!

As we come in uncle is blowing the trumpet. His cheeks are as big as a balloon. He opens his eyes and sees us, then closes them again. He just plays on as if he has not seen us. I want to go to him immediately because I know this person who is playing the trumpet in my home. I know him. He's my uncle. And my friends must see that I know him, as soon as possible. But I cannot go to him. He is playing the trumpet and I do not know what he will do if I go to him.

He is not playing a smooth song. He keeps on playing and then stopping. And then starts all over again. There is a wide book before him on a shining silver stand. And when he stops, Uncle seems to read from the book. Then he closes his eyes again and plays. Sometimes he plays the same sound over and over again. Then suddenly he starts a song and I wish he would play it forever. But then he stops and starts all over again.

'Who is he?' asks Doksi loudly in my ear.

'My uncle!' I shout back.

'He says it's his uncle,' Doksi shouts to Wanda.

'When did he come?' Doksi asks again.

'I don't know,' I say. 'He was not here when I left for school this morning.'

'He does not know!' shouts Doksi. 'The man was not here this morning when he went to school!'

I look at my friends. They are standing in a row behind me. We are looking at Uncle playing his trumpet. It's right in my home.

* * *

'It must be hard, hey?' Uncle says. 'It must be hard when a writer keeps looking up at the ceiling without looking down. Either the ideas are not coming, or the mind has wandered.'

This jolts me out of my thoughts and I become aware again of Uncle sitting at the opposite end of the table. He is leaning forward on the table towards the candle so that he can read the newspaper he has spread before him. He had put the candle in the middle between us so that we could share the light, as he had said. He is looking at me now, and I am embarrassed. There is a little smile on his lips, and in his eyes. I would be laughing and smiling with him without a care if I didn't have to be doing this home-work. I smile back at Uncle a little. He looks down at the paper.

'Places I would like to visit'. I am really not sure which places I would like to visit. I have cousins in Durban. Maybe that's the place I would like to visit. But I am not sure why I would like to visit Durban. Besides that I want to visit my cousins . . . . Mistress Khumalo had said it should be because of something very important we want to see that we want to visit a place. Why should I be thinking of visiting another place when Uncle is here visiting? It might seem as if I want to chase him away. But if Uncle is here visiting, it should be important too if I want to go to Durban because my cousins are there. I look at the ceiling. But I remember Uncle. He should not catch me look-ing at the ceiling. I look at the candle in the middle between us. We are sharing its light.

'Ah, now you are looking at the candle,' says Uncle. 'Perhaps part of the problem may be that there isn't enough light in here.' Uncle snaps his fingers and goes out of the living room. He returns with a paraffin lamp. 'If you have to be a scholar,' he says, 'then be a real one. Have enough light whenever you read. Only words that are glowing with light will get into your head. Then you can think clearly.' He is again sitting opposite me. The light of the candle has disappeared into the bigger light. Big things swallow small things.

It is strange. As soon as there is more light, I begin to write. Ideas just come out. *The place I would like to visit is Durban. I would like to visit Durban because my cousins are there. There is Sizwe; there is Vusi; there is Nomanlanga. And my aunt is there. Only her husband I do not know. (He is dead). That is why I want to visit Durban. Durban is the place I would like to visit. When I'm there, there will be cousins to play with. And we will be visiting other relatives there. There is the sea too. And we can all go swimming. A beach full of relatives. That is really why I want to visit Durban. Durban is really the place.* Ideas are following each other like ants, and the essay is coming on.

Maybe it's because of Uncle's suggestion about the light, I don't know. Things will always happen this way. When someone says to you: 'If you do this or that, then this or that will happen.' If you really like the person then whatever he says will happen, will indeed happen. When my mother says: 'You're a good boy, you'll do well at school,' I usually get all my sums correct. But sometimes she's angry and says, 'You are a nasty little pig, whatever comes in through one ear, goes out through the other ear.' Then, true to her word, I get to school and nothing stays in my head.

I am wondering what more to say now. Uncle is reading his paper again. Mother went out about an hour ago to deliver yet another baby. She asked

Uncle so many questions this afternoon when, coming back from delivering a baby, she found him with me and Doksi and Wanda talking and laughing in the living room.

'Oh, my little brother,' she said when she saw him. 'Why didn't you tell us you were coming?' And she embraced him and kissed him, and all the time she kept on saying: 'Oh, my little brother.' And there were tears in her eyes and she kissed him again and again. Then she went to make him tea and Uncle followed her into the kitchen, and Wanda and Doksi and I stayed behind in the living room blowing into the trumpet in turns.

'How is Mother?'

'I think she's fine.'

'How is Father?'

'I think he's fine.'

'Think? You say think?'

'Well, I'm not sure how they are right now, since I am not with them. But when I left them six months ago, they were fine.'

'I am shocked! Oh, Lovington, I am shocked. You have not seen Mother and Father for six months?'

'I do send them money regularly.'

'Money! That's what a typical young man of today says when he wishes to avoid responsibility. First you disappeared for five years, and when you reappeared you stayed for a month. And now you've been gone again for six months. And all we hear about you is from the papers. Do you know what hopes they put in you when you were born?'

'*Sisi*, please, not again.'

'I was doing my last year of training when you were born. Exams were around the corner, yet every month end I would leave Bridgeman Hospital and

take a train all the way home to Bloemfontein to help
mother take care of you. And she used to say: 'This is
our last one, he will take care of us.' And you were so
weak. I don't know what would have happened if it
were not for my training. And then you disappear.
Five years! And when my husband dies, we don't
know where to get you. Fancy disappearing for five
years and leaving Mother and Father all alone. How
are they dealing with the congregation?'

'They were managing.'

'Does she still start the hymns?'

'I should think so.'

'What a congregation! Father has had so many
complaints. But he deals with them. But why, why,
why, Lovington? You have given them trouble for as
long as I can remember.'

'I've told you all I had to follow my calling. And
everybody was saying I should have a teacher's cert-
ificate to fall back on in case something went wrong.
A talent is a talent. I had to follow my talent.'

Mother just clapped her hands and did not reply.
And Uncle kept on saying: 'You don't have to do
that, *sisi*, you don't have to do that.' And there was
the clinking of cups and saucers.

'And the cattle?' Mother said after a long silence.
'When are you driving the cattle away from home?'

Uncle laughed and said girls were hard to come by
these days. And then there was talking and laughter
in the kitchen.

I no longer look at the ceiling, nor do I look at the
light. I look at the piano behind Uncle. He is looking
down at his paper. Then he looks at me and our eyes
meet. And I look beyond him quickly. Uncle laughs

and says: 'How's the going?'

'I'm thinking,' I say.

'Do you know that what comes out of that piano can take you places?' Uncle laughs and then says: 'Bring your atlas here and let me show you some of these places.'

Uncle comes to sit next to me and we look at the map of South Africa. 'Show me Bloemfontein . . . yes . . . . That is where your grandmother and grandfather are. Your uncles. Your younger mothers. They are all there. That is the centre of your life too. Your mother had to come home before you were born because you were her first born. And that is where I buried your umbilical cord. Right there in the yard. Wherever you are in the world, you must return to that yard. Now show me Johannesburg . . . yes . . . . That is where Uncle bought his trumpet. Now look at this: Ladysmith, Pietermaritzburg, Durban, East London, Port Elizabeth, Cape Town, Kimberley, Pietersburg, Middelburg, Witbank, Pretoria, Springs, Germiston. All foreign names; but that will change in time. This whole land, *mshana,* I have seen it all. And I have given it music. You too must know this land. The whole of it, and find out what you can give it. So you must make a big map of the country, your own map. Put it on the wall. Each time you hear of a new place, put it on the map. Soon you will have a map full of places. And they will be your places. And it will be your own country. And then you must ask yourself: what can I give to all those places? And when you have found the answer. you will know why you want to visit those places.'

Uncle is snoring in the other bed. He disturbs my thinking. But I think. It is nice to think of nice things when one is in bed and it is dark in the bedroom and things that have happened become nicer. And everything is happening over again. And you are lying there in bed not moving, and yet you are also in there in what is happening although you are still in bed not moving.

Uncle is playing and stopping, playing and stopping, and suddenly he flings his arms open. The trumpet is in the other hand and Doksi and Wanda and I are looking at him. But he is looking at me and he says: 'Ah! Who is this? Who is this? What do we have here? A man or a boy? Let's see if I can still lift him up.' He is tall. He lifts me up but not for long. I can feel the trumpet under my armpit. He holds me together with the trumpet, then he brings me closer to him and bites my ear. I was afraid he would do that for one of the things I remember most is that Uncle would bite my ear whenever he was happy. Perhaps it was okay when I was young, but now I am older and it embarrasses me. Especially with friends around. He puts me down and embraces me and says: 'You are too light for a boy of eleven.' And I say: 'This is Doksi and this is Wanda.' And Doksi becomes brave and says: 'What is this?' I say: 'Stupid, this is a trumpet.' Uncle says to me: 'Here, blow.' I blow and only wind comes out. 'Harder!' Only wind comes out and each time this happens everybody laughs. Doksi blows and the trumpet goes piaoo yaoo yaoo! and we laugh. 'Now here's a trumpeter in the making,' says Uncle. Wanda says: 'It sounded like a fart.' Doksi says: 'Shush! How can you say that in front of a grown-up.' 'Not to worry boys, not to worry,' says Uncle. 'A fart is a fart whether one is young or old. But remember,' — and he looks serious — 'never turn away from ugly things.' And while Wanda is trying to blow the trumpet and only letting out air, Uncle asks if I can play the piano. I say a little and I go to the piano and play a boogie woogie. Then Uncle plays with me but he is so loud that I don't hear the piano any more and I stop playing, but Uncle plays on and on. When he stops he says: '*Mshana,* when I play this note here on the piano there is a sound as if something like a penny is in here under this note.' I say: 'Yes, one day when I was silly I put a penny in there and could not take it out.' Uncle says it must be taken out because it interferes with the music, and he says: 'Now watch this, boys.' Uncle moves his hands over the piano notes, especially over the note where I had put the penny. He begins to speak in a language we cannot understand. His eyes have turned red and his hair seems to spring up. Then he says: 'Come up! Come up! . . . Come up! Come up!' And it is a wonder, a wonder, for the penny is coming up slowly. The penny is coming up slowly. Then it falls down on the floor. It is a wonder and I don't know what to say. Wanda and Doksi also don't know what to say. It is a wonder and Mother comes in, and Mother comes in, and Mother comes in. And there is Mother, and she embraces Uncle. Mother is here, Mother is here . . . .

I wonder where Uncle is. I have not really seen him today. When I left for school this morning, he was fast asleep. Mother said not to make a noise because Uncle was on holiday; he needed peace. I had to wear my shoes in the kitchen. When I rushed home at the eleven o'clock break I did not find him in. The news of the trumpet had spread, and half of my classmates had come home with me to see the trumpet. I pulled the trumpet from under the bed and would not let anyone touch it. I wanted to blow it, but I was not sure if only wind would come out. If I blew and only wind came out, then I would have no right to boast about the trumpet. I had told these children that Uncle spent half the night teaching me how to play the trumpet. Lies sometimes catch up with a person. And I told them I could not blow now, lest I give Uncle my germs.

When I came home after school there was still no Uncle. I tried to play some songs on the piano so that I could be good when Uncle played with me. I struggled with 'Nonsukulu'. I had never played it before. I played a few notes over and over again just as Uncle does until I knew them. I then passed on to others. That way I got to know how to play the song. When Doksi and Wanda came, I told them I would not come out to play. I told them not to disturb me for I was learning how to play a song; that learning how to play a song is real sweat. They left, saying I was behaving like a white man. I did not care, for Uncle had said learning a song is real sweat. And I was sweating. The best way to avoid endless struggle, Uncle had said in the dark when we were about to sleep and I was asking him many questions, is to struggle very hard for a short period of time. The big struggle makes future struggles much lighter. So I would need to put aside two or three years of hard work learning how to read music. Then I would play easily for many more years. Everything had to be struggled for. Uncle said he would give me books from which I could learn to read the language of music.

When Uncle does not appear for supper, Mother begins to complain: 'Fancy disappearing on the first day of his visit! For all I know he is gone. Once a disappearer, always a disappearer!'

'But,' I ask, 'could he go and leave his trumpet?'

'As far as I know he knows nobody in this township.'

I wash my hands and sit down to eat. We are quiet, Mother and I. Then she says: 'He has always been a bad example! Kept us one hundred percent worried. Staying away from school. Disappearing on Sundays and shaming my father before an inquisitive congregation. And he had such a beautiful voice when he really wanted to sing.'

'I'm sure he will be coming soon,' I say.

'How can you be sure? You don't know your uncle.'

How could I be sure? Some things one is sure of, yet one is not so sure, but one is sure all the same.

When I have finished washing the dishes, Uncle still has not come.

Now I am alone, for Mother has just been called out again to deliver a baby. I am in the dark and I am thinking of Uncle. I am thinking of when it was Sunday, and we were visiting Bloemfontein, and Uncle had lifted me high up so that I sat on his shoulders, and he held my legs and we went through the streets of Batho Township. The morning was warm and blue with the sky. The streets were full of people, especially women carrying bibles and hymn books. Many women would stop us, saying to Uncle: 'Hello, Lovey! And he would say: 'Hello, my darlies!' And they would say: 'What's this little picture of you on your shoulders?' And he would say: 'This little picture on my shoulders is my *mshana*.' And they would say: 'Oai! What can you tell us? You've been hiding your child and then having a free ride on us!' And then they would say: 'You do look like your uncle. Look at those lips.' And Uncle would say: 'What's the use of looking at lips from a distance?' Then he would bend his knees, and I would be kissed so many times. And after kissing me, some would say: 'Oh, Lovey, how I miss you! How about a little loving?' And Uncle always said: 'Okay, darly, I'll come round sometime this week.' And they would say: 'I can't wait.' And he would say: 'All good things have to be waited for!'

Sometimes we would come across men who were sitting on benches close to the walls of their houses. They would be reading the *Golden City Post* or the *Sunday Times*. After greeting, Uncle would say: 'So what does the white man say today?' 'The usual thing,' they would say. 'So why keep on reading?' 'To make myself angrier and angrier!' And the men and Uncle would laugh. Then they would lift up a canned-fruit bottle with a brown liquid in it and offer it to Uncle. And Uncle would squat without putting me down, take the bottle, shake it and then drink. And soon Uncle would be smelling of sorghum.

And there was the man who was polishing his shoes. He spat at his shoes and then applied polish to them with a cloth. He kept on spitting and applying polish, spitting and applying polish. When he finished, his shoes were shining like a mirror, and Uncle was singing like a gramophone. And smelling of sorghum. And the smell was coming up to me on his shoulders.

And late in the afternoon we were walking back, and Uncle was running and jumping like a horse saying: *'Koqo koqo koqo koqo!'* And I would laugh.

He was stumbling all over the place. And he kept on saying: 'Sorry *mshana,* we'll be home soon.' And he was stumbling. Like many other men in the streets; with dogs barking at them. And I held on fast to his face. And he said: 'I can't see!' And my hands went down. And he said: 'Peace, peace, ease up, I can't breathe!' And I let his nose be and held on to his neck. And he said: 'Peace, peace, don't strangle me!' So I let his neck be and held on to his hair. But he said: 'Peace, peace, I'm being scalped!' Then I let his hair be and put my hands on his mouth. All along I was scared because he was not walking straight, and he stood still at intervals to get his balance. And he kept on mumbling, 'Mm mm mm mm mm mm mm!' But I held on fast to his mouth.

When we entered the yard, I saw my mother come out of the house, running towards us, my younger mothers behind her. Grandmother was looking from the kitchen window.

'Fancy,' mother was saying. 'Taking the child away for the whole day. Bring him down! Do you hear what I say? Bring him down!' And my younger mothers were shouting also: 'Poor thing, he must be famished!' And then they let loose a tirade upon Uncle.

Uncle knelt down and I jumped off. My feet were stiff. Mother took my hand. And one of my younger mothers kissed me, while another one was pushing in my stomach and feeling it. And while Uncle was kneeling Mother pushed him back and he fell on his back, and just lay there looking at the sky.

'So this is what you do to me,' he said. 'So this is what you do to me.' Mother dragged me towards the kitchen. Before I turned the corner I saw Uncle rising up like an old man. His hands and his feet were on the floor and he was like a cow getting up from the ground.

In the kitchen Grandmother put me on her lap and covered me with her hands and was moving to and fro and sideways saying: 'Child of my child. Child of my child.' Ever so softly. And my cheek was resting on her breast.

'Hurry with the food before he sleeps,' Mother said to my younger mothers. 'My child has no uncle. Hurry with the food before he sleeps.'

'Lovington!' Grandfather bellowed from the living room. He always sat there alone. 'I will not give up on you. Come here at once. And bring your Bible along!'

I fell asleep on Grandmother's lap long before the food came.

Uncle is not here. Let me sleep. Tomorrow will be Wednesday. Then it will be Thursday. Then it will be Friday. Then it will be . . . .

'Just because your uncle is here,' says Doksi, 'you don't care for us any more.'

'You will remember us when he is gone,' says Wanda. 'And when you do we are going to look away from you.'

'What have I done?' I ask.

'You'll see, just wait until he is gone.'

'You'll see.'

'My uncle says if a friend turns away from you when all is nice, you must start wondering if he is a friend, because when things become dangerous, will he be there?'

'I'm not turning away from you,' I say. 'You are turning away from me because you won't come into my house with me to see my uncle play.'

'I won't come in,' says Doksi.

'What's there to see?' asks Wanda. 'I'm going to play my uncle's penny whistle.'

We are standing at the gate of my home. It is after school. Uncle is playing the trumpet in the house and I want to go in to see him play. But what these two

are saying is not fair. I'm still their friend. But when
two people say one thing and you, alone, say another,
it begins to look as if they are right and you are
wrong. And when they are friends it is worse because
you want to be with them, because you are friends
with them, but at the same time you want to do what
you want to do. If I want to do what I want to do, I
should do it and still be friends; and if they want to
do what they want to do, they should go and do it,
and we shall meet tomorrow and still be friends.
When one friend wants to do this, and another friend
wants to do that, each should go ahead and do it.
It's not the end of the world. After all, friends
do most things together. But even though I feel
this way, I do not say so, for I would rather be
defiant.

I say instead: 'The trumpet is the king of sounds
and the penny whistle says "Hello sir" to it.'

'It depends,' says Wanda. 'When you want some
kind of sound, that sound is the king.'

'Nothing can beat the trumpet,' I say.

'Let's go, my friend,' Wanda says to Doksi. And he
puts his arm round Doksi's shoulders. Doksi does the
same to him and they walk away from me.

I shout at them: 'When the trumpet and the
penny whistle are playing together at the same time
which one do you hear, and which one do you not
hear?'

Doksi turns his head over their joined shoulders
and says: 'I'm going to play my brother's guitar!'

I'm surprised by Doksi since I have never heard of
this guitar before. He did not talk about it on Monday,
and did not talk about it on Tuesday, and did not talk
about it this morning. Nor has he ever talked about it
ever before. So where does this guitar come from? I

want to ask him. But I don't. He is friends with Wanda and they are walking away, their cases hanging from their free hands.

I am left wondering about Doksi. Sometimes he is with me, sometimes he is with Wanda. Perhaps if I want him to be on my side, I should get him first. Then he and I will be two, and Wanda will be one, and Wanda will be left wondering if *he* is wrong and *we* are right.

Doksi. He has no uncle, anyway.

They walk away. I want to be with them; but there is a trumpet in our house.

I walk into the house, and find that Uncle has someone with him, and I know this person immediately.

I know him because everybody knows him. Everyboy knows him because each time there is a school vacation, brother Mandla walks up and down the streets of the township carrying a megaphone and speaking into it, calling all small boys and girls to come to Charterston High School every morning from ten to twelve, to learn how to draw.

And there would be many small boys and girls walking with brother Mandla up and down the streets, calling all small boys and girls. And the numbers would swell at each and every street.

We loved to learn how to draw, but we also liked just to be at the high school. One day we were going to be students there, but drawing brought us there sooner. And we felt we were grown-ups somehow, and we would walk like the big students, and speak English. At first there would be many children learning how to draw, but as time went by there would be fewer and fewer until brother Mandla said: 'Now I have the chosen few!' Brother Mandla was always

there to teach how to draw Every day. During the
weekend before the schools re-opened there would be
an exhibition in the Charterston Community Hall.
And two days before the exhibition we would be
walking up and down the streets with brother Mandla
calling on all parents, brothers, and sisters to come to
the exhibition.

Uncle is playing his trumpet. Brother Mandla is
drawing at the table. Uncle has taken his shirt and
vest off, and they are hanging from each side of the
back of the chair closest to Uncle. Brother Mandla
has his shirt on but he is sweating and many parts of
the white shirt are wet. Uncle is sweating too. Brother
Mandla keeps looking at Uncle and then at the drawing
on the table. He looks and draws, looks and draws.
Uncle: the sweat on his face and body is like a river.
He keeps playing a note on the piano and then saying:
'Toh toh tah lah lah lah-ah-ah!' and then plays on the
trumpet. Then he looks at the music sheets on the
silver music stand and takes a pencil and rubs off
something, then turns the pencil round and writes on
the music sheets.

'Phew!' says Uncle. 'Improvising on this piece is
going to be very difficult.'

'Difficult?' says brother Mandla. 'I thought that
in improvisation you are free to play what you want.
Now stay in that position for a while.'

'Ah!' says Uncle. 'That's a misconception. You see,
I have put so many transitions in this song, that even
in the improvisation I need to be moving from scale
to scale and from rhythm to rhythm.'

'So?'

'You see, when you are improvising you are free.
Completely free. But I'm telling you, you've got to
learn to be free. You've got to struggle hard for that

freedom. You see, if I can give you this trumpet and say to you: play something, you'll soon tire of playing anything, because your playing will have no direction. Unlearned freedom frustrates; nothing elevating and lasting ever comes of it.'

I look at Uncle. He is looking at his music sheet intensely. Brother Mandla lights a cigarette. His fingers are black from the charcoal he is drawing with. His cigarette too is soon stained black. Then he rubs on the drawing with his thumb. They don't seem to have seen me. I look at Uncle again. When I left for school this morning, he was sleeping. I thought there was the smell of sorghum in the bedroom, but I was not sure.

It is quiet for a while, and I go nearer the table to see what brother Mandla is drawing. I am surprised because what he has drawn there is not Uncle as I had assumed. In the first place, the trumpet is too huge. The part that brings out the sound is so open that it is almost half the size of Uncle. And the rest of the trumpet is completely covered by Uncle's big hands and thick fingers. And Uncle's lips seem to have become part of the hands and seem to be swallowing the trumpet. And his blown up cheeks have become the whole face. And his eyes are a deep line across the cheeks. His nose is facing up as if when he breathes he will suck in everything. I don't see why brother Mandla keeps saying to Uncle: 'Just hold it there for a while!' because it's not Uncle he has drawn there. I want to say so. I'm not sure. But I say it.

'That's not Uncle!'

Only then do they notice me. Brother Mandla laughs. Uncle leans over towards the table and laughs also.

'I think I agree with my *mshana*,' says Uncle.

'But I'm telling you,' says brother Mandla. 'This is you!'

'*Mshana,* tell brother Mandla why this is not me.'

'Well, everything is so huge. It's not real.'

They laugh.

'But,' says brother Mandla, 'this is how you are when you play the trumpet. When you play you *are* exaggerated. You are bigger than what you normally are because you have become all those who are listening to you. This is the only way I can express it. We all go into you and swell you up as we cheer you and you take us all in, and you become stronger and stronger the more you play. And we all become powerfully one. I've heard you play, man. I've followed you to five cities. And when I saw you yesterday walking through the small streets of small Charterston, looking like you wanted to meet someone, I knew my ancestors were with me. They brought to me the man I have always wanted to meet, because he has always turned my drawings and sculptures into sound. My brother, art makes ordinary things extraordinary.' And brother Mandla is looking at his drawing all the time he is speaking, puffing all the while.

'Ja!' says Uncle, sitting down on the sofa near the window and spreading his arms along its back. The trumpet is in one hand while the other he occasionally uses as a fan. 'You know,' he says to brother Mandla. 'One never stops learning. I've read so many things and studied so many things, but I have never sat back to consider how my art relates to the other arts. I've learned so much from you, my brother, since yesterday. What are you doing in this small town?'

'Where should I be?'

'Well, for one thing, here you have fewer people to stimulate your mind, nothing much is happening.

And then, this being a small place, you can feel the
foul breath of those stupid Boers going down your
neck much more than you can in a big place like
Jo'burg.'

'Let me tell you something, my brother,' says
brother Mandla. 'I have lived in Johannesburg. That's
where we all run to when we do not have enough
excitement at home. It was good, I learnt many
things. I rose to win the Artist of Fame and Promise
Exhibition Prize. And there was the glare of newspapers and recognition in the street. And there were
the parties in white suburbs. But one night I just
walked out of one of those parties, leaving all the
noise behind me. And I walked all the way home to
Orlando East, getting there at four in the morning.
And I took out my tools and carved what I called
'The Hunchback'. I worked at it continuously for two
weeks. It was small; no more than ten by four inches
of marble. You see, I did not mind the glory. But
there was something missing: there was no history to
it. It was one of those things I had stumbled across by
chance. It did not consist of anything in me or in the
surroundings I live in day in and day out. I felt I was
an eagle that never learnt to fly and when eventually
it was taught how to, it was taught to fly like a butter-
fly. There was no tradition.

'That's how "The Hunchback" came about. It was
a man with a grotesque hunch on his back. But that
hunch was the lightest part of the sculpture. The man
was groaning, not under the weight of useless flesh
on his back, but under his drum of human skin, filled
with air. I could not stand it. That's what we all are
when we have given everything away to the white
man's cities. We groan so pathetically under the
emptiness of our minds. And there is nothing so grotes-

quely tragic as an empty tin that has only a small
grain of sand in it. It rings all the more horribly. Here,
in this little town, I do not have to pretend. I am
nothing, and that is where I begin, rather than from
an imagined somethingness. My mind can never rot
here because I've learnt to humble myself before
the people, beginning from the somethingness that
has always sustained them.'

'Ja!' exclaims Uncle, polishing his trumpet with a
handkerchief. 'Is that why you mix with the likes of
Nzule?'

'Oh, that one,' says brother Mandla. 'He is a tragic
reminder. The lost glory and the emptiness of the
present. I accept him, without becoming him.'

'Do I have much to fear from him?'

'Well, who knows? Who knows what he might do
when he gets to know? He might feel that you violated
a code of honour. I mean, there we were yesterday
night at the Stoneyard drinking and everybody
entertaining you. And then you trip him up and take
his feet from under him.'

'If he threatens me I'll have to find a way.'

I think I had better change my school uniform, and
then go out to play.

We are coming from school, my friends and I. As
we approach Mayaba Street,.we can see that Nzule is
standing at the corner. His arms are akimbo. He keeps
looking up towards us. Then he looks down towards
the Jew's store. Then he looks in the general direction
of my home. He keeps looking at his wrist-watch. He
crosses the street and comes back again, his arms still

akimbo. We pass him, keeping a safe distance.

After we have passed Nzule we don't talk. We had been talking very nicely, kicking things and chasing a girl or two down the street. But now we are quiet. We don't even talk about Nzule. Who wants to talk about Nzule? He might hear you. We part.

I turn the handle of my bedroom door. Nothing. I put my case down so that I can use both hands to turn the handle down. Nothing. The door is locked. This is funny. This door has never been locked before. I am surprised that it could ever be locked. Yet I am pleased somehow that it can be locked. But who has locked it? Only my mother's bedroom can be locked. Since father died, though, it has never been locked. I look at Mother's bedroom door. Its key is not there. Perhaps it is Uncle who has locked the door. But why should he?

It's so hot!

I put my case against the wall, close to the door, and go to the kitchen to drink water. As I'm drinking, I see a faint shadow pass, and from the corner of my eye I see a person going out of the kitchen door. It is Uncle. He passes next to the window before which I am standing, on his way to the toilet. Gosh, his fly is open and his belt is dangling before him like a snake. I think that if Uncle is going to be sleeping in the bedroom when he comes back from the toilet, and does not want to be disturbed while he is sleeping, I had better go and put my case inside before he locks the door again.

I open the door. It is dark in there, for the curtains have been drawn. But there is enough light. It is hot. And the dull light and the heat are just what would make one want to sleep and not wake up. And there is perfume. I have been in such dull, curtained heat

before, but I don't remember when. I know that I
had loved to feel the sweat all over my body, and that
the heat was uncomfortable yet pleasurable, and
Mother was close to me and was hot and I was hot
and the room was hot. The sun could not come in
because of the curtains but the room took as much
light as it wanted.

I put the case into the bedroom close to the door
alongside the wall. I am about to step back out of the
bedroom when I look at my bed, and there is a
person there. It is a woman. She is lying on her back,
her head resting on her hands on the pillow. Her eyes
are closed, and she is big. I am looking. I cannot go
away, although I want to and I have to, but I am
looking. She is so smooth. All over. So brown! It is
hot, the curtains are drawn, and she is brown. And
her breasts are lying there on her. The hair under her
armpits! She is lying there on my bed. And I have
never seen thighs. Never knew they could be so big.
The only time I have seen them, is when they were
drawn up against a tight skirt, and I would look and
look and concentrate, wondering how big they would
be if I really saw them. And the skirt was gone now,
and here were the thighs on my bed, and they are
strangely joined together by hair that's a triangle. She
is all so brown, all so moist, and I am looking. I've got
to go now. I've got to go. But I can't. My heart is
beating fast, and I am trembling, and I feel hot now,
very hot. I don't know what to do. Brown woman,
brown woman, you're on my bed! She raises one of
her legs and the triangle disappears from view and she
speaks, not opening her eyes:

'Are you back?' she says. 'I was thinking you were
never going to come back. And I would be stranded
in someone else's house.' She is smiling.

Slowly I close the door. I rush into the sitting room and close the door behind me. And I listen. Uncle passes. I hear the bedroom door open and then close. And I can hear the key turn. I am trembling and I am hot. I go out quietly to the kitchen. The upper part of the kitchen door that leads outside is open. I lean on the lower part and look at people and things outside. Nzule is still at the corner. He is looking towards my home, his arms still akimbo.

'What did you see?' Uncle asks in the dark; in our bedroom, after he has blown out the candle. 'What did you see?'

What can I say?

'What did you see?'

I saw Wanda. I saw Doksi.

'What did you see?'

At the eleven o'clock break today, Wanda and Doksi came to me with a group of boys and they were shouting and arguing, and when they got to me Wanda said: 'Tell them! Tell them your uncle is also a magician. Tell them!'

I told them.

'You see.' He looked at them. 'They didn't believe me. Tell them again.'

I told them again.

'Tell them your uncle and mine are great friends.'

I told them.

'Tell them your uncle is teaching me how to play the trumpet, every day. He says I am a born player.'

I told them.

'Tell them he says he will be my friend forever.'

I told them.

'Your uncle said me and him will be in the newspapers together, didn't he?'

I said that he did.

I just went on telling them as I was told to tell
them. I just went on agreeing to everything. Sometimes
you have to agree with the claims of your friends
because that is the best test of friendship. So I agreed
and agreed. And when I had agreed enough, Wanda
said:

'Okay now, my friend, let's go!' And he covered
me with his arm across my shoulders and led me
away. Suddenly he remembered something, stopped
and looked back, then said: 'Doksi, come, you too
are my friend.' Doksi came and Wanda covered him
with the other arm. And Wanda was in the middle,
leading us away. He said to cover him with our arms
and we did.

'What did you see? Look at the spirits travelling
along the wall. They want the truth, *mshana*. What
did you see?'

I look at the lights that keep coming and travelling
along the wall close to Uncle's bed. They travel along
that wall, and then turn at the corner where that wall
meets the wall along which is the door. The lights go
towards the door, but before they reach it, they disappear. Then more lights come. Sometimes there are
no lights for a long time. Then they come again.

'You see,' says Uncle. 'It's just like I said yesterday.
The spirits will visit us until you tell what you saw
this afternoon. Nobody can ever lie to them, because
spirits can never be deceived. What did you see?'

I saw the woman on my bed. I saw thighs. I saw
breasts. And there was sweat there where the breasts
parted, and sweat over the breasts. And there was sweat
going down her sides. Rivers. That's what I saw. And

I was hot. Oh brown woman, I wanted to do anything for you. You will be happy. That's what I saw. But I do not say this to Uncle.

'What did you see?'

I cannot tell you, Uncle. But I do not say this to him.

'What did you see?'

There are more lights on the wall. The spirits are looking at me. They say: 'Speak speak speak. What did you see?'

'What did you see?'

Oh big woman! Oh brown woman, moist. I saw you.

There are more lights travelling along the wall. Spirits . . . .

I became aware of those spirits yesterday night after I had entered the bedroom to sleep and I found Uncle, dressed strangely, sitting on the floor on a small mat that had many bright colours and designs on it. He wore clothes of shining cloth: black, green, and gold. He wore on his head a big cloth that had been turned into a hat, just like the hat Indians wear. And he was sitting on the mat just like Indians do.

'Sit there in your bed,' he said when I came in. Then he blew out the candle. And he began speaking in tongues. Then he said: 'Tell me what you desire. Anything.'

I thought for a while and then said: 'Many toys. A train set. Because I like to travel far.'

And Uncle spoke in tongues again. 'Bim sala bim!' is all I think I heard, because that's how we say Indians speak.

'No, you cannot have that. Look at the wall. Do you see the lights on that wall? Those are the spirits of our ancestors. They are visiting us. I have the power to call them and to speak to them. They say ask for other things.'

I looked at the wall. Spirits! They were there. Coming and going.

'I want a trumpet,' I said.

Uncle spoke again in a strange tongue.

'No!' he said. 'No. They say ask for something else.'

I thought, and then said I really did not know what I wanted.

'That is exactly what they are saying too. They say you really do not know what you want, and that is very dangerous for someone who is going to be a man. They say they know what you want, but that you are going to have to find it yourself. They say you have a good mind. They say it is a big mind that can take in many things. They say you have a good heart too. They say you must travel a lot. See the world. They say travel always renews a mind and a heart, so that they can take in more of the world. For the world is endless and the more of it you take in, the wiser you are. But you will be the wisest if you know that you cannot take in the whole of it. It is impossible. So you must travel. Know people. And the more new people you know the more you are likely to know what it is you want in this world. You cannot find what you want without people. You will find it with them and among them. And once you find it, it is no longer yours. It belongs to them among whom you found it. And you belong to them, and they belong to you.

'Every night you will see the spirits on the wall. I will tell them to visit you every night. Talk to them. Ask them anything. The more you see them, the nearer you will get to finding what you want.'

Then Uncle spoke in the strange language again. And then said: 'Go to sleep now.'

I crept into bed. I saw the spirits on the wall.

Haven't they always been there? I was not sure. It did
not matter, they were there now and they would be
there every night. They came and went, came and
went.

'What did you see?'

There is Gwendoline. She is sitting in the front desk
of the middle row. I am sitting at the third desk behind
her. She is sitting with a boy she does not like, and I
am sitting with a girl I do not like. We have told each
other often that we don't like the people we are sitting
with in class, and that we would have much preferred
to be sitting together since we were going to be together till the end of time. I can see Gwendoline's left
side. I can see the end of the little line where her lips
meet. I can see her high cheek bone. I can see where
her left eye ends, almost like the end of the lips. I can
see where her hair ends just below the top of her
neck: so neat, so well combed. I'm looking at Gwendoline and I feel a pain inside me. I don't know what
to do. Mistress Khumalo is talking about David and
the Philistines, but I really can't hear what she is
saying. I can see only Gwendoline, and can only feel
the pain inside of me. Gwendoline, oh Gwendoline, I
will no longer chase you down the street. No more.
That is how I feel this morning. Last year when we
met at night in the street, and you were going home
from the shops, and I was still on my way there, you
suddenly rushed at me, kissed me and ran away. I was
angry, and I said: 'Bitch! What did you do that for?'
while I groped for a stone in the dark. I did not find
one and you ran away. Gwendoline, let's meet again
in the dark. I will kiss you too. Let's meet. No more

chasing down the street. Let's go to a distant tree just outside the township, and sit in the shade and be green. And I will hold you, and we will talk about the future. Gwendoline, my room can be locked.

Doksi, Wanda and I are walking out of the school yard. School is out. There are many children who are merry and are shouting: '*Woza* week-end!' The week-end *has* come and I must meet Gwendoline and tell her that the week-end is here. I have a plan which I have been thinking of the whole day. I will give her the time and the place, and on Sunday afternoon we will walk away to a distant tree. I can see Wanda is uneasy for he is part of the plan. He would have to go to Twala's Store just across the street and buy some sweets, and then give one to Gwendoline and another to Mapula. He would have to; his tin had rolled away from the traffic island, and we had a pact. But Wanda is afraid. He had told Doksi that he had stolen the money to buy the sweets. But to me, he had said his uncle gave it to him from the goodness of his heart. Wanda is afraid to buy the sweets, and he is afraid of giving the sweets to Gwendoline and Mapula, and he is afraid of telling Gwendoline of the time and the place I am to go to with her to a distant tree. But we had a pact. And if Wanda did not follow the pact, we would tell; and everybody would laugh at him, and nobody would trust him. A pact is a pact.

I locate Gwendoline. She is standing at the corner across the street, just opposite Twala's Store. She is with her younger sister, Laurata. I try to show Wanda where Gwendoline is, but it is not easy for now I see her, now I don't. There are too many children going up and down like bees. While I'm trying to point Gwendoline out to Wanda, we hear the sound of a car hooting continuously. The car is coming fast up

Letsapa Street. Children are scattering out of the street. It is Ngwenya's taxi. He drives ever so fast. He is swinging his sjambok from the window with his right hand. As soon as the taxi has passed, the children run back into the street like flowing water coming together again after it has been disturbed. Every child likes running away from Ngwenya's taxi, and then coming back on to the street again after he has passed, and then waving fists at him. But right now I don't like it because I have lost Gwendoline.

Something else attracts our attention. There is a crowd of children and grown-ups just beyond Twala's Store. There is some excitement. As we get nearer we hear some children saying:

'There's going to be fire!'

'Nzule has run home to fetch his weapons!'

'Nzule's going to kill him!'

'And all he has are stones!'

'If I were this fellow I would run away!'

'What will he do with stones?'

'Nzule will bring him down to earth!'

'That's right, these famous people come here and think they can do whatever they like!'

Wanda, Doksi and I push our way through the crowd and there, in the centre, in a somewhat large clearing, is Uncle. There is a pile of stones next to him. And next to him is a woman. Oh, my God, it is that woman. The one who was on my bed. Only yesterday she was on my bed. Is it Uncle Nzule is going to be fighting? What for? Oh no, Uncle! I must go to Uncle and tell him there is not a chance. Not a chance in the world!

'If it were my uncle I would tell him there's no way,' says Doksi.

'Mine would fight back,' says Wanda.

'Tell him,' says Doksi. 'Tell him, please.'

Oh Uncle, I don't know what to do. There are all these people watching, and there is danger coming.

'Please tell him,' says Doksi. 'There is no chance. Tell him, please!' Doksi looks like he is beginning to cry.

'Mine would fight back,' says Wanda.

Then the crowd around Uncle moves away from him somewhat, as it's done in the films when there is about to be a shooting. And it's because they want to see Nzule who is now coming out of Mbatha Street into Letsapa Street. At the corner of the two streets he stops to dance. He is singing. He has got a cowhide shield in his left hand, and a knobkerrie in his right hand. The crowd is cheering him. He stamps his feet on the ground like a horse and scrapes the soil back like a bull. Then he springs forward as if to charge. A woman comes out of the house on the corner. She stands by the gate and shouts at Nzule:

'You troublemaker! Take your fights away from here! It's always you! What's special about this corner? What's special about this house of mine? You always have to come and fight in this area, putting the fright into all of us. Away, mule, away!' She waves her fists at him, but does not come out of her yard. People laugh, for Nzule is not paying any attention to her. He just keeps on stamping, scraping and charging. Nzule is invincible with those weapons of his. Then he moves forward towards Uncle.

There is excitement now. Nzule is standing about ten yards away from Uncle. Some little boys are jumping into the air with excitement. There are some teachers also in the crowd, for school has just come out. Uncle and Nzule are facing each other and the big woman is holding Uncle's left arm with both hands.

'You shamed me!' shouts Nzule at Uncle. 'You

shamed me, and you will pay for it. As for you, shameless woman, now is the time. Choose! But make the wrong choice, and you are in it with him.'

'It doesn't have to be this way,' says Uncle.

'What other way is there?'

'Just turn around and walk away.'

'Turn around and walk away,' he says. 'It's all very nice for you. I struggled so much to get this girl. Even teachers have been wanting her. But she chose me. When am I going to get a high school girl again? And then you come and spoil everything in one night. And then you say: "Turn around and walk away." It's my knobkerrie that wants to walk away with you.'

Many people in the crowd laugh. Uncle shrugs his shoulders. He says something to the big woman, and she moves away from him. Now there is Uncle and Nzule facing each other. Anytime now there is going to be fire. I don't know what to do. But I know that it will be a disgrace if Uncle loses. What will the trumpet matter then? What will my friends think of me?

Uncle picks up a stone from his pile. Nzule laughs. Uncle suddenly makes as if to throw the stone and the laugh disappears from Nzule's face as quickly as it had come, and he raises his shield to cover himself. But Uncle does not throw the stone. And that is a mistake because Nzule charges as he raises his shield. I want to look away because soon it will be over, but I don't. Nzule is almost upon Uncle, and the distance between them is too close for Uncle to throw the stone effectively. Oh no, Uncle spins round on his foot and runs. The crowd parts before him, and Nzule is right behind lunging and missing, lunging and missing as Uncle picks up speed. The people are laughing. How can they?

'David is running!' children are chanting. 'And Goliath is upon him.' According to the syllabus, every Standard Four class is learning about David and the Philistines in the Scripture lesson. But I knew that David would run. Most of the people are laughing. How could they enjoy this?

Uncle is running up towards Mbele's Store in the direction that Ngwenya's taxi took. He is moving away from Nzule with each stride. He must run. He will rather run and be a coward than be hit. But I am not sure. Perhaps it would have been better to fight. Uncle soon reaches the Domestic Science school which is about one hundred and twenty yards away from Twala's store. Nzule is about twenty-five yards behind him. Uncle keeps looking back over his shoulder. Strange, he seems to be smiling! Everybody is running behind them. The whole township seems to be there. And the whole township is laughing.

At the end of the divided street, very close to Twala's Store, Uncle turns left and runs across the street towards the Domestic Science school. Then suddenly he increases his speed as he turns left again. Now he is going back in the opposite direction. And Nzule is running towards him, trying to cut him off. Uncle is running along the fence of the Domestic Science school. Nzule is going to intercept him. Uncle makes as if to throw the stone again. But he does not throw it. Nzule slows down to cover his face with the shield, but again no stone is coming and he accelerates to meet Uncle. They are about to meet. Uncle is running fast, and Nzule is running fast. Nzule lifts his knobkerrie. He lunges! Oh, Uncle! But Uncle crouches, and the knobkerrie lands on a fence and there is a noise like a golf ball being hit, only this noise is harder. There is a shout in the crowd, and everybody is running down again. Uncle turns right and is running across the basketball field towards the passage between the tennis courts and our school. I do not follow them. I run down along Letsapa Street. By the time I reach the corner, Uncle has already reappeared and is running up Twala Street towards Twala's Store again. Nzule is far behind now. And Uncle is running towards his pile of stones.

Where is Doksi? Where is Wanda? I have lost them. There is so much running around. People have become bees, and there is jubilation. The sky is raining with people's laughter. And Uncle has now got to his pile of stones. This time Uncle lets his stone go, and as it hits Nzule's shield, he has already picked up another stone and it is so fast it goes voong-ng-ng! as it flies through the air. It hits Nzule's shield. Nzule stops. And as he stops, another stone is coming and he jumps away from it in time. Nzule is breathing hard now. And when I look at Uncle again I see that he is no longer alone. Doksi is next to him! And he is also picking up a stone and Uncle is telling him to get away, and pushing him away with the other hand. But Uncle cannot keep Doksi away because Nzule is coming nearer. Uncle throws a stone; and Doksi throws a stone. There are tears in Doksi's eyes. Nzule has more stones to face now and he is beginning to step backwards a little. I am running now towards Uncle and Doksi, and I get there at the same time as Wanda. Nzule has many more stones to face now. We are moving towards him. And the crowd is laughing. Let them laugh. Their laughter sounds different when one is fighting. It makes one want to throw more stones. Then Nzule turns to run, and now Uncle is behind him. And there is once again jubilation. Now there are more stones being flung at Nzule; there are countless children throwing stones now. And Nzule has put his shield in such a way that it is protecting the back of his head, and he is running in the same direction in which he had been chasing Uncle. He is running wildly and does not see that there is a car coming towards him. The car is hooting. It is a taxi. Nzule does not see it because he keeps looking back to avoid stones. When he does see the taxi it is almost upon him. He dives to the side of the street like soldiers do in films when a grenade has been thrown at them. Just in time. The taxi goes on towards the children. We scatter like chickens. And Uncle is shouting: 'Who is that shit of a driver? Who is that shit of a driver?' But we are not interested in the taxi. We know it is Ngwenya; we enjoy scattering before him. We just wave our fists behind him as if we are angry. And when we turn to Nzule again, he is far away. He turns right into Bantu-Batho Street and disappears behind the Domestic Science school.

I feel sorry for Nzule. I feel like crying. I really feel like crying. He is no hero anymore. He had run away from the policemen. Now he is running away from stones. I did not like the way he looked when he was running away. Oh Nzule, I want to be friends with you. I want you to come to my home, and I will go to your home, and we will do many things together. Nzule, you are still invincible. I will tell any visitor from the big cities that you are the one. You are the best. The terror of Charterston. Our own terror.

'Fancy!' Mother shouts. 'Just fancy a big man like you. A whole grown-up fighting in the streets. Where is your self-respect?'

Uncle does not answer. He eats his supper quietly.

'Just fancy! What a disgrace! Today I asked for a special day's leave from the clinic so that I can spend this Friday, the whole of it, with my brother. And what does he do? He gets up as if he was in an hotel and disappears. Look!' Mother gets up from the table and opens the canopy of the stove. 'Look! Here is your lunch. Here is my day's good cooking. I thought I would sit the whole day with my child's uncle and talk and be happy. And what's my reward? Disgrace. What will the people say? It's the brother of the nurse, they must be saying. And what example were you being to this *mshana* of yours?'

'*Sisi,*' says Uncle 'What was done had to be done.'

'You mean I had to be disgraced? Fancy!'

I am thinking that it was not right. It was not right what Uncle did to Nzule. And I am wondering where he is now. I am wondering what he will do to us when Uncle is gone. It was not right. But I don't say anything.

'Well,' says Uncle. 'Just come to think of it, a little disgrace once in a while is in order. Or else you'll forget what disgrace is like. That's how you learn to keep your name respected. By being disgraced somewhat. You must be tested all the time.' Uncle puts food into his mouth and licks his fingers.

'Listen to him,' says Mother. 'What does he know about respect? This child of yesterday. I changed his nappies, and he is teaching me about respect. Let me ask you: what's the use of being in the papers if you cannot maintain self-respect? What do you know about respect?'

'As for my *mshana,* he learnt a lot. I taught him that in this world one has to fight sometimes, and that when one does fight one must do it very well.

'Did you see, *mshana?* Did you see how a man who

thinks too much of himself is a defeated man? He was too sure of his superiority. Did you see? When he came round that corner dancing and impressing people, I knew he was a defeated man. Study your enemy, *mshana*, and know him well. Self-righteousness and the feeling of superiority are the weakness of the powerful. If you know that, you can defeat them with the simplest of things.'

'Don't say such things to the child.'

'He's a man.'

I'm fingering my food and mixing *papa* with some meat and gravy. I am not looking at Uncle as he talks to me. Why does he look at me? Why address me? He should be looking at Mother. I cannot look at him. Mother will think I am listening to him. She'll think I am not respecting her; that I am taking sides. We are quiet for a while.

'Eat quickly,' says Mother to me. 'And then wash the dishes.'

'I will help you, *mshana*,' says Uncle.

'You will do no such thing,' says Mother. 'I am living with this child and he should learn to carry his own responsibilities.'

'And after helping you with the dishes we are going to clean up our bedroom and then have a good bath afterwards.'

'At nine? So late at night?'

'The room must be clean, and we must be clean.'

'Surely it could wait for tomorrow. At nine? At night?'

'At any time of the night!'

'That boy must be tired. He must go to bed now!'

'He's a man.'

'That there is my son!'

'O-o-o! When I am here, I have complete responsibility over him.'

'Since when have you been so responsible?'

'Even if you changed my nappies once, I am that boy's uncle.'

'Oh, you!' exclaims Mother putting a bottle in front of Uncle. 'Here's some honey, I know you've always liked it. See, it's still in the honeycomb. Got it from the priest's wife yesterday.'

'Do you remember when I disappeared with him for a whole Sunday?'

'Only a fool could remind me of that day,' says Mother as she leaves the kitchen carrying her cup of tea. She is smiling.

Uncle winks at me.

I'm in my small bathtub, and Uncle is in his big one. The water is fine, and the sides of the metal tub are no longer very hot. I can hold on to the sides now. I feel very relaxed, for Uncle has said he and I are men. When he took off his trousers a few minutes ago and was completely naked, I was very embarrassed. I looked at him all over except down there. My eyes just could not look down there.

'Now, now, now, *mshana*,' Uncle said. 'Come here and stand opposite me. Come on, don't be afraid. Now look!'

I looked at his eyes.

'Look!'

I looked at his feet.

'Come on now, look!'

And I looked. And saw. I started laughing. I don't know why, but I just laughed. Then Uncle laughed too. And we laughed very much.

'We are men,' said Uncle afterwards. 'Now jump into your bath.'

I have just got into the bath and I feel happy. I am just splashing water lightly over my body. Uncle is doing the same. In fact I am doing what Uncle is doing. But I look at him out of the corner of my eye before I do what he is doing. I have a question in my mind.

'Uncle,' I say. 'Supposing he had found you at a place without stones?'

'A good question,' he says. '*Mshana,* God's world has so much in it, but we have lost the ability to live by it. Let me tell you something. Remember the king of the Basotho, King Moshoeshoe? Remember how he defeated the Boers by rolling rocks at them from the top of the mountain of Thaba Bosiu? Their guns, their cannons, were nothing compared to the terrible descent of rocks. You must know that mountain all your life. It is the fortress of the greatest wisdom: living with the Earth. Now, supposing King Moshoeshoe lived in the desert with his people, what do you think he could have done, with the Boers just one sand dune away? Who knows? But I believe he could have found a way of raising a sandstorm. The Boers wouldn't have been able to see. Their guns would have jammed with sand, and their lungs would have been full of sand. They would have been falling and falling, and the vultures would have been circling high up in the sky ready to eat up Boer soldiers killed by sand. So you see *mshana,* I could easily have blinded the fellow with sand. You see, for him everything was in his weapons. *Mshana,* the simple is always decisively surprising.'

'Uncle, tell me a story.'

'No, not now, *mshana.* Not until we are clean. We

must get on now and wash ourselves.'

But I am full of things to say, full of questions to ask, yet I am not sure what those things are, and what the questions are.

'Uncle,' I say. 'Where is your band?'

'Oh, those? I left them in Johannesburg.'

'Won't they go without you?'

'That would be the day! Know what I said to them? I said: "Gents, I'm going to Nigel to see my *mshana*, wait until I return. My *mshana* comes first." '

I smile.

Then Uncle quickly leans across the space between our tubs, puts his hand round my neck and pulls me towards him. I lose my balance and splash water. But Uncle does not care. Soon I feel the hot breath of his mouth against my ear and then pain.

'Echooo-oo!' I scream.

'Ah!' says Uncle, releasing me. 'That was a fine tasty ear.'

'Uncle, why do you like to bite my ear?'

'Because you are the only *mshana* I've got. And I said to my band: "I'm going to see my *mshana*." They were surprised. And I said: "Always call on your relatives when they are nearby. You are not alone in this world. Everywhere you go, your people will take care of you." Now let's wash before the next question.'

I want to ask about the big woman. I have many questions. I want to know why I felt so hot when I saw her. I want to know exactly what she was doing there on my bed. But I should not ask, I suppose. Even if it is so nice now, I suppose I should not ask.

'Now listen,' says Uncle. 'We have been talking too much. Our business now is to clean ourselves. Listen carefully. What we are going to be doing now you should learn to do every Friday night to the end of

your life. This is the washing away of the week. You
have been accumulating all kinds of things during the
week, both clean things and dirty things. But you
never know what is really dirty and what is really
clean when you are accumulating them. This is the
time to wash away the dirt and to keep what's useful.

'The head, *mshana*. That is the dirtiest part, for the
mind takes in everything it comes across. And it is hard
to wash away things that are in the mind. That is why
the washing away of the dirt of the week must be
done every Friday. Every Friday you wash away a
little bit, wash away a little bit until the end of your
life. Perfect cleanliness is what you can't do without
in the world, *mshana*. Now watch and follow me.'

We wash the head and the face three times. Then
the body twice, and the legs and the feet three times.
Then Uncle puts on his gown to throw the water out.
He comes back and wraps me up with a clean white
sheet. Then he takes off his gown and wraps himself
up with a clean white sheet too. And we sit down on
the mat facing each other. I sit like Uncle, with my
feet together and my hands resting on my knees, which
I try to keep on the floor just like Uncle's. Uncle
leans over towards his bed and takes out two books
from under his pillow. The candle is on the floor
between us.

'Now we are cleaning the soul,' Uncle says. 'Let's
be silent for a while and think of all the things we
have done this week.' Uncle puts the two books
before him on the floor and closes his eyes. I close
my eyes. Wanda had said that one should never close
one's eyes in the presence of someone else for one
never knows what that person can do to you. He said
that's what his uncle had said. We had agreed with
Wanda, Doksi and I. Wanda had said the world was

tough and we had nothing to trust but ourselves. But Doksi had a question, and he asked Mistress Khumalo during the Scripture lesson, why it is that people have to close their eyes in church when they pray. Mistress had said we can only see God when we have closed our eyes. And we can only know ourselves when we have closed our eyes, and that closing one's eyes in church is also an act of trust. If you close your eyes you can be at the mercy of those who have not closed their eyes, so we all trust each other to close our eyes, and our lives are in one another's hands.

Where is Uncle? Is he still in front of me? I trust him. But I cannot see him. I don't know whether he is there where he was when I last saw him with my eyes open. I know that he is there. I cannot prove it, neither can I disprove it. But he is there. I'm sure. I can see only the orange light of the candle. Or is it yellow light? It is one or the other. Or it is both. Strange, I can see even with my eyes closed. Do eyes ever close then? It can't be. Even when I'm asleep? What is it that sleeps then? It must be the mind that sleeps, and the eyes just stay open even with the eyelids over them because these eyelids cannot shut out the light of the candle. Where is God? Is He the light? For that is all I can see with my eyes closed. But the light is from the candle. Unless God is everything that makes one see, God must be light because the spirits on the wall are light. No. Candlelight is candlelight. I don't know.

'Look here, *mshana*,' says Uncle with a hissing voice.

I open my eyes and the first thing I see is Uncle's shadow dancing behind him on the wall. Then I can see that Uncle is holding a book in one of his hands and the book is held very close to the candlelight. Light makes one see clearly.

'*Mshana,* look at this book. Can you read it?'

I look. It has funny handwriting. It's like short lines drawn across the page with dots at the end of each line. Some lines are straight, others are curved.

'Is this a book?' I ask.

'Of course it is.'

'It can't be.'

'Why?'

'Because books are written with words that one can see.'

Uncle lightly coughs out a laugh. It is a laugh that is a strong hiss.

'Do you know what a dog is saying when it barks?'

I think. Then I shake my head.

'Do you know what a cow is saying when it says, "Moo!" and another one says, "Moo!" in reply?'

I shake my head.

'Do you wish to know?'

I cough a laugh like Uncle for I am not sure.

'I think it would be nice to know what a cow is saying, and what a dog is saying,'

'Sure,' says Uncle, 'it would be very nice to know. But we can never know because animals don't know how to write. We can only guess what they are saying, but we can never know for sure. But because we don't know, it does not mean that they are not saying anything. So when you see this book and find that you do not understand what is written in it, that does not mean that the book is not a book. It is a book. Only it is written in a different way. It is written in a different way because it is written in a different language. But unlike the case of animals, it is possible to learn another language, spoken by other people, if you really want to.

'Now what you see here is a language called Arabic.

This book was written a long time ago by a great scholar. A learned man. He wrote about the history of the world. He wrote it a long, long time ago. And we can still read this book today because he wrote it. And because he wrote it we can read about the great empires of Africa. Although they are no longer there now, we know that they were once there. And that is good because we know where we come from. So we can know where we are going. And we all have to rise up again in this world because we were all once a very great people. And we can only rise up again if we know. So we must always find time to know. Whether you go to school or you don't you must find time to know. Then you can never be deceived. Once you know you can never be deceived. But when you know, never deceive.

'Now know something about your uncle. Most of the time, *mshana*, people are what they are because of what they are born into. So you see, when your uncle was young, he used to travel with your grandfather because your grandfather is a priest. A priest of the Presbyterian Church. So we used to travel by train, by bus, by car, by bicycle, and sometimes we would walk long distances. And I was carrying things for your grandfather and helping him to set up the altar wherever he was to preach. And why did your grandfather do all this travelling and haul me along too? He believed he had something important to give to the people. You should have heard him preach, *mshana*, with that huge growling voice of his. If he was an animal he would have been a lion, your grandfather. And those eyes of his would be blazing, and the people shouting 'Amen!' throughout the service. Mhm? He believed he was giving them something that would make their lives meaningful. He was giving

them the Christian God; he was giving them the story
of Jesus. Mhm? The miracle of His birth, the prophetic
justice of His death, and the miraculous redemption
of His resurrection. And after every service he would
whisper into my ear: 'After me, you will be.' I loved
to see the people moved. I envied your grandfather
for the power of his voice and the strength of his
conviction. Young as I was.

'So even when I grew up, when the fascination of
his words vanished for me, when the plans that he
had for me became an unbearable prison, and I re-
belled; even when my rebellion took me to the bottom
of life; even when I was finally rejected by him and
he had given up hope, I never lost the inspiration of
his zeal. I never lost the urge to find meaning.

'But what had he given to the people all those years,
mshana? Nothing beyond what he also gave me; the
flame of his life. We would be inspired by him, but
not convinced. His message did not reverberate with
the strength of our experience. He skirted our lives
like a train avoiding another train at a siding. There
would be echoes from one train to the other, but
they were still separate trains. Prayer must fill us with
the zeal to change the quality of our lives in every
respect. If it does not do that it is a waste of time.
And this means that prayer must deal with our lives
and hammer home to us the need to go out there and
smash everything for change. And if God does not ask
us to do that He is not our God.

'*Mshana,* I have what he never had, your grandfather.
I have always been close to people. And when I rebell-
ed I was with them even more. Yet just at the time
when they too were about to destroy me I disappeared. A voice told me I now had everything, yet
still had absolutely nothing. And I knew without

knowing how I came to know, that no matter how much energy of life there is in you, if that life is unreflective then it is merely a bundle of life without any aim, without any direction. It is a bundle of life that still has no place in the history of the world. I had to find time to know.

'I did find time to know in the vibrant world of Fordsburg, in Johannesburg. And for five years I accumulated knowledge in the home of an Indian Moslem who taught me how to read Arabic. And I have since found more than he, because he too like your grandfather was trapped: trapped in his religion.

'Look at this. Here is another language I am learning.'

I look and I see that Uncle is showing me the second book. I can see that the writing is different from the other one, but it is still strange. I can see birds; I can see animals; I can see drawings of people sitting; I can see snakes, and many other things I cannot recognise.

'This,' says Uncle, 'is the Egyptian language. In this language, *mshana,* is written all the ancient wisdom of Africa. Know that. From Egypt we gave our glory to the world. Now it is time that we got it back. I am learning this language so that I can find more by myself. There must be no-one between myself and this wisdom. The coming glory should be mine. It should be ours, *mshana,* and all that will be in the way of our glory must be smashed. So it is always good to know why you smash something before you smash it. We will smash things in our way because they are in our way, and we know where we are going, and we have to get there because we *want* to get there. I found my music too, and I try to smash things with it. And as the music smashes something, it builds something else.

'*Mshana,* history will always clean your soul, and knowledge will enter it when it's clean, and settle forever.'

Suddenly Uncle blows out the candle and in this sudden night of darkness I hear the curtain rings screech on the curtain rod. Moonlight comes in, in blue or in shining gray, and a dark figure descends just in front of me, and the whiteness of Uncle's sheet emerges from the moonlight. And he says:

'*Mshana,* are you clean?'

'Yes Uncle, I am clean.'

'Do you feel clean?'

'I feel clean, Uncle.'

'One of the most awe-inspiring things in the world, the most destructive and yet the most creative in its promise of newness — because that's how the world must have come about, *mshana* — is the volcano. Do you know a volcano?'

'Yes,' I say. And that is true because the *Student's Companion* had taught me that. So did the book of animals and the world and people and fish, which Father bought me when I was very young. I too have books.

'Yes,' says Uncle, 'it gathers force over a long period of time, and when there is too much of it, the volcano shoots it out with such violence that millions and millions of tons of earth are moved. The greatness of the earth!

'Think of a volcano, and think of the history of peoples; of the transitions, the upheavals that come and go, for they are bound to come, and they are bound to go. Think of it. Close your eyes and think of it . . . .

'Say volcano.'

I say volcano.

'Say volcano.'

I say volcano.

Then we say 'volcano' for a long time until there is a heaviness behind my eyes and a pain in my throat. I am tired. But I try to say 'volcano' as long as I can. I'm not sure now whether I'm saying 'volcano' or not. But I'm sure of Uncle's voice. His voice is a distant rumble now. I just hear a distant rumble. It is a rumble upon a rumble. There is rumble upon rumble in my head. And soon I see a sky full of aeroplanes and jets spinning and diving menacingly over the township. The people in the township are standing in the streets. They are standing still, not moving, caught in movement but still. Everything is still and the people's faces are frightened for the only things that can move are the jets in the sky. And there are many in the sky like hundreds of vultures. The planes are faster and the people are at their mercy and there is the look of fear in the eyes of the people.

Then all of a sudden, the people are moving, they are running all over. I am with them now although I don't know from where it was that I was looking at them before. We are moving now and we are a mass of people and we do not care where we are going. We see towns and factories on the way. We just go and go, not caring where we are going. But after we have passed a place there would be nothing left: no grass, no houses, no stone upon stone, no brick upon brick, nothing. Only the rivers can resist us for after we have passed a stream or a river it fills up again. Each time there is nothing behind us after there had been something before us, we shout with the voice of a throng. And there is thunder in the sky and the jets break into more and more pieces and we shout once more with the voice of a throng. And there is thunder in the sky and our voices are the sky and there is thunder and rain.

When I open my eyes I am in my bed. It is morning and the light of spring is coming in through the parted curtains. I don't know how I got into bed. Uncle is still on the floor sitting still. His lips are moving. He is whispering things I cannot understand or hear very well. Slowly he opens his eyes. Slowly he rises to his feet. Then he turns round to face the window and the morning coming in through it. And he raises his arms high before arching back so far that his spine looks like it may break. And when he is far back he starts saying: 'The light has come. The light has come. The light has come . . . .' He says this until he is standing still and his hands are hanging at his sides. Then he goes into bed. Soon he is breathing slowly and deeply. Today he does not snore.

I get up. And when I open the top part of the kitchen door and look out at the day I wonder why Uncle went to sleep when he should be getting up. For the world is beautiful. The morning is cool and the sun is just up there above the trees behind the clinic. It is green. It is blue. The world. It is also red from the roofs of houses. There are so many colours in the world. Perhaps Wanda was right about the sky being full of colours. And there are our neighbour's doves flying across the sky. The sound they make as they fly is like the sound you make when you bend a book somewhat, pressing its pages between your thumb and your pointing finger. And then you let your thumb let go of the pages one by one but very quickly. A kind of purring sound.

In the streets there is not a single dog. Dogs like to sleep at this time of the day, enjoying the rising morning sun after they have found a warm spot somewhere.

But some boys are already practising football moves in the streets. They have no work to do in the house for they have sisters. And there is no school today. People are slowly coming out of their houses. They are dressed beautifully, for they are going to town for some shopping, or to Springs, Benoni, Germiston, Johannesburg, to visit friends and relatives for the week-end. They walk so slowly for it is not to work that they have to be rushing.

In the distance on the road to town, when cars pass a certain spot, there is a blinding flash of light from their windscreens as the sun hits them. What a blinding flash! Coming and going so instantly. Coming and going like the spirits on the wall. The world is so wonderful!

Oh, what can I do for Mother?

It is Saturday evening. I am kneeling just in front of Mother. She has put her feet in a basin of hot water. She likes to do this because she walks a lot, delivering babies. I'm kneeling just in front of her, and I keep scooping up water with my hands and pouring it down her legs. She keeps warning me not to tickle her under her feet when she lifts them up and I have to massage them for a while before putting them back in the water. While I am busy soothing her legs Mother is knitting. She says she is making little socks for little feet, little mittens for little hands, and a little bonnet for a little head. She says they are for a baby that she delivered last week.

Uncle is sleeping. I only saw him once today. And I'm not happy with him. My spirits are low because of him. Perhaps Mother can see that; which is why she keeps saying: 'You don't look happy. You must tell me what's wrong with you.'

Whenever she asks this I concentrate all the more on her feet, or I look up at the ceiling, trying to avoid the question.

'It's me who's asking you, not the ceiling,' Mother says. I think it is better for me to tell her soon because once she decides that I'm not well she will not hesitate to take out a bottle of castor oil. And no matter how much I may protest she will maintain that it is impossible to pretend one is well when one is ill, for the illness will stand out like an ostrich hiding its head in the sand.

'It's Uncle,' I say.

'Uncle?' she exclaims. 'How can that be? There never was a nicer Uncle in all the world.' She looks at me with a smile on her face; the kind of smile that speaks. The kind that says: 'Oh, you foolish little darling.' She strokes my head briefly.

I hesitate. How can I complain to someone about her own brother? I think she can see that I'm uneasy because she says: 'Okay, then, let's hear what your horrible Uncle has done.' She is still smiling that smile, so I know that she does not believe Uncle is horrible.

'This morning when you went to town, you remember? You said I should stay at home and not go anywhere just in case Uncle gets up and wants something.' Mother keeps saying 'mhm! mhm! mhm!' each time I finish a sentence.

'But Uncle just slept on and on, and I thought he would never get up. So I got bored and went out to play football in the street. But as we were playing I heard Uncle's trumpet. We all heard the trumpet. So we all abandoned the game to go and see Uncle playing the trumpet.'

'Did he let you?' says Mother with sudden interest.
I look up at her. She is really interested. So since she
is interested I decide to enjoy telling her this story.

'Wait! Wait!' I shout, raising my hand at her as if to
stop her in her tracks. 'I will tell you in time.' But I'm
angry for I realise that I don't have many more details
to keep her in suspense.

'So we all ran home. By the time we got here we
were breathing hard and sweating. So I led them into
the dining-room. I opened the door, and there was
Uncle practising. But he stopped immediately and
looked at me with blazing eyes, and his uncombed
hair looked like it was standing up, ready to jump out
of his head. Then his lips began to tremble and I
could see that Uncle was angry.

' "Get out!" he roared at me, looking only at me and
not at the others. I looked back at him hoping he was
just joking. But he was not.

' "GET OUT! OUT!" he screamed.'

'What a terrible man!' said Mother, stroking my
head again. She had stopped knitting.

'I cried immediately. But Uncle had no mercy.

' "OUT!" he screamed for the last time. By the time I
closed the door I couldn't see him because my eyes
were full of tears. But the other boys were giggling.
They tried to squeeze out of the door at once, all
the while giggling. But I was crying. I felt so ashamed.
They ran out of the kitchen, out of the gate, and left
me alone.

'I walked out and leaned against the gate outside.
Then the music of the trumpet started again. I was
busy wiping tears off my eyes when brother Mandla
came.

' "What's the matter little man?" he asked.'

Mother laughed. I looked at her, and she pinched

my cheek.

' "Why are you crying?" asked brother Mandla. But I could not answer him. How could I? My heart was sore, and my spirits were low, for I had been let down by an uncle.'

Once more Mother chuckled a little and stroked my hair.

'Brother Mandla went into the house. A few seconds later the trumpet stopped playing. Then Uncle's voice cut through the air. This time he sounded very mad, like a dog that has a worm under its tongue.

' "GET OUT! Can't a man practise in peace?"

'After a while brother Mandla came out of the house. Unlike me when I was kicked out, brother Mandla was smiling. When he reached me at the gate he patted me on the shoulder and said: "Did you go in there?"

'I nodded.

' "Don't disturb him," said brother Mandla. He gave me a penny and walked away. And Uncle's trumpet kept on playing and playing and playing . . . .'

As I finish telling the story of my sadness I also finish soothing mother's feet with water, for the water has been growing cooler and cooler. I push the basin away and start drying Mother's feet with a towel. Mother takes the towel away, puts it under her feet. Then gently she rests my head on her lap and starts stroking my hair. Then she starts parting my hair and scratching and scratching; then moves on to another part of my head, blowing with her breath, parting the hair and scratching and scratching.

'Your uncle is just like your grandfather,' says Mother ever so softly. Her voice, her warm fingers, and the scratching make me feel like sleeping. There is a tickling sensation behind my neck.

'Every Saturday afternoon your grandfather used to lock himself in the sitting room. And none could enter there. And your grandmother would say to us; "Children, if you don't want trouble go and play far away; your father is thinking." When he was thinking, your grandfather did not want to be disturbed. Sometimes, when you do something that you really like, something important, you want to be alone. It's not that you do not love people any more, but because you want to prepare yourself to love them more and better. So you have to be alone. Your uncle then wanted to be alone so that he can make us better music. That's why Mandla was smiling; he understood what your uncle was doing.'

And as I am sinking further into sleep I embrace my mother around her waist, and I'm thinking that Uncle and I were alone last night, and it was wonderful; and I wouldn't have wanted us to be disturbed.

'Up! Up! You two, get up! Sunday morning is shining!' It is Mother. She shakes me saying: 'The roosters have long, long been up!' Then she crosses the floor and shakes Uncle saying: 'Shame on you. Up! Up!' She parts the curtains. The sun comes in. There is no way we can sleep now.

'Why so early, *Sisi?*' asks Uncle.

'The service begins in an hour and a half,' says Mother.

'But surely you know I don't go to church.'

'Oh yes, you have to, child of my mother. You have come to a praying woman's house. Besides, I told the priest's wife I'd be bringing you along to meet them. So let's not get into an argument over this.' Then mother leaves our bedroom saying there is enough hot water in the big pot for both of us to wash, and wash quickly.

I have to get up and wash quickly because I am the cross-bearer in church. Father Zama, the priest, always wrings our ears when we are late. I don't like him very much. He will sometimes give a boy a slap across the face right in the middle of a service should a boy lose concentration, no matter how slightly. And Michael too, the head server. I hate him for he too will slap a boy across the face. The congregation nods whenever that happens because a server has to be exemplary. He has to stay awake and concentrate.

I look at Uncle across at the other bed. He smiles at me. Deep down in me I don't want to smile on account of his behaviour towards me yesterday. But since I understand, I smile. I'm glad because I'm thinking it is good to understand, because then one can do the right thing. If I did not understand I would just go on and be angry. And Uncle and I would go on being angry forever.

As we leave the gate uncle puts his arm around me and says: 'Well, *mshana,* sometimes we have to sacrifice ourselves to the desires of loved ones.'

'Let's be hurrying now,' says Mother.

We hurry. I am carrying under my arm my red cassock and my white surplice. Mother is carrying her Bible and hymn book. Uncle had refused to take Father's hymn book. In the streets there are many other people who are going to church. Everybody is well dressed. Church bells are ringing. But some people are not going to church. There are some people already playing dice under the big tree at the corner of Moshoeshoe and Letsapa Streets. There are groups of men just standing and talking. Others are reading newspapers. Many people look at us as we pass them. But they are really looking at Uncle.

'When are you going to play for us?' some ask.

'One of these days,' Uncle says. And everybody laughs.

Occasionally a woman would greet Mother who would ask: 'How is the child?'

'He has a little cough, but otherwise he is all right.'

'Keep him warm. I'll be coming to weigh him one of these days.' Then Mother turns towards Uncle and says: 'You know, since you came, the mothers have always asked me to name their children. When they ask me I say: "Let him be Lovington." ' They look at each other. Mother looks away and says: 'Let's hurry, it will not be long before the last bell rings.'

When we reach the church I leave Mother and Uncle because I have to go to the vestry to dress up. Many of the girls look at Uncle. They smile at him, and Uncle nods as he holds Mother's arm, leading her into the church.

It is Holy Communion and I am kneeling just next to the left side of the altar. Sometimes I look at the altar and fix my eyes on the lacing that's covering it. That lacing was made by Mother, and she crocheted **ALL SAINTS CHURCH** on it. Sometimes I look at the people coming up to the altar to receive the Body and the Blood of Our Lord. They are so meek. They clasp their hands near their chests, and when the Body comes they raise their heads slowly and part their lips slightly to let out their tongues on which the priest puts the Body. Then they close their mouths. They don't seem to be chewing, for Mother says the

Body just melts in one's mouth.

Mother Dineka is playing the church organ. She is so black. She is so kind when she sees me. She likes to say: 'Here is my man, here is the nurse's son.' And I always look at one of her protruding teeth. But in church she never knows me. She is playing the organ. Playing softly. She is pumping the organ with her feet and looking up at the ceiling, her eyes closed. And the music is coming out of her fingers. The church sings and, with a clear voice, Uncle sings too.

The priest is giving the Body and I can see that there are flies that keep buzzing around him. He has to wave them away with the hand that's holding the Body. But more flies come. And then, above the slow, low music of Communion I can hear a buzz. It is mixed with the music. Bees! Then some people kneeling before the altar to receive the Body and the Blood begin to duck. The men duck under their jackets. Some people are waving away frantically. Some men in the church start closing windows. There is no song now, but a growing roar of people. Some people are running towards the door. The bees are all over now. And all the people who have come to receive Our Lord are leaving without Him. I stand up because there are also some bees buzzing around me. The priest has put down the Lord on the altar and is covering his head with his big surplice. He is wearing trousers underneath. There is confusion now. People are screaming, mothers and fathers and children are running away. Brothers and sisters and children. Everybody wants to leave the church fast.

Uncle has got me. He has Mother in the other hand, and he is pushing through the crowd. Outside there are more bees and people are running away and each one has a few bees buzzing after him. Uncle has given his jacket to Mother to cover her head. I have lifted my surplice and Uncle is pulling us forward. We are not running but trying to move fast. We are following the people who are running up Mayaba Street towards home. Along the way are some men who are kicking a boy on the pavement. They are the church deacon and three warders.

'He is the one,' they keep saying as they kick the boy. 'He is the one who disturbed the priest's bees.' The boy is bleeding. But the men go on kicking him. They don't mind the bees that are buzzing around them. They are just kicking and the boy is asking for forgiveness. His face is bloody. The men kick him again and again.

'That's enough!' shouts Mother. 'Do you want to kill him?'

But the men go on kicking the boy.

'Do something,' Mother says to Uncle.

I can see Uncle is not sure what to do. He keeps looking at the men kicking and then at the street with people running. And I can see that Uncle is looking at a car that is coming fast along the street against the people who are running. They are jumping on to the pavement. Uncle pushes us to the pavement, but he does not leave the street, and he waves down the car. People are screaming as they look at him standing in the road and the taxi coming fast. But it screeches to a stop very close to him. Uncle opens the door and says to us: 'Come in quick.' And Mother keeps saying: 'Save the boy.' But Uncle is pushing her in and Ngwenya is shouting that he wants to take off; he is losing time. Then Uncle cannot come in. People have opened the other doors and bundled themselves into the taxi. There is no room anymore. Ngwenya takes off and the force of the car springing forward forces the doors to close with a bang and the people who were trying to enter jump away from the car just in time.

Mother keeps saying: 'My brother, my brother, wait!' But Ngwenya will not wait. I try to look through the rear window to find Uncle. But it is not easy to see him. There are too many people in the street and there is much confusion. My neck becomes painful as I strain to look back. But when I finally see Uncle, I have only a brief glimpse of him pushing the church deacon away from the bleeding boy, while the other three men continue to kick and kick.

Soon Uncle is off my mind, for I'm thrilled. I realise that I'm thrilled. I'm in Ngwenya's taxi and people are scattering before us. So this is how it looks when we are scattering away before Ngwenya's taxi? We pass the church. We see the priest disappearing into his mission house. His wife is just behind him. And there are many other people behind her. I can see that there is some smoke next to the beehive. We drive past. Ngwenya is hooting and people are scattering before us.

When Uncle finally comes home, he finds us waiting for him at the dinner table.

As he comes in he says: 'And to think that I did not want to go to this church in the first place.'

Mother does not say anything.

'And then I get stung, and I almost get into a fight with *some men of God!* '

We are quiet. Uneasy.

'Okay then,' says Mother, 'the bees stung you, but you should have done something for that poor boy.'

'So that's it?' exclaims Uncle. 'Let me tell you something. There are too many problems in the world.'

As he talks he does not look at Mother who has accused him; he looks at me who has not accused him.

'There are too many problems in the world,' says Uncle. 'And one has to choose which ones it would be useful to be involved in. Besides, sometimes problems come to you when you least expect them, and then you are powerless and you don't know what to do. At least I got you into a taxi away from danger. You should be grateful for that. As for the boy, I could not do much for him. I tried though. I was just too confused.'

We are quiet for a while. Then Mother rises from her chair and approaches Uncle.

'Now,' she says, 'let's look for that sting. How many stung you?' Uncle does not answer. Mother begins to part his hair, blows, then searches trying to find a bee sting. Uncle closes his eyes. I'm thinking that he must be enjoying Mother's search for the bee sting. But I'm also thinking that I understand. I understand about the boy. But I'll not tell Uncle that I understand. I'm thinking there must remain a question in his mind.

I have been sleeping. Soon after lunch I went to sleep because I was drowsy. I left Uncle alone reading the Sunday paper. Mother had to go away in the middle of lunch to deliver a child somewhere. I have just been awakened by a great noise outside. There is a lot of music, many voices of people, and screams and laughter. I get up and rush out of the bedroom. It's all happening right in my home. Uncle has opened the front door and the front gate and is on the veranda playing his trumpet to the background of gramophone music. He has put the gramophone on the chair. The gramophone is playing, and Uncle is playing, and people are dancing in the street, and a few are in the yard dancing on our little lawn. They are mostly people of our neighbourhood. There are some I do not know. I am watching from the door. Then I walk out of the house and stand next to him. I know what I am going to do: I'm going to wind the gramophone for Uncle.

The song ends and Uncle says I should play the record again. As I am rewinding the gramophone Uncle raises his hands into the air and says: 'Welcome!' And there is a shout of applause from the crowd.

'Welcome!'

And there is another shout.

It is about four in the afternoon, but the people seem not to care about the sun. I am winding the gramophone. I am wondering what Mother will say if she comes now and finds Uncle playing her gramophone. She never allows me to play it except on special days. She says it was the first thing she bought after marrying Father. She says we must play the gramophone only when we remember him.

Then Uncle is not looking at the crowd anymore. He is looking beyond them at the wide open space spreading far out to the main road in the distance. It is the road that goes west to town and then to Johannesburg, or east to Balfour and then to Durban. There are three men walking fast across the field.

'Call those people!' Uncle shouts. 'Call those people. Get them here!'

And everybody is looking at the people Uncle is talking about. The three men are dressed the way miners dress. They are wearing big, baggy, multicoloured trousers, big boots, sleeveless vests, and their arms are full of bangles. One is playing a guitar, another is playing a concertina, and the third is playing a mouth organ. They are probably returning to the mines after a weekend in the township. They are walking at a very fast pace, and they are playing their instruments all the while. Then suddenly they stop and walk backwards for a while and then forward again. They are doing the *setapo* dance.

Everybody is shouting at them. They are turning now and are coming towards us. I start the record. And soon Uncle is playing the trumpet. He waits until the record has started and then plays along with it. And there is dancing again. The crowd is increasing. I am proud. I am proud that they have come to my home. When the miners reach us they do not stop their music; they play on. And there is the gramophone, there is the trumpet, there is the concertina, there is the guitar, there is the mouth organ, and there is the voice of people singing. People are sweating, the sun gleaming off their faces. And everybody is doing the *setapo* now.

Mother appears from the back of the house. She is in her white, starched uniform and is holding a suitcase full of medicines and bandages and needles. She looks and then shakes her head, and then walks away to disappear into the house. The song ends. It is time to rewind. Uncle gives me another record to play. Then he goes to the miners.

'Please sing with us,' he says.

They say their shift starts in about five hours' time and it takes them three hours of walking to get there in time.

'Never mind,' says Uncle. 'Here is another shift. We shall find a way to get you to work on time. Start a song.'

Uncle waits until they have started the song. He lets the song go for a while. He is listening. Concentrating. Then he puts his trumpet to his lips and blows. I put the record on. Uncle flags me down. But the record is on. I let it go. And soon there is the gramophone, the trumpet, the concertina, the guitar and the mouth organ. If only I could play the piano, I could have had it wheeled out of the house. And everybody is dancing. The crowd is big now. The whole township is here. Mother reappears carrying a tray with a huge jar full of cool drink. She must have made it from the many bottles of *Exa* in the house. There are many cups and glasses on the tray. She places the tray close to the gramophone and then pours the drink into the cups and the glasses. She is passing the drink around now. People pass the glasses along when they have finished and Mother moves around refilling glasses and cups.

Then there is the sound of cars hooting. They are coming round to pass close to my home. It is a wedding procession. The bride and the groom are in the front car and they are waving. They are wearing white gloves. There's waving in the other cars too. It is a long procession. And the paper ribbons decorating the cars are fluttering in the air. But the people dancing in the street do not move away. The cars are hooting. More than twelve of them. But the people do not move. The cars hoot. And there is the gramophone, the trumpet, the concertina, the guitar, the mouth organ, and the hooting cars. The cars have stopped now, for the people are dancing and will not make way for them.

Then the bride and groom are out of their car. And the bridesmaids and their escorts are out of their cars. They bring their heads together. When the heads part,

a wedding song has started. And there is the gramophone, the trumpet, the concertina, the guitar, the
mouth organ, the hooting cars, and the wedding
song. And the *setapo* dance is raising dust into the air.
And Mother is passing cool drink.

The sun is going down.

Oh, Uncle, everybody is here.

The Music of the Violin

Vukani was doing homework in his bedroom when voices in the living room slowly filtered into his mind. He lifted his head to look up, as if to focus his ears. No. He could not recognise the voices. Now and again the hum of conversation was punctuated with laughter. Then he grew apprehensive, the continuing conversation suddenly filling him with dread. He tried to concentrate on his work. 'Answer the following questions: How did the coming of the whites lead to the establishment of prosperity and peace among the various Bantu tribes?. . .' But the peace had gone from his mind. The questions had become a meaningless task. Instinctively he turned round to look at his music stand at the foot of his bed. Yesterday he had practised some Mozart. Then he saw the violin leaning against the wall next to the stand. Would they come to interrupt him? He felt certain they would. He stood up, thinking of a way to escape.

There was another peal of laughter from the living room, and Vukani wondered again who the visitors were. As he opened the door slowly he was met by another thunderous roar. Escape would be impossible. He had to go through the living room and would certainly be called by his mother to be introduced to the visitors, and then the usual agony would follow. A delicate clink of cups and saucers told Vukani the visitors had been served tea. Perhaps it was coffee. Most probably tea. Visitors generally preferred tea. Another roar. His father and the male visitor were laughing. He knew now that the visitors were a man and a woman, but he did not know them. Curious now, he opened the door another inch or so, and saw the woman visitor who sat close to where the passage to the bedrooms began. Vukani's mother, in her white nursing uniform, sat close to the woman in another heavily cushioned chair. They were separated by a coffee table.

'I couldn't make it at all to the meeting last Saturday,' said Vukani's mother.

'Which meeting, dearie?' asked the woman.

The men laughed again during their own conversation.

'Don't you laugh so loudly,' Vukani's mother shouted.

'You see,' Vukani's father was saying. 'I had caught the fellow by surprise, as I usually do.'

'That's the only way to ensure that the work gets done,' said the other man.

'Indeed,' agreed Vukani's father.

'So?' asked the other man.

'So I said: "Show me the students' garden plots." I saw a twitch of anguish cross his face. But he was a clever fellow, you see. He quickly recovered and said: "Of course sir, of course, come along." So we went. There was a wilderness around the school. These bush schools! I wouldn't have been surprised if a python had stopped us in our tracks. So, after about two hundred yards of walking and all the wilderness

around us, I began to wonder. So I say to this teacher:
"Mr Mabaso," — that was the fellow's name — "these
plots, they are quite far aren't they?" "We're just
about there, sir," he said.'

'Man alive!' exclaimed the other man. 'This story is
getting hot. Let me sip one more time.' There was
some silence while the man sipped his tea. Vukani's
mother also lifted her cup to her lips. The women
were now listening too.

'So,' continued Vukani's father, 'we walked another
two hundred yards and I turned to look at the man.
"We're just about there, sir." I only needed to look at
him and he would say: "We're just about there, sir." '

Everybody laughed. 'You see, the fellow was now
sweating like a horse.'

'So?' asked the woman visitor, laughing. She was
wiping her eyes with Kleenex.

'Then this fellow, Mabaso, shows me a hill about a
mile away and says: "We're going there to that hill,
sir, the plots are behind it. You see, sir, I figured that
since the wind normally hits the hill on the side we
are looking at now, I should have the plots on the
leeward side to protect the plants." What bosh!'

There was more laughter and the male visitor said,
in the middle of laughter: 'Beatrice give me some
Kleenex, please.' His wife stood up and disappeared
from Vukani's view. She returned soon. Vukani heard
a nose being blown.

'Please don't laugh, fellow Africans,' said Vukani's
father. 'The man is a genius. What's this poem by the
English poet? "The man blushes unseen in the wilderness." He knew I would not go any further. So I
really have no proof that there were no garden plots.'

'Of course there weren't any,' asserted Vukani's
mother.

'Of course there weren't,' everybody agreed.

'You school inspectors,' said the male visitor, 'have real problems with these bush schools.'

'You don't know, you!' agreed Vukani's father. 'We just can't get it into these teachers' heads that we have to uplift the Black nation. And we cannot do that through cheating and laziness. We will not develop self-reliance that way. That fellow was just not teaching the students gardening, and that is dead against government policy.' Vukani shut the door. In spite of himself he had been amused by the story. He went back to the desk and tried to continue with the homework. He could not. What about going out through the window? No. That would be taking things too far. He wondered where Teboho, his sister, was. Probably in her bedroom. Teboho and their mother were having too many heated exchanges these days. Their mother tended to make too many demands on them. Vukani wished he could go and talk to Teboho. They had grown very close. Then he suddenly became frantic again and went back to the door. He had to escape. When he opened the door, as slightly as before, it was the woman visitor who was talking.

'You just don't know what you missed, you,' she was saying. The men laughed again.

'Please, you men!' appealed Vukani's mother. But they laughed once again.

'Do you want us to leave you and go to the bedroom?' threatened Vukani's mother. 'And you know if we go in there we won't come out.'

'Peace! Peace!' said Vukani's father. 'Peace, women of Africa!' Then he lowered his voice as he continued to talk to the other man.

'Now, come on, what have I missed?' asked Vukani's mother eagerly.

'Well, you just don't know what you missed,' said Mrs Beatrice, pulling the bait away from the fish.

'Please don't play with my anxiety.'

'I want to do just that,' said Mrs Beatrice, clapping her hands once and sitting forward in her chair, her legs thrust underneath. She kept on pulling down her tight-fitting skirt over her big knees. But after each effort the skirt slipped back, revealing the knees again.

'You women are on again about the Housewives' League?' remarked Vukani's father, interrupting the women.

'Day in and day out,' said the other man, supporting Vukani's father.

'Of course yes!' said Mrs Beatrice with emphatic pride.

'Forget about these men,' pleaded Vukani's mother, 'and give me a pinch of the story.'

'Mother-of-Teboho, you really missed,' Mrs Beatrice started. 'A white woman came all the way from Emmarentia — high-class exclusive suburb, mind you — to address the meeting on Jewish recipes. Came all the way to Soweto for that. It was wonderful.'

'Was it not Mrs Kaplinsky?'

'As if you know!'

'Ha, woman! Please, give me! Give me!' begged Vukani's mother with great excitement, clapping her hands repeatedly. 'I'm fetching my pen, I'm fetching my pen. Give me those recipes.' But she did not leave to go and fetch her pen.

'I'm selling them, dearie. Business first, friendship after.' They laughed.

'Ei! Women and food . . . ' exclaimed the other man.

'What! We cook for you men,' retorted his wife.

'Exactly,' concurred Vukani's mother. 'More tea?'

'No thanks, dearie.'

'Hey you men, more tea?' But the men were already back to their conversation, and burst out laughing. Vukani's father answered while laughing, suddenly coming into Vukani's view as he brought his empty cup to the coffee table between the women. 'No thanks,' he was saying. 'No thanks . . . he he he hehe-heee . . . that was a good one . . . no thanks . . . what a good one.' Then he took out a handkerchief from the pocket of his trousers, wiped his eyes, wiped his whole face, and then wiped his lips. 'A jolly good evening, tonight,' he remarked. Then he went back to his chair, disappearing from Vukani's view.

'Thanks for the tea,' said the other man, blowing his nose.

'Teboho!' called Vukani's mother. 'Please come and clear up here!' Teboho appeared carrying a tray. She had on denim jeans and a loose blouse.

'That was a nice cup of tea, Teboho,' said the other man. Teboho smiled shyly.

'When are you going back to 'varsity?' he asked.

'We have six more weeks,' replied Teboho.

'You are lucky to have children who are educating themselves, dearie,' said Mrs Beatrice.

'Oh, well,' said Vukani's mother, shrugging her shoulders as Teboho disappeared into the kitchen. There was some silence.

'Sometimes these South African Jews sicken me,' said the other man reflectively.

'Why?' the two women asked.

'Well, they're hypocrites! I mean look, they say they were killed left and right by the Germans, but here they are, here, helping the Boers to sit on us.'

'How can you say such a thing?' asked his wife. 'People like Mrs Kaplinsky are very good friends of ours. Some of her best friends are Africans.'

'Because she gives you recipes?'

'Food, my dear husband, belongs to mankind, not just to one race.'

'Yes, exactly,' agreed Vukani's mother. 'Like art, literature and things. Completely universal.'

'Well! . . . ' said the man, but he did not pursue the matter further.

'In fact this reminds me,' said Vukani's mother with sudden enthusiasm, her eyes glittering. 'Instead of sitting here talking politics, we should be listening to some music. Have you heard my son play? He plays the violin. A most wonderful instrument!'

'Yes,' said Vukani's father, 'you know . . . .'

Vukani swiftly shut the door, shutting out the living room conversation with an abruptness that brought him sharply to himself as he moved to the centre of the room. He began to feel very lonely and noticed he was trembling. It was coming now. He looked at the history homework on the desk; then looked at the reading lamp with its circular light which seemed to be baking the open pages of the books on the desk with its intensity, so that the books looked as if they were waiting for that delicate moment when they would burst into flame.

Then he thought of Doksi, his friend. He wondered where he was and what he was doing at that moment. Friday evening? Probably watching his father cutting the late evening customers' hair and trimming it carefully while he murmured a song, as always. Doksi had said to Vukani one day that when he was a grown-up, he would like to be a barber like his father. Doksi seemed to love hair. Vukani remembered his favourite game: a weekly ritual of hair burning. Every Saturday afternoon Doksi would make a fire out in the yard and when it was burning steadily, toss knots of hair into it. The hair would catch fire with a crackling brilliance that always sent him into raptures of delight. He never seemed to mind the smell of the burning hair. One Saturday after his bonfire Doksi had said, while making the sign of the cross over the smoking fire: 'When God had finished burning hair He thought that it was good.' Vukani had playfully accused him of sacrilege. But Doksi, suddenly looking serious, had said: 'Dead things catch fire.'

Now, Vukani was suddenly fascinated by a desire to see the books on the desk aflame. Perhaps he should lower the lamp: bring it closer to the books. It was a silly idea, yet he lowered the lamp all the same. But the papers shone defiantly with a sheen. It was futile. Then he saw his violin again, and felt the sensation of fear deep in his breast.

He looked at the violin with dread, as something that could bring both pain and pleasure at once. It was like the red dress which Miss Yende, their class teacher in Standard Four, occasionally wore. She had once said to the class: 'When I wear this red dress, children, know that I will not stomach any nonsense that day. Know that I will expect sharp minds; I will expect quick responses to my questions; and I will expect absolute seriousness. And I shall use the stick with the vengeance of the God of the Old Testament.' That dress! It was a deep, rich, velvety red that gave the impression that the dress had a flowery fragrance. Yet, because it signalled the possibility of pain, it also had a dreadful repulsiveness.

Vukani tried to brace himself for the coming of the visitors. It was always like that. Every visitor was brought to his room, where he was required to be doing his school work or practising on the violin. Then he had to entertain these visitors with violin

music. It was always an agonising nuisance to be an
unwilling entertainer. What would happen if he
should refuse to play that night? He knew what his
mother would say. It was the same thing every time.
His eyes swept round the room. He was well provided
for. There was the beautiful desk on which he did his
work; bookshelves full of books, including a set of
Encyclopaedia Britannica; a reading lamp on the desk;
two comfortable easy chairs; a wardrobe full of clothes;
his own portable transistor radio; a violin and a music
stand; a chest full of games: Monopoly, chess and
many others. His mother never tired of telling him
how lucky he was. 'There is not a single boy in the
whole of Soweto — including here in Dube — who has
a room like yours. Can you count them for me?
Never! This room is as good as any white boy's. Isn't
it exactly like Ronnie Simpson's? You yourself, you
ungrateful boy, have seen that room when we visited
the Simpsons in Parktown North. Kaffir children!
That's what. Always ungrateful!'

What did all this really mean to him when it brought
so much pain? Vukani remembered what teacher
Maseko had said at assembly one morning: 'Children,
I would rather be a hungry dog that runs freely in the
streets, than a fat, chained dog burdened with itself
and the weight of the chain. Whenever the white man
tells you he has made you much better off than
Africans elsewhere on this continent, tell him he is
lying before God!' There were cheers that morning at
assembly, and the children had sung the hymn with a
feeling of energetic release:

> *I will make you fishers of men*
> *Fishers of men*
> *Fishers of men*

> *I will make you fishers of men*
> *If you follow me.*

Three weeks later teacher Maseko was fired. The
Principal made the announcement at morning assembly. He spoke in Afrikaans, always. Concluding the
announcement he said: 'Children, a wandering dog
that upsets garbage bins and ejects its dung all over
the place, is a very dangerous animal. It is a carrier of
disease and pestilence, and when you see it, pelt it
with stones. What should you do to it?'

'Pelt it with stones!' was the sombre response of
the assembled children that morning. Vukani wondered whether teacher Maseko was that dog. But how
could anybody pelt teacher Maseko with stones?

Vukani heard another roar of laughter from the
living room. But why did his mother have to show off
at his expense in this manner? That Friday, as on all
Mondays, Wednesdays and Fridays, he had carried his
violin to school. The other children at school just
never got used to it. It was a constant source of
wonder and ridicule. 'Here's a fellow with a strange
guitar!' some would say. Others would ask him to
play the current township hits. It was so every day.
Then one day his violin had disappeared from class
while he had gone out to the toilet. He was met with
stony faces when after school he pleaded for its
return. Everybody simply went home and there was
no sign of the violin. What would he say to his music
teacher in town? What would he say to his mother?
When he went out of the classroom he found Doksi
waiting for him. They always went home together,
except on the days when Vukani had to go to town
for his music lessons after school.

'Doksi,' he said. 'I can't find my violin. Somebody

took it.'

'These boys of shit!' Doksi cursed sympathetically. He had not waited for details. He knew his friend's problem. 'Do you suspect anybody?'

'I can't say,' replied Vukani. 'The whole class seems to have ganged up on me. There are some things that will always bring them together.'

'Even Gwendoline?' asked Doksi with a mischievous smirk on his face.

Gwendoline was the frail, brilliant, beautiful girl who vied with Vukani for first position in class. Vukani had always told Doksi that he would like to marry her one day. And Doksi would always say: 'With you it's talk, talk all the time. Why don't you just go to this girl and tell her you love her? Just look at how she looks at you. She is suffering, man!'

'Look,' said Vukani, 'this is no time for jokes. My violin is lost.'

'The trouble with you, Vukani, is that you are too soft. I would never stand this nonsense. I'd just face the whole class and say: "Whoever took my violin is a coward. Why doesn't he come out and fight?" I'm sure it was taken by one of those big boys whom everybody fears. Big bodies without minds! They ought to be working in town. Just at school to avoid paying tax. But me, they know me. They know what my brothers would do. My whole family would come here looking for the bastards.'

'Let's go and tell the principal,' suggested Vukani. The principal was one of those Vukani had entertained one day in his bedroom. 'But maybe we shouldn't,' said Vukani changing his mind.

'Let's go and find out from the girls sweeping your classroom,' suggested Doksi. They went back.

Most of the children had gone now. Only those

whose turn it was to clean the classrooms remained. The girls were singing loudly and the room was full of dust.

'Leave it to me,' said Doksi.

There were four girls in the classroom. Gwendoline and Manana were as old as Doksi and Vukani. The other two girls, Topsana and Sarah, were much older.

'Hey you girls,' shouted Doksi, squaring his shoulders and looking like a cowboy about to draw. 'Where is the bloody violin?' The bigger girls simply laughed.

'And who are you, toughie?' said Sarah, pushing a desk out of the way for Topsana to sweep.

'Hey you, Vukani,' called Topsana, 'I want to soothe your heart. I've long been waiting for this moment. Come and kiss me.' The smaller girls giggled and Vukani regretted that they had come back. 'I mean it,' said Topsana. 'I know who took your violin. It's safe. You'll find it at home. I made them promise to take it there. There now, I want my kiss. I want to kiss the inspector's son.'

Meanwhile, Doksi turned to the younger girls: 'Hey you, what is the joke? What's there to laugh at?'

'Hha!' protested Manana, sweeping rather purposefully. 'Laughing is laughing.'

'I can show you a thing or two,' Doksi said. 'Punch you up or something.'

'Doksi,' appealed Vukani. 'Please let's go.' Doksi clearly felt the need for retreat, but it had to be done with dignity. He addressed all the girls with a sweep of his hand: 'You are all useless. One of these days I'll get you. Come on, Vukani, let's go.'

The walk home for Vukani had been a long one. Better not to tell the parents. If Topsana had been telling the truth, then he should wait. Nobody asked about the violin that night. But he would never forget

the morning following that day, when his mother
stormed into his bedroom, black with anger. She
simply came in and pulled the blankets off him. Then
she glared at him, holding the violin in one of her
hands. Vukani had felt so exposed, as if his mother
would hit him with the violin. It was very early in the
morning. His mother was already dressed up in her
uniform, ready to go to work. If she was on day duty,
she had to leave very early for the hospital.

'Vukani!' she shouted. 'What desecration is this?
What ultimate act of ungratefulness is this? Is this to
spite me? Is this an insult? Tell me before I finish you
off.'

'What's happening, Dorcas?' Vukani saw his father
entering the bedroom.

'Can you believe this? I found this violin on the
doorstep outside as I was leaving for work. Can you
believe this?'

'Vukani,' said his father. 'What on earth should
have made you do such a thing?'

'I didn't put it there, *Baba,*' Vukani replied.

'Nonsense,' shouted his mother. 'You don't have to
lie. Ungrateful boy, you have the nerve to tell your
parents a lie.'

'Wait a minute, dear, maybe we should hear what
he has to say.' Vukani had nothing to say. The deep
feeling of having been wronged could only find expression in tears. He heard the violin land next to him
and he recoiled from its coldness. He also heard his
mother leave, saying that he was crying because of his
sins. She never knew what had happened and seemed
not to care.

But that was last year. Today he had been humiliated
again in public, and there were people in that living
room who wanted to humiliate him again. Right

inside his home. It was all because of this violin. The homework had made him forget the latest ordeal for a while. The homework was like a jigsaw puzzle; you simply looked for pieces which fitted. All the answers were there in the chapter. You just moved your finger up and down the page until you spotted the correct answer. There was no thinking involved. But now it was all gone. It was not South African History, the story of the coming of the white man, he was looking at; he was now faced with the reality of the violin.

There was that gang of boys who always stood under the shop veranda at Maponya's shopping complex. They shouted: 'Hey, music man!' whenever he went past their 'headquarters' on his way home to Dube. That very Friday they had done more than shout at him from a distance. They had stopped him and humiliated him before all those workers who were returning from work in town.

'Hey, music man!' the one who seemed to be their leader had called. Vukani, as a rule, never answered them. He just walked on as if he had not heard anything. But that afternoon as he was coming up from Phefeni station and was turning round the corner to go down towards the A.M.E. church, it was as if the gang had been waiting for him.

'Hey, music man!' This time it was a chorus. A rowdy chorus. Out of the corner of his eye Vukani saw two boys detach themselves from the gang. He dare not turn to look. He had to act unconcerned. He tried to quicken his step as imperceptibly as possible.

'Music man! Don't you know your name?' They were behind him now. Crossing the street had been no problem for them. They simply walked into the street and cars came to a screeching halt. They were the kings of the township. They just parted the traffic

as Moses must have parted the waves of the sea.
Vukani wanted to run, but he was not going to give
himself away. If he ran and they caught up with him
they could do a lot of harm to him. He had had that
feeling once — of wanting to take advantage of something weaker than him — when he'd found a stray
dog trying to topple a garbage bin. If the dog had
stood its ground and growled, he would have been
afraid. But the dog had taken to its heels, tail tucked
between legs, and Vukani had been filled with
the urge to run after the dog, catch it, and beat it to
death. A fleeing impala must excite the worst destructive urge in a lion. Vukani had once seen a film in
which a lion charged at a frightened impala. There
had been a confidence in the purposeful strides of the
lion, as if it felt this was just a game that would surely
end with the bringing down of the prey.

A hand grabbed Vukani's collar from behind and
jerked him violently to a halt. The leader of the gang
came round and faced him. He held Vukani by the
knot of his tie. He was short but heavily built. He
had puffed up cheeks with scars on them. His blood-
shot eyes suggested the violence in him. He must have
been four or five years older than Vukani.

'Spy!' the leader cursed, glaring at Vukani. 'So you
are special! So we had to cross the street and risk
death in order to talk to you. You don't know your
name, music man? Every day we greet you nice-nice
and you don't answer. Because you think you are
being greeted by shit. By scum, hey? Why, spy? Are
we shit?'

'Ja! Just answer that,' said the fellow behind. 'Are
we shit?' Vukani tried to free his neck.

'Shit!' screamed the leader. 'We just wanted to talk
to you nice-nice. That's all. We just wanted to dance

to your music a little. Dance to your guitar a little. But no. You don't even look at us. Do we smell, music man? Do we smell?' There was a crowd of workers now who were watching the spectacle quietly.

'Shake him up, Bhuka!' was the chorus from the rest of the gang about thirty yards away at the shop.

'What are you rogues doing to this poor boy?' asked an old lady who had a bundle of washing on her head.

'Shut up!' said Bhuka. 'Go and do your white man's washing, he'll want it tomorrow.' Some in the crowd laughed at this.

'Dogs of the street! Don't talk like that to your mother. Whose child are you?'

'I'm your child,' said Bhuka with a certain flourish. This time more of the crowd laughed.

'He's the child of his mother!' said the boy behind Vukani. None laughed at that one. He was in the shadow of his leader.

'You are laughing,' said the woman, bravely addressing the crowd. 'You are laughing at this boy being harassed, and you are laughing at me being insulted by these street urchins. I could be your mother, and this could be your son. *Sies!* You rogues, just let decent people be.' The woman then left, taking Vukani's hopes with her. But she had not left Bhuka unsettled. He had to move his prey to safer ground. Too many lesser animals could be a disturbance. He tightened his grip around Vukani's tie pulling him across the street towards the 'headquarters.' Vukani looked at the fist below his chin, and saw that it had a little sixth finger. There were two shining copper bangles round the wrist.

Part of the crowd left, but another part wanted to

see the game to its end. They followed the trio to the shop. The gang then had Vukani completely encircled.

'Do you have a sister?' Bhuka snapped. Vukani had trouble breathing now. Bhuka realised this and loosened the grip. Vukani thought of Teboho at home. If she came here she would fight for him. 'I asked you a question. Do you have a sister?' Vukani nodded. 'Hey man, talk! Is your voice precious. His master's voice!'

'Yes,' answered Vukani in a whisper.

'I want to fuck her. Do you hear? I want to eat her up thoroughly. Do you hear? Tell her that.' Bhuka paused and jerked Vukani to and fro so that Vukani's head bobbed. He then stopped and glowered at Vukani. 'And what song will you play when I am on top of her?' There was a festive laugh from the crowd. Bhuka looked round with acknowledgement. 'Tell me now, can you play *Thoko Ujola Nobani?*' It was a current hit.

Vukani felt tears in his eyes. He winked many times to keep them in. Why couldn't they just leave him alone? That day would be final, he would simply tell his parents that he did not want to play the violin again. If they still insisted he would run away from home.

'Please leave me alone,' he heard himself say.

'I asked you. Can you play *Thoko Ujola Nobani?*' Vukani shook his head.

'Why, music man?'

'I'd have to learn how to play it first. I can't just play it like that.'

'Next time you pass here you must be knowing that song. And come with your sister.' Then he gave Vukani a shove at the chest, and Vukani reeled backwards and fell on his back. But he still held on to the violin.

'Next time we greet you nice-nice, you must greet nice-nice.' Vukani got up timidly and hurried away, glancing back occasionally. Somehow he felt relieved. It could have been worse. The stories he had heard about the violence of this gang were simply unbelievable. He felt deep inside him the laughter that followed him as he slunk away. Just after passing the A.M.E. church he saw the rubbish heap people had created at the corner and wished he were brave enough to throw the violin there.

'My son,' his mother had said one day when Vukani complained about the harassment he suffered as a result of the violin, 'you should never yield to ignorance.'

'But maybe you should buy me a piano,' Vukani had said. 'I can't carry that in the street.'

'If Yehudi Menuhin had listened to fools he wouldn't be the greatest living violinist. A violin you have and a violin you will play.' That's how it had ended. But his agony continued, three times a week.

Then the door opened. 'Here he is!' said Vukani's mother as she led the visitors in. His father took the rear. Vukani looked blankly at the homework. Question three: Who introduced the European type of education among the Bantu? . . . But Vukani felt only the solid presence of four people behind him.

'Vuka,' said his mother. 'I did not hear you practise today.' It was not clear from her voice whether she was finding fault with her son or was just trying to have something to say by way of introduction. Vukani turned round and smiled sheepishly. They all looked at him as if they expected him to defend himself, their eyes occasionally going to the table as if to see what he was doing.

'Are you doing your homework, son?' asked the male visitor.

'E!'

'Good, hard working boy!' he said patting Vukani on the shoulders. Vukani felt in that hand the heaviness of condescension.

'He's a very serious-minded boy,' added his mother with obvious pride.

'You are very happy, dearie, to have a child who loves school,' observed Mrs Beatrice.

'And here is my Mozart's violin,' said Vukani's father, pointing at the violin against the wall. He took the case, opened it and took out the violin.

'Vuka!'

'Ma!'

'These visitors are the mother and father of Lauretta. Do you know her?'

'No, I don't think I do,' said Vukani shaking his head.

'But you are at the same school together! Surely you know Lauretta, the daughter of Doctor Zwane. Stand up to greet them.' Now Vukani remembered the girl who was well known at school for her brilliance. She was two classes ahead of Vukani. But Vukani wondered if she could beat Gwendoline. Vukani greeted the visitors and went back to his seat.

'Vuka, you will play the visitors something, won't you? What will you play us?' asked his mother. Vukani looked at the violin in his father's hands. He was explaining to Dr Zwane the various kinds of violins.

'This type,' he was saying, 'is very rare. You do not find it easily these days. Not at all.'

'It must have been very expensive,' observed Dr Zwane appreciatively. 'One can judge from its looks.'

'Five hundred and fifty rands down,' butted in Vukani's mother.

'Made to specifications. You just tell them how you want it and they make it. This is special.'

'One has to pay to produce a Mozart,' said Vukani's father with finality.

'We had Lauretta started on ballet recently,' said Mrs Zwane, as if suggesting that they were also doing their duty. 'I'm happy to note that she seems to be doing well. All these things have to be taught at our schools. You school inspectors have a duty to ensure that it happens.'

'Indeed,' agreed Vukani's father. 'But do you think the Boers would agree? Never. Remember they say Western Civilisation is spoiling us, and so we have to cultivate the indigenous way of life.' The conversation was stopped by Vukani's mother.

'Okay now,' — she clapped her hands — 'what will you play us?'

Vukani's father brought the violin to Vukani who took it with his visibly shaking hands. He saw the red, glowering eyes of Bhuka that afternoon. He heard the laughter of people in the streets. He remembered being violently shaken awake by his angry mother one morning. He remembered one of his dreams which came very frequently. He was naked in the streets and people were laughing. He did not know how he became naked. It always occurred that way. He would be naked in the streets and people would be laughing. Suddenly he would reach home and his mother would scold him for bringing shame to the family. But the dream would always end with his leaving home and flying out into the sky with his hands as wings.

Vukani found he had instinctively put the violin on

his left shoulder. And when he realised that, he felt its irksome weight on him. What did people want of him? He did not want to play. He did not want to play. And for the second time that day, he felt tears coming to his eyes, and again he winked repeatedly to keep them from flowing. This was the time.

'Mama!'

'Yes son.' But Vukani did not go on. His mother continued. 'Why don't you play some selections from Brahms? You know some excerpts from his *only* violin concerto? Perhaps Mozart? Yes Mozart. I know that sometimes one is in the mood for a particular composer. What about Liszt? Where are your music books? There is something on the music stand; what is it? Ahh! It's the glorious, beautiful Dvorak! Tum tee tum! Tum tee tum!' She shook her head, conducting an imaginary orchestra. 'Come up and play some of this Dvorak.' Vukani wanted to shout but his throat felt completely dry. He wanted to sink into the ground. He tried to swallow. It was only dryness he swallowed, and it hurt against the throat. Standing up would be agonising. His strength and resistance were all gathered up in his sitting position. All that strength would be dissipated if he stood up. And he would feel exposed, lonely and vulnerable. The visitors and his parents soon noticed there was something amiss.

'What is it Vuka?' asked his mother. 'Is there something wrong?'

'Nothing wrong, Ma,' said Vukani, shaking his head. He had missed his opportunity. Why was he afraid? Why did he not act decisively for his own good? Then he felt anger building up in him, but he was not sure whether he was angry with himself, or with his parents together with the visitors, whose visit was now forcing him to come to terms with his hitherto unexpressed determination to stop doing what brought him suffering.

At that moment there was a dull explosion seemingly coming from the kitchen, of something massive suddenly disintegrating into pieces. There was a moment's silence, then Vukani's mother muttered: 'The bloody street girl has done it again,' and she stormed out of the bedroom. Her voice could be heard clearly in the kitchen: 'Awu, Lord of the heavens! my ... my expensive ... my precious ... my expensive ... this girl has done it again. Teboho! Has the devil got into you again? Do you have to be breaking something everyday?'

'It slipped out of my hand,' said Teboho in a subdued voice.

'What kind of hands do you have?' said her mother shrieking with anger.

'It was a mistake,' replied Teboho, her voice now a pitch higher.

'What a costly mistake! Oh, my God. What a costly one! I gave Mrs Willard three hundred rands to bring me this set from Hong Kong when she went there on holiday. And I've pleaded with you countless times to be extra careful with the china!'

'Ma, I didn't just dash the pot to the floor . . . .'

'And such care doesn't cost much. How many households in the whole of Johannesburg, white and black, can boast of owning such a set ... a genuine set? Will you not appreciate that? Don't just stand there . . . .'

'Mama, can you please stop that.' Teboho's voice sounded urgently restrained.

'Is that how you are talking to me?'

'You don't want to listen to anybody. You just

came in here shouting.' Teboho's voice was loud with a note of defiance. It seemed to have lost all restraint.

'Is that how they teach you to talk to your parents at the University?'

'Mama, that is not the point.'

'Are you arguing with me?'

'I'm not . . . .'

'Then what are you saying?'

'You're always telling us not to break dishes, not to scratch the furniture, not to break your house plants, there are so many things one cannot do in this house . . . . Haven't you been showing more interest in your dishes than in your children?'

'What?'

'I'm not going to say anything more.'

'What decent girl, but a slut, can talk like that to her mother, and there are visitors in the house?'

'Mama, will you stop!' There was the sound of a slap. Another explosion. Lighter this time; perhaps a glass.

'You've slapped me!' screamed Teboho. 'I'm leaving this house; you can stay with it. If you want to be a slave to things; then do it alone.' There was the sound of a little scuffle, followed by hurrying footsteps. Then the door to Teboho's bedroom banged shut, rattling some cutlery.

Vukani's father was about to leave for the kitchen when he met his wife at the door. She brushed past him into Vukani's bedroom, grinning at the visitors.

'I'm sorry for that unfortunate diversion,' she said. 'Children can be destructive. Since Teboho went to that university in the north she has some very strange ideas. Opposes everything. Defiant. Can you have your own child calling you a white black woman, a slave of things?'

And then she mimicked Teboho's voice: ' "That's how it's planned. That we be given a little of everything, and so prize the little we have that we forget about freedom." Fancy. Forgive me; but I had to remind this show-off girl that I was her parent.'

There was a moment's silence of embarrassment. The adults all exchanged glances. A wave of sadness crossed Vukani's mother's face. But it did not last.

'One can never know with children, dearie,' observed Mrs Zwane, breaking the silence.

'Indeed!' said her husband. There was another silence.

'Well, Vuka,' said Vukani's father at last. 'Can you heal our broken spirits?'

'Yes!' agreed his mother. 'We have been waiting for too long.'

Vukani thought of his sister. He wanted to go to her. They were very lonely. Their parents disapproved of many of their friends. Even Doksi. His mother had said he should have friends of his own station in life. What would a barber's son bring him? All this had brought Vukani and Teboho very close. He decided then that he would not let his sister down. But what could he do? He thought of dashing the violin against the wall, and then rushing out of the house. But where would he go? Who did he know nearby? The relatives he knew lived very far away. He did not know them all that well, anyhow. He remembered how envious he would be whenever he heard other children saying they were going to spend their holidays with their relatives. Perhaps with a grandmother or an uncle. He remembered once asking his mother when were they ever going to visit his uncle. His mother had not answered him. But then there was that conversation between his parents.

'By the way,' Vukani's mother had started it, 'when did you say your sister would be coming?'

'Next month.' There had been a brief silence before his father continued. 'Why do you ask? I have been telling you practically every day.'

'I was just asking for interest's sake.'

'Well,' his father had said, putting down the *Daily Mail* and picking up the *Star,* 'I just feel there is more to the question than meets the eye.'

'You think so?'

'Yes, I think so.' There had been silence.

'Relatives,' his mother had come out eventually, 'can be a real nuisance. Once you have opened the door, they come trooping in like ants. We cannot afford it these days. Not with the cost of living. These are different times. Whites saw this problem a long time ago. That is why they have very little time for relatives. Nuclear family! That's what matters. I believe in it. I've always maintained that. If relatives want to visit, they must help with the groceries. There I'm clear, my dear. Very clear.' Vukani's father had said something about 'Whites are whites; Africans are Africans.' But Vukani's aunt never came. Nobody ever said anything about her. Yet, Doksi liked to say: 'It's nice to have many relatives. Then when you are in trouble at home, you can always hide with one of them. And your father will go from relative to relative looking for you. When he finds you, he will be all smiles trying to please the relatives.'

'Vukani!' called his mother. 'We are still waiting. Will you start playing now?'

Vukani stood up slowly, feeling every movement of his body, and walked round to the music stand. Then he faced his mother, and something yielded in him.

'Ma, I don't want to play the violin any more.'
There was a stunned silence. Vukani's mother looked
at her husband, a puzzled expression on her face. But
she quickly recovered.

'What?' she shouted.

'I don't want to play the violin any more.' Vukani
was surprised at his steadiness.

'This is enough!' screamed his mother. 'Right now
. . . right now. You are going to play that violin right
now.'

'Now you just play that instrument. What's going
on in this house?' His father's voice put some fear
into him.

'Wait, dearie,' pleaded Mrs Zwane. 'Maybe the boy
is not well.'

'Beatrice,' answered Vukani's mother, 'there is
nothing like that. We are not going to be humiliated
by such a little flea. Play, cheeky brute!'

'Today those boys stopped me again. . . .' Vukani
attempted to justify his stand.

'Who?' shrieked his mother. 'Those dogs of the
street? Those low things?'

'What's bothering him?' asked Dr Zwane. Vukani's
mother explained briefly. Then turning toward her
husband she said: 'As I told you the other day, he
keeps complaining that people laugh at him because
he plays the violin.'

'Jealousy!' shouted Mrs Zwane. 'Plain jealousy.
Jealousy number one. Nothing else. Township people
do not want to see other Africans advance.'

'Dear,' answered Vukani's mother, 'you are showing
them some respect they do not deserve. If you say
they are jealous you make them people with feelings.
No. They do not have that. They are not people: they
are animals. Absolutely raw. They have no respect for

what is better than they. Not these. They just trample over everything. Hey, you, play that instrument and stop telling us about savages.'

Vukani trembled. He felt his head going round now. He did not know what to do to escape from this ordeal. The tears came back, but this time he did not stop them. He felt them going down his cheeks, and he gave in to the fury in him: 'I do not want to play ... I do not want to play ... not any more! ...' Then he choked and could not say anything more. But what he had said had carried everything he felt deep inside him. He felt free. There was a vast expanse of open space deep inside him. He was free. He could fly into the sky.

Then he heard Dr Zwane say: 'How difficult it is to bring up a child properly in Soweto! To give him culture. African people just turn away from advancement.'

Those words seemed to build a fire in Vukani's mother. They sounded like a reflection on her. She let go at Vukani with the back of her hand. Vukani reeled back and fell on the bed letting the violin drop to the floor. It made no noise on the thick carpet. Then she lifted him from the bed, and was about to strike him again when Teboho rushed into the bedroom and pulled her mother away from her brother.

'Ma! What are you doing? What are you doing?' she screamed.

'Are you fighting me?' shrieked her mother. 'You laid a hand on your mother. Am I bewitched?'

'You never think of anybody else. Just yourself.'

'Teboho,' called her father. 'Don't say that to your mother.'

'Please, dearie, please,' appealed Mrs Zwane. 'There is no need for all this. How can you do this to your children?'

'Sies! What disgraceful children! I am a nursing sister, your father is an inspector of schools. What are you going to be, listening to savages? You cannot please everybody. Either you please the street, in which case you are going to be a heap of rubbish, something to be swept away, or you please your home, which is going to give you something to be proud of for the rest of your useless life!'

'Dorcas! That's enough now,' said Vukani's father with calm, but firm finality. Vukani's mother looked at her husband with disbelief, a wave of shock crossing her face. She looked at the visitors who stared at her. Then she turned for the door and went to her bedroom, banging the door violently. Soon there was bitter sobbing in the main bedroom. Then it turned into the wail of the bereaved.

Fools

When I first saw him in the waiting room on platform one at Springs Station, I wanted to know him. He was tall enough: about two-thirds of a door. There was no doubt from his fine, slender shape that he was in good physical condition. He wore an overcoat that was a very good fit. It was the fashionable kind: charcoal black, with slits and useless buttons on the sides. The brown legs of a well cut pair of trousers emerged just below the knees and rested neatly on shiny, brown Barker shoes. The heels of the shoes were iron-tipped, for they rang on the cement floor as the boy paced up and down the waiting room. There was a detachment about him that I found impressive: such detachment as I had never seen in any of our young men in all the countless years I had been teaching. I wondered who he was, and where he came from.

But why couldn't he sit down on the bench? He seemed much preoccupied with something; somewhat excited in fact. The look on his face was so intense that his already dark face seemed to grow darker the more he paced up and down. His big eyes seemed to glow like two lit windows in the dark, and I wanted to look into them. He kept looking at his watch, muttering to himself as he did so. He wouldn't look at me. Yet, I felt sure that he was fully aware of me. I was quite sure that he was looking at me out of the corners of his eyes. Despite my interest in him I gradually began to feel vaguely resentful of those stolen bits of attention. Surely there was no need for this kind of behaviour, considering there were only two of us in the waiting room that early morning. He had not even said a word to me. And when I realised that, I suddenly felt a growing urge to unsettle him; to torture him with a bold stare. So I fixed my eyes on him; ready for him. If he just dared cast a more obvious glance in my direction, he would find a smirking face saying to him: Yes, I'm looking at you, young man! After all, if fate had brought us together so early in the morning, why shouldn't we have been getting to know each other like good people?

He had found me there. I had been sleeping on the bench, trying to catch up on sleep that had been interrupted very early that morning by bad dreams. Luckily, the bad dreams ensured that I would certainly catch the first train to Nigel so that I could make it for school assembly at eight. I was huddled up on the waiting room bench with my hands tucked warmly between my thighs, when the heavy noise of a huge suitcase being dropped on the floor woke me up. It was as if a locomotive had blundered into the waiting room. I opened my eyes just in time to see the young man open his left armpit to let his travelling rug drop on to the bench, just opposite me. Then he bent his knees so that he could gently drop a grass-woven provision basket he held with the right hand, and then with the free left hand release a leather brief-case that had been squeezed under the right armpit. I sat up, hoping to welcome him. But I had to wipe off drooling spittle from my left cheek, and was trying to clear my eyes. We looked at each other. I saw something like a shadow pass across his face. Then he lowered his eyes towards my hand which was rubbing against one of the thighs of my faded corduroy trousers. I looked down too, and saw the silvery drool there on the trousers along the tiny corduroy furrows. I rubbed more vigorously until there was only a spot of wetness and no more silver. When I looked up the young man had turned away and was gazing through the huge windows at other platforms, and beyond at the shunting yards. Did he think I was a tramp? I wanted to prove him wrong. I was not some homeless, starving wanderer drooling all over the place. But before I could do anything, he started pacing up and down the waiting room, and I soon became so interested in him that I forgot all about my own resentment.

He seemed the assertive type, all right. There are young men whose assertiveness is so transparently the effort of an immature cock trying to crow with a deep voice, but only managing an annoying gurgle. But this young man seemed to have a turbulence in him that was much more than that of a boy whose armpits were beginning to grow hair.

I looked at him, and saw how, as he paced impatiently up and down, he was unaware of the game he was playing with his shadow: how it seemed to move away from him, only to follow him. Then he would turn to chase it and trample on it whenever he came under the lamp in the middle of the waiting room.

I decided I would talk to him. After all, hadn't I been chewing food for many more years than he? I knew all the ways of chewing and swallowing, so I could afford to make some concessions, and gain authority in the process. Besides, maybe I had unsettled him enough by now.

'You must be from school,' I said, clearing my throat and looking suggestively at his baggage. I was thinking also, that this was about the time when most boarding schools were closing for summer.

I don't think he ever expected me to talk to him, for my voice jolted him. He swung his face in my direction as he stopped on his shadow. The confusion on his face was soon replaced by a look of reluctance. But he forced himself to reply.

'What did you say?'

Now, there is nothing so terrible as having to repeat something after you have been uneasily trying to make easy conversation. The superficiality of it all shines through.

'You must be from school,' I repeated, once more looking suggestively at his baggage.

'Yes,' he said. He still stood on his shadow.

'Where?' I asked.

'Swaziland,' he said, turning away without resuming his pacing. He seemed to have been showing some special interest in the train that was on platform five. It was the long-distance train that had arrived from Breyten at the same time as I got to the station at five o'clock. If he was from Swaziland, then he was definitely from that train. The steam engine that had been pulling it from Breyten was being replaced with an electric locomotive, and that would haul the train on its last leg to Johannesburg.

'Swaziland!' I exclaimed, trying to sound very interested. 'I must say you are lucky. You are very lucky that your father sent you there. You see . . . .'

'I don't have one,' he cut in.

'What?' I asked.

'A father,' he said.

'Oh, then it was your mother who was wise,' I said.

'She had nothing to do with it,' he answered with unmistakable annoyance.

'Well, whoever . . . .'

'It's not a question of "whoever," ' he cut in again. 'It was my uncle.'

'Well, whoever . . . .'

'I told you it was my uncle,' he said with finality. I was rather unnerved by his hostility. Surely I had done nothing to deserve it. But I would not give in to a bed bug. I had to control things: stay calm yet be firm. Pretend I didn't notice anything.

'Well,' I said, 'then your uncle is a wise man. You see, there is no education for us in this country. In the Protectorates, you can get a better education. In fact, a good education.'

'Of course,' he said looking at me directly for the first time, 'it does not take much political intelligence to come to that judgement. You see, that's our problem. The damage was done way back in 1953. Now it is 1966. Yet, we keep complaining as if the injustice began yesterday. The obviousness of analysis! The lack of new insights! Old complaints uttered as if they were revolution itself! And now, November 30, 1966: yet another summer, and our minds continue to languish in an eternal winter. It saddens me.'

I looked at him, and felt somewhat overwhelmed. I told myself that if the young man thought he could defy or humiliate me, he was wasting his time. I had had so much abuse heaped on me in the last few years, that I persuaded myself I could only be more fascinated than annoyed by his attitude. I would try to make him think I felt his sting: just to let him feel the sweetness of victory. After all, since we were going to be on the same train, it would not do to be rash. I had to concentrate on getting to know him.

It's amazing how this kind of rationalisation had become so instinctive with me! I suppose that's what made me seem so resilient, so understanding, and so compassionate: all of which offered refuge to my growing inability to assert myself.

I looked away from him, and really noticed, for the first time that day, the world around. Although the sun had not yet come up, its light was gradually filling the sky from the east. There was much shunting activity in the railway yards; and much smoke and steam coming in huge clouds from the stacks and the numerous valves of locomotives. A gentle breeze blew the smoke towards cottonwood trees that lined the boundaries of the station. And the branches seemed to suck in the smoke as it disappeared through the green leaves into the dark centre of the trees. Some of the smoke wafted in huge tufts into the sky and spread, so that it reflected the red light of the yet unseen sun. And there were birds too; and many doves cooing. Their cooing mingled with the hum of the early morning traffic and the whistles of the trains. Some sparrows were hopping on the platforms, and down among the rails. I felt refreshing coolness in the air which made me wonder why the young man did not take off his overcoat. I suppose it was the habit of all travellers: if it's a long journey, summer or winter, just dress heavily.

I became so wrapped up in the solace of the morning that I did not even hear or see our train rolling in. A commuter train speeding out of Springs to Johannesburg reminded me why I was at the station. When it was gone I noticed that the long-distance train at platform five was moving, and that

the boy had walked out of the waiting room and was
standing just outside, looking at the train. Then he
looked back at the waiting room as if he wanted to
go back in there, but changed his mind. He looked
up at the sky, then at his shoes, then sideways, and
everywhere but at the train he seemed to have gone
out to see. And as the train gathered speed, I noticed
a white handkerchief being waved in our direction.
The boy finally made himself notice the handkerchief.

Even from the distance of about fifty yards, I
could see her full face, for she had brushed her hair
back, and the puff at the back of her head flared out
like the black crown of a Zulu hairdo. I saw in her
dark, softly beautiful face, a look of compassionate
superiority. Although she was smiling, she seemed
unhappy, as if she was smiling out of a sense of duty.
She seemed to be waving not so much to say goodbye
to the boy, as to keep the future open. She seemed
to be trying to humour him.

At last, the young man took his right hand out of
the overcoat pocket, but only to wave as if he was
shooing a fly away from his face. He put his hand
back into the pocket, and spun round to return
to the waiting room. But just as he reached the
entrance, he turned his face briefly towards the waving
girl. The girl stopped waving and looked. She waved
again. When her train finally took a bend, she withdrew her head from the window. The anxiety in her
movements was unmistakable; but she seemed impatient rather than alarmed. The train disappeared. It
left a silence which was not so much in the surroundings of the station, as in the fact that I had just been
witness to a strange yet significant event. I had just
encroached upon a moment of intimacy which gave
me a much greater sense of victory over the young

man, than his arrogance towards me could ever give him. I could not help feeling that there had now been two people that morning who had understandingly, perhaps not condescendingly, tried to make the young man feel important. He shuffled back into the waiting room, seemingly in a trance. I don't think he was even aware that he was sitting down. It was just then that I stood up.

'It's no use sitting down now,' I said. 'Our train's here.' Certainly, I enjoyed having said, 'It's no use.' I think I had a grudge against him for his not having sat down to talk to me earlier. He turned his face up to me. It was not impatience I saw there now; nor was there any self-righteous arrogance. There was a vacuousness in his face that gave me the impression that I might as well start burying him. His very dark face had become faintly gray. But all of that look of helplessness did not invoke even a slight pang of sympathy in me. Even if that dignified, defiant detachment I had seen earlier had returned I would have had absolutely no use for it. I went towards him and the semi-circle of his baggage around him, picked up the big suitcase and the travelling rug, and struggled into the train. He surely followed, for the door of the carriage closed with a bang even before I sat down in the train. Then I saw him ease himself on to the seat opposite me. There were only the two of us in that second class carriage, and we were quiet for some time, feeling each other's heavy presence. Again I looked him in the eyes, wanting to be much heavier for him than he could ever be for me. He avoided my eyes and looked out through the window. But I felt quite sure that he really was not seeing anything out there. I made the next move.

'Your girl?' I asked. He jerked his face away from

the window, and looked at me. It was as if I had unexpectedly jabbed him with a knife.

'I didn't hear you,' he said with meek alertness.

'Your girl?' I repeated.

Then he did what I had not at all expected: he
smiled his agreement. I smiled too. And then, almost
as if there had been a signal, we both broke into
laughter. I wasn't really sure what was happening, but
we both had a good laugh. I felt grateful.

'So,' I said, wiping away tears with my handkerchief. 'There is so much between you and that pretty,
waving girl that you will not think of her without a
smile. And then a laugh!'

He nodded, and we laughed a little more.

'Where is she from?' I asked after a while.

'Soweto,' he said. 'Emdeni North.'

'Is she also going to a boarding school in Swaziland?'
I asked.

He nodded. Then he looked at me with a steady
gaze. He seemed to have recovered completely from
the waiting room incident. He looked relaxed and
confident again; but something of the intimidating
look I had seen earlier still remained. He looked at
me as if he was trying to make up his mind about
something.

'You know,' he said, 'I have a question to ask you.'

I smiled my permission for him to go ahead.

'Are you the teacher?' he asked. 'Are you really
Teacher Zamani?'

He quickly swept his eyes all over me. Instinctively,
I brought my thighs together, hoping that the wet
spot of my drool would disappear from view. I dared
not look down to verify. I could see that he was looking at a shadow of me. He looked at me as if he had
the right to say anything to me and I was obliged to

listen. But I was not going to allow a small boy to ask me my name before I had asked him his. He was not going to take advantage of me.

'And who might you be?' I asked.

'So I was right,' he said. 'I thought so when I first saw you in there.' He pointed with his head towards the waiting room. 'Not only do I know you, Teacher Zamani, I have also heard a lot about you. I even know your nickname: Panyapanya. The name still seems appropriate for your eyes still blink as continuously as ever.' He chuckled, while I seethed inside. But a deep sense of powerlessness made me sit back and listen. There was something in him that drained me of any will to challenge him.

'You were the terror of schoolchildren,' he said. 'I knew about you long before I even set my eyes on you. That was when I was a mere seven-year-old at Emzimkhulu Lower Primary School. That was, let's see ... eleven years ago. Time flies! And you were there at the higher primary: Zakheni Higher Primary School. You were teaching there. And I know that you are still there. You know, whenever we thought of you, us toddlers at Emzimkhulu, we dreaded the possibility of passing our exams and moving up towards you. It was said you could beat a child until his skin peeled off.

'The children used to say: "Panyapanya will let you lie face down on a bench, and then have the bigger boys of the class hold your arms and legs fast. And then he will get hold of his notorious cane, Happy Days, with his right hand; and with the left, he will flick his fingers just over your buttocks as if he was seasoning them with salt and pepper. And then the cane will rain down on you." That's what the children used to say. And we would invent all kinds of stories

to illustrate your brutality.' He paused and looked at
me as if he had made the world's greatest revelation,
and then asked: 'Do you still peel off skins?'

I decided to feel amused. He seemed so sure of
himself. He had asked a good question, of course. A
perfectly good question: 'Do you still peel off skins?'
I didn't do it anymore. I stopped about three years
ago. But the urge was there to begin again with that
boy sitting in front of me. He was just the kind of
boy I liked to break. But what was special about this
one was that he was articulate. That was harder to
deal with. Usually, my students expressed their protest
through such impotent acts as shuffling their feet on
the classroom floor, wasting shoe leather and their
parents' money. Or they would refuse to raise their
hands when asked a question; or they would hand in
half-done homework in which case, I figured, they
were working for their own failure. You don't win
against a teacher unless he gives you permission to
win. So as long as they continued to perform these
silly acts, I knew I had defeated them. But this fellow
before me was articulate. I would never have known
how to deal with him. It is harder to deal with words.
You don't see them. They may infuriate you, frustrate
you, move you to tears; but you cannot handle them
and throttle the life out of them. Now here was a new
specimen who fascinated me. I would let this cock
crow on. But I wondered why he spoke to me the way
he did. It was as if he had the right to speak that way.

'Well,' I said, 'whoever you are, young man, I want
you to realise that you have been disrespectful
towards me from the moment you set eyes on me this
morning. You have still not even greeted me.'

'You will certainly be pleased to know who I am in
a moment,' he said sharply.

I looked at him, becoming more and more anxious. Who was he? I asked myself. Just then the train slowly began to move. I was grateful for that, for we both looked out to see the place we were leaving behind us. The sun, too, had finally come up. It was just behind the trees and the tall buildings of Springs. But soon I became conscious that the boy was not looking outside as I was: he was staring fixedly at me. I tried to pretend I was not aware of him. He seemed to be waiting for my response to his challenge. Perhaps out of some desperation to make sense of what was happening, I suddenly went back in my mind to the waiting room when I first saw the boy. And I realised that within the space of about twenty-five minutes I had seen his restlessness, his impatience, his arrogance, his humiliation and agony, his helplessness, his joyfulness, and his amazing recovery through aggression and intimidation. All within the space of about twenty-five minutes! Wasn't I dealing with a madman? Was it really sanity I had just been witnessing? I took out a packet of cigarettes and offered him one. The vehemence of his refusal seemed to confirm my impressions.

'No,' he said, after shaking his head first. 'I don't smoke; never have; will not now, nor in the future, for ever and ever!'

'Amen!' I said spiritedly, with all the enthusiasm and fascination of discovery. My hands were shaking as I lit my cigarette.

'That,' said the young man with a contemptuous gesture towards my cigarette, 'is one of those things that have for ever been destroying people!' It was amazing! His face had once more grown dark with anger. I was pleased, though, that my cigarette had taken him away from me and my past.

'I believe in science,' he said. 'Scientists, after rigorous experiments, have shown the harmfulness of smoking. Who are we to ignore their findings? They have shown too, that our people are terribly undernourished. Very little protein in their diet. But no, not only are their bodies wasting away every day, they have to destroy their lungs also. And all the white man has to do afterwards is just push us over. Look at the human wrecks they throw away to the homelands to die. Finished bodies, finished lungs, finished minds, finished spirits. All because we have been enemies to science!'

'How would those people have known about your science?' I asked.

'That is the wrong I intend to put right,' he said. 'I want to spread knowledge and science to the people. And the best place to begin is where I was born. I am coming back to Charterston to bring light where there has been darkness. And this light is destined to spread to the whole country.'

'So you are the political type?' I said. 'You turn everything into politics.'

'I have seen your type too,' he said. 'Masters of avoidance. They refuse to see connections between things. And then they condemn us, not out of conviction, but out of a cowardly desire to stay out of trouble. They don't even need to smoke; they have been destroyed by their own fear of living . . . .

'Some of them, like you, are paid to be killers of dreams, putting out the fire of youth, and to be expert at deflowering young virgins sent to school by their hopeful parents.'

I pulled hard at my cigarette, and then belched. The wind must have come from deep down in my stomach, for I could feel the roar down there. And the belch came out with all the smoke in my lungs. I could taste the acid, and the smell of last night's beer. It was all mixed with the smoke, the disgust in the boy's face, and the contempt he clearly had for me.

'What a cross I have to bear!' he said with a deep sigh. He shook his head slowly as if he was looking at the very essence of futility. There had been a tinge of sorrow in his voice, as if he was on the verge of crying. At that moment I felt so drawn to him. There may have been a touch of insanity in all this, but there was also a restlessness more powerful than the urgings of adolescence. His eyes, his face, drew me to him; not because of the same pain and helplessness I had seen in them in the waiting room, but because I had a real feeling that I had before me, for the first time in my life, someone who genuinely felt sorry for me. At that moment I was seized by a deep feeling of contrition. So rarely in my life had I felt so small before a young person. When he did speak again, it was with a very quiet voice.

'You are fifty-five years old,' he said. 'I know that.' I stared at him.

'Your father-in-law was Reverend Shezi,' he said. 'I know that too. I know so many things about you. I know that when you first came to Charterston, fresh from Ohlange Teacher Training School, you were a young man of thirty-two, full of new ideas, and dying to change the township and put some life into it. I know that.'

'What else do you know?' I said, not really wanting to hear more, pretending I was really above all this foolishness.

'You started the boy scout movement, and taught preparedness. Did you ever ask yourself what you were preparing those boys for?'

'At least I did something,' I said.

'It probably no longer matters to you now. But what does matter is that the local churches began to compete for you, as they always competed for the allegiance of handsome young teachers. More converts were enrolled that way. My research confirmed all that. But it was Reverend Shezi who was the most imaginative. A true product of the Anglican church: table manners and speaking English through the nose. Who else could his daughter, a registered nurse, be married to in small Charterston if not to a young, handsome teacher? Isn't that so, Teacher? Isn't it, Teach?'

There was a triumphant gleam in his eyes that I found overwhelming. 'I cannot allow you to parade my private life in some train,' I said trying to sound indignant. But the more I tried to say something, the more powerless I felt. He ignored me.

'I know what you did to Reverend Shezi's church,' he continued, as I sighed visibly. I genuinely wished I were younger. 'Who was a credit to his church, but almost its disgrace? Answer the question fully . . . . It was Teacher Zamani, treasurer of the All Saints Anglican Church. Why did you embezzle church funds? You explained it, of course, to someone. You embezzled church funds not because you needed the money, but because you wanted to express your disgust with the Church of Christ. You despised the church and Christians. You said you wanted to ruin the church and bring it down to the poverty that it preached.'

'You ought to show a little respect for me,' I said.

'But your embezzlement never really became public. You wanted to destroy the church slowly and quietly, but you could never stand up for your political morality. You did not have the moral courage to stand exposure. And the clever priest was going to protect you. All you had to do was marry his daughter. And there was the white wedding of the year. The biggest Charterston had ever seen. The teacher and the priest's daughter! What a fine couple! A fine pair! A fine pair stepping into a loveless, childless future.'

'What gives you the right to talk that way to me?' I asked. He spoke as if he had every right in the world.

'How foolish of you,' he said. 'You should have prepared the people first. How can you struggle without them? You used the wrong methods for the right ends. And then you did not have enough courage. If you fear the consequences, then it is best not to do anything. If your sense of public esteem was going to be much stronger than your convictions, then you could not afford a war whose methods would have diminished your moral credibility in your own eyes. As for me, I'm going to avoid all your mistakes.'

It was funny how meek I had become. The accuracy of his observations made me numb. But I was too startled to figure out just how he came to know me so intimately. I felt so naked before him, like a frog that was being dissected alive, and there was nothing in the world it could do about its misfortune. I felt that his power over me must have had something to do with some connection between us that I was not aware of. But I didn't have long to wait for the revelation.

'And that Teach, is the story of your life. Yes, I can see you probably suspect who I am. That is the story of your life as told by you to my loving sister. You know her? Mimi? I'm Zani Vuthela, the brother of that bright little girl whom you subdued with the story of your misfortunes. What girl would not give

in, completely overwhelmed, to the passionate con-
fessional of her legendary teacher? Tell me? What
girl? What girl would not be flattered by this gift of
recognition?'

So my life was bare now. Not just my crime against
his sister, but the whole of my life.

'Do you see this briefcase, Teach? In it is her letter.
I received it two years ago. A year after she bore your
child. In it she was letting out to me, for the first
time, the tragic poetry of her disillusionment. She has
such a beautiful way with words! You did not completely destroy her. What a terrible lesson you are!'

Then he seemed at a loss for words, and looked at
me as if he was not so much wronged as greatly disappointed.

'Why?' he asked. 'Why?'

It was perhaps my deeply felt contrition that had
enabled me to listen to all this with such stoicism.
But an ember of anger glowed in me against the kind
of fate that would so unexpectedly bring such revelat-
ions about my life in some train one morning. Under
such circumstances, one recognises the need and the
urge to say something no matter how feeble. But it
had to be something that would recognise the legitim-
acy of revelation, the whole source of his authority,
while preserving whatever modicum of honour was
left in me.

'You ought to show a little respect for me,' I said
again.

He sighed. Another long deep sigh which hinted at
the futility of my response. It told me that I was a
snake that wanted to strike again, but had no more
poison left, and that, possibly, the poison was gone
forever. Then he looked away from me towards the
window and whatever he could see out there from the

moving train. I looked at him, wanting to say something more. But I could only look at him. I recognised
what I had been seeing all along in him in that waiting
room: his sister Mimi. I had been seeing her smooth
ebony skin; her high cheekbones; the almost perfectly
round nostrils of a rather flat nose that twitched
frequently with an intimidating suspiciousness; her
lips that always seemed about to break into a smile and
didn't, only remained enticingly potential. But it was
her eyes, big and almost transparently brown, that gave
her most of her aura. I know, for I had seen her grow
up, and I saw her for a whole year in my class when I
taught her in Standard Six. She was one of those girls
teachers always talked about in the staffroom.

But where the aura around her seemed fragile, her
brother's was solid. And this gave him a face in which
there constantly alternated the colours of compassion
and cruelty, ease and restlessness, innocence and
maturity. It was a taffeta of moods, giving that face
an intriguing flux which made you scrutinise it, hoping
it would eventually yield something constant; something you could possess, because everything seemed
finally to resolve itself into what was explainable.

Where had he been all these years? His sister had
spoken of him with much pride and fondness. And
whenever I pressed her for information, she merely
smiled as if she had something valuable to keep from
me. But I always knew when, like her, he had come
out top of his class; when he had broken the school's
record in the hundred yards dash; when he had scored
a goal in a soccer match. I heard also of his skills as a
debater; of his love for poetry, science and mathematics. His sister once told me that he wanted to
study nuclear physics and astronautics. It had all
seemed nothing more than the flights of wild ambition,

and the enthusiasm of a proud sister extolling the imaginary virtues of her brother. But now that I saw the young man before me, I was struck by the actual heavy possibility of achievement.

Looking at him I felt profoundly low and despised. I had felt this way many times in the last three years, but only now did it seem as if I had a clear intellectual understanding of my condition. It was then that I began to feel a compulsion to justify myself. I felt a vehemence in me that could not find words. Then he spoke again.

'Charterston!' he said. 'Charterston Township! Indeed, I'm returning to your stagnant isolation!'

I looked outside and saw what he was referring to. Our train had long left the mainline to Johannesburg with its maze of crisscrossing rails, and was now on its lone line to Nigel.

'Yes,' he said, 'I'm coming back.'

I felt, at that refreshingly timely moment, that it was now my turn to feel profoundly sorry for him. He seemed so sure of himself, so rich with determined conviction. How would he receive the pain of having his certitudes tested?

As I looked out at the receding telegraph poles and trees and bridges, and at the stillness of the sky above, I could see how much light there was now. The sun was rising fast. I couldn't help wondering, after the sudden swiftness with which the darkness had been swallowed, what the light of day would show us.

It was six forty-five when our train arrived at Nigel Station. I had an hour and a quarter to get home, pick up my books, and then rush off to school in time for the assembly at eight o'clock. As soon as the train stopped, I stood up and picked up Zani's large suitcase and travelling rug. But I only just managed to heave the suitcase off the train. The thing was too heavy. It would have been foolish of me to carry such a heavy object when the fresh, vigorous young man I was helping strode along comfortably.

'Have you got bricks or something in this suitcase?' I asked with a smile, and just managed to rest the suitcase on the platform without dropping it. Zani followed me off the train, put the provision basket on the platform, and looked at the length of the train we had just come out of. He swept his eyes all over the station like a detective who had to note every detail of the scene of a crime. Only about six other passengers got off the train. They all came from the third class carriages. There were no whites from the white section of the train. Many passengers were waiting, though, to take the train on its way back to Springs. And all the while that Zani was looking he was nodding his head slowly like a doctor who had finally recognised all the symptoms.

'No change,' said Zani eventually. 'No change. Still the same old Nigel. Small, isolated, dull. The only change I can see mirrors the very sickness of the land. The last time I was here seven years ago, there was only one foot-bridge crossing the rails. Now we have our own separate one. What progress!' He looked up at the sky for a moment, and then at me, all the while nodding.

'Yes,' he said. 'I do have bricks in this suitcase, Tee. But they are bricks of a certain kind. With them I do not build houses; I build the mind.'

I was surprised that he responded to something I had said so casually. He even seemed not to have heard me.

'You are a very serious young man,' I said.

'Times demand it,' he said, and picked up the heavy suitcase. He started walking away towards the bridge which had the NON-EUROPEANS ONLY sign.

That's it! He just walked away, as if fully expecting that I would pick up the rest of his luggage and follow him. The cheek of it! I had a distinct feeling that I was being treated like a puppy. It was the tormenting consciousness of all I was expected to do: the damning inevitability of having to bend and pick up the provision basket, and then to lumber without dignity after my master, the builder of his own mind. But I did just that. I followed him with meek obedience as if he was a magnet. Was it some natural ability in him to lead? Was it the arrogance of a strong personality? It was probably both. But I was sure there was something else; something so crushingly familiar. It seemed the same kind of moral ransom I had to pay my father-in-law. How many errands did I have to do for him? He owned me! He ran my life. He ran my house. Yes, that's how I felt as I followed that boy towards the bus stop: profoundly humiliated. Or was I just being overly sensitive? Perhaps.

When I finally caught up with him, he was waiting at the bus stop. But there was no bus. All the other passengers had simply gone to the three taxis that had been waiting at the taxi rank some twenty yards away. Two taxis took off just as I joined Zani. The remaining one, obviously waiting for us, I recognised as belonging to Ntate Pikinini, who had been running his taxi for as long as I could remember, and was known by everyone in the township.

'Well,' I said to Zani, 'school starts in an hour, so we may have to take a taxi. Besides, the bus is not

here, and from what I know of these early morning
buses to the station, it may not come at all. I suggest
we take a taxi.'

'A cheaper ride is worth waiting for,' he said.

'Well,' I said, 'there is also the convenience that a
taxi will take you home with all your luggage. Straight
home.'

'Such conveniences are not important. What matters is the principle,' he said. 'We waste too much
money. The fact of the matter is that I will get home.'
He looked up at the sky. I put his things down and
walked away to the taxi, leaving him looking up at
the sky.

'I greet you, Teacher,' said Pikinini as I got into his
taxi.

'I greet you too,' I said.

'Is the young man over there not coming?' asked
Pikinini.

'Let's go,' I said. 'That there, is a young man with a
worm under his tongue.'

I looked at Zani as we drove off. He was still looking
at the sky. Of course he knew we were looking at
him. He suddenly seemed so lonely. He was part of
the loneliness and desolation he had recognised a
few minutes before. And there would be a desolate
silence there until the next train came after an hour,
for only then would there be a bus. And soon, it
would be very hot. And he was still wearing his overcoat. I continued to look at him until he looked like a
small pole in the distance. And I began to feel a deep
loneliness within myself too. Perhaps I should have
tried to persuade him. Perhaps I shouldn't have left
him alone there. I should have offered to pay his taxi
fare. But why should I feel any obligation towards
him? Wasn't he bearing his cross? Perhaps that's the

problem: some of the weight of the cross was my own.

Nosipho, my wife, was coming out of the gate on her way to work when Pikinini stopped in front of our house on Ndimande Street. It was such a shock for me to see her, for it suddenly dawned on me that since leaving hurriedly for Springs the previous afternoon, I had not once thought of her. She looked so beautiful in her starched, white nursing uniform, and her black cape with the scarlet lining. Not once had I thought of her. She looked at me once, hesitated briefly, and continued on her way to work. How despicable I was! What a despicable man!

I got out of the taxi and called out to her. She just walked away. She walked away with that briskness that nurses are known for. My beautiful wife!

'Nosipho!' I called out again, and began to run after her. 'My sister! My wife! Wait for me!'

She walked on.

'You will not even say "where have you been?" ' I said, catching up with her.

She stopped for a while; and then walked on. I followed. I followed in the same manner that I had been following a mere boy some twenty minutes ago. The image of him alone at the bus stop at the station lingered vividly in my mind. I felt his loneliness. But I felt lonelier than he: it was a loneliness that comes from being among people who were silent, perhaps amused, witnesses to my misfortune. There were many people in the streets going to work. Some men, particularly young ones, were laughing, but women shook their heads pityingly. There were schoolchildren too in their uniforms, going to school. Soon I would be standing with the other teachers before them at assembly. Some stood and watched, while others passed discreetly, not wanting to be recognised by me. They should not have bothered. In my abject state of contrition it mattered little to me what impression all those people had of me. I just wanted to look at Nosipho; to look at her brown face. If only I could touch that face with my hand.

Someone had made a fire at the rubbish dump on the corner of Chwayi and Ndimande Streets. It was one of the many rubbish dumps in the township that people had created themselves because of a terribly inefficient municipal rubbish collection service. And when the horrible smell of rotting things became unbearable, people simply decided to set fire to the heaps, thus burning all the children's and dogs' shit, dead cats, old shoes and clothes that had become indistinguishable from the rotting fermentation of bones, food, twigs, soil, and grass. Thick acrid smoke was spreading into the streets. And it was in that smoke that Nosipho decided to stop. But when she turned to look back, it was not at me. She looked past me towards the insistent sound of a voice I had until then been hearing very faintly.

'You haven't paid me! You haven't paid me! . . .' It was Pikinini.

I noticed that he had been following me, driving in reverse, and shouting to me as he leaned out of his window. Pikinini stopped his car about three feet from me. As I was looking at him, Nosipho walked past me towards the taxi.

'Please,' she said to Pikinini, 'take me to Dunnotar Hospital. I will pay for everything.' Then she went round to the front passenger seat. Pikinini shook his

head and drove away into the location. He still had
more passengers to collect before setting out once
more.

I stood there in the thickening smoke until the
acrid smell made me choke and gasp for breath. I
walked out of the smoke in a daze. It was habit that
made me turn at the right corners on my way to school.

'Meneer,' said the principal, 'I have called you to my
office to have a very serious word with you. And you
will know that this is one of the so many times that
I'm having a serious word with you. Let's do things a
little differently this time. Since I have a feeling that
perhaps you think I'm persecuting you, I suggest you
go ahead and tell me what it is I've called you for.
Guess your own guilt, as it were.' Then he looked at
me as if I should admire him for his new, very in-
novative teaching method.

As I stood before him at his desk, I looked behind
him at a picture of Dr Verwoerd hanging on the wall
and gazing down at Principal Lehamo. Dr Verwoerd
was smiling, but it was a cold smile, tinged with a
hint of malice. The principal had put it up there soon
after the prime minister's assassination. On the morning after Verwoerd had died, the principal had
given an inspired eulogy of the dead man at assembly.
A man with a fine intellect, the principal had said. A
man whose strength of mind and character stood
before the world as a shining example of leadership.
He alone in the world could crack a granite rock in
order to dig a cave of safety for his children, his
nation. And then he closed the cave with a granite
door, and he stood facing the world with his back

to the granite door, and said to the world: "Dare me to alter my vision!"'

'Mr Zamani,' said Principal Lehamo, 'you are not saying anything. Let me tell you once more that it is because of the patience of the school board that you are still teaching here. Sooner or later I'm going to be forced to resort to my ultimate powers. I'll fire you without an ant's weight of regret. Yesterday afternoon there was a staff meeting which you knew about. We were finalising preparations for the examination next week, and were going over all the examination questions. You were not there; nor did you have the courtesy to inform me you were going to be absent; nor did you leave your examination questions with me or with one of your colleagues. We cannot continue to work like that. You are cheating the African child.'

My mind shut him out as it began to recall the strange events of that morning. There had been Zani and Nosipho. And now this. All within the space of about five hours. I felt no desire to say anything. I was conscious of my eyes blinking so much that I was not sure whether I was about to cry or not. I didn't cry. It was just one of those rare moments when I became conscious of the habit of blinking. I looked at the portrait of Verwoerd on the wall and saw how small the principal was under that gaze; so small under that cold shadow of granite. An impulse told me to go out, to go back to my class and resume the interrupted history lesson. I yielded to the impulse.

'Mr Zamani!' called the principal. 'Mr Zamani! Mr Zamani! My authority demands that you come back in here and stand before me! Mr. Zamani!'

It must have been the children, when they stood up for me as I re-entered the classroom, that restored

my senses to me. And as I looked at them standing
before me, waiting for my signal to sit down, I felt a
glow of love for them. It was the same quality of love
and joy that I had felt the day before after I had
received the telegram to go to Springs. How could I
express it? I told them to put away their textbooks of
South African history. I told them to sit down and
close their eyes and empty their minds of all thought.
I told them to think of endless darkness and then,
gradually, to let a ray of the light of time travel
through the darkness. Some of them giggled. What a
prize of giggles! Was it the joy they should take
in making new worlds? I told them to see in the ray
of light people: many people. Kings, queens, soldiers,
goldsmiths, uncles, mothers, and many people building and planting. I told them to see teachers and
children in schools. And when there were people and
buildings and monuments and fields and the sea and
ships and the sun and the moon and the stars and old
men and old women telling children stories of the
past, I told them the story of the glories of Ancient
Egypt.

I worked until late that day; until well after the
other teachers had gone home; well after the children
whose turn it was to clean up the school had gone.
My children would get their exercise books tomorrow.
I prepared my examination questions, and tomorrow's
lessons. I felt I wanted to work for ever and ever. It
had been a long time since I had felt so much energy
in me. And when I finally left the school at a quarter
past eight, I felt the vitality of summer seeping into
me. There was a rich smell of summer darkness hanging
in the evening air. It was the smell of leaves: the green
leafy hedges around the school; the tall gum trees
surrounding the netball field; the cottonwood trees

along Letsapa Street, and the peach trees in the yards of
the township. Why had I not felt this energy last night?

There were still many people in the streets. Somewhere in the darkness of Twala Street there was the
voice of a child counting for hide and seek. At the
corner of Letsapa and Mbatha Streets three girls were
playing *bhathi* under the street lamp. The two on the
outside were such accurate throwers! The one in the
middle never built a column of more than four tins
before it was brought down. I wondered if they had
any homework.

After I had passed the girls, I noticed that there
was some commotion further down, at the corner of
Nala and Moshoeshoe Streets. People were crossing
and recrossing the intersection. Cars were honking.
Men were coming out like miners from the beer hall at
closing time. I could see so many shadows of people
passing before the headlamps of stationary cars. They
looked like huge dark twigs.

'Hold him!' some men were shouting. Some five
men detached themselves from the crowd. They were
struggling with a man who held a knife in the air. The
other men were trying to push him away, and to
bring down his arms so that they could get hold of
the knife.

'Let me finish him off!' the knife wielder kept on
saying.

'Calm down now!' the men were pleading with
him. 'We don't want a corpse here!'

'Can you let someone tell you that you have the
mind of a chicken?' asked the knife wielder, heaving
wildly to free himself from the tight grip of the men.
He heaved hard and repeatedly, like someone trying
to push a car that is in gear. The fury of it made some
onlookers laugh.

'He drank of me!' shouted the man. 'I bought him all the liquor. Was it right of him then to insult me? Please, just let me put him off to sleep.'

As the men dragged the knife wielder further and further away, I turned my attention to the crowd which had gathered.

'What happened?' I asked someone who recognised me.

'Someone has been stabbed, Tee,' he said.

I forced my way to the centre of the circle to see what first aid I could administer. Two men were attending to a third who was lying on the ground on his back.

'People of the township, move back to give him some air, please!' one of the two men appealed to the crowd.

'People of Charterston, please!' said the other, whom I knew immediately. It was Buti, the weight-lifter and body-builder who had won the Mr Charterston contest some four years ago, and was still the champ, for there had never been another contest. He was getting ready to lift up the victim when he saw me.

'Tee,' he said, 'you've come at the right time. What do you think of this wound?'

'People, move back, please,' appealed the other man. 'We want to have more light from the lamp.'

'My god!' I muttered under my breath as I looked closer at the victim. It was Zani.

His shirt, soaked in blood, had been torn in half and then used as a bandage to cover the knife wound on his upper left arm. The shirt was soaked with blood. I carefully undid the rough knot to check the extent of the bleeding. I looked at the wound. It was not so deep, and the blood had already begun to coagulate.

'Not bad,' I said to Buti. 'He'll be all right.'

'That's what I thought,' said Buti. 'I was about to take him home.'

Then I looked at Zani. He was so undignified in the grip of his fear. He was breathing hard and fast like a chicken that is being slaughtered with a blunt knife, when the knife keeps on going to and fro in a cutting motion without piercing or even grazing the skin of the throat. He looked so undignified. All the self-confidence, the self-assurance of that morning had evaporated. All the human attributes. And what was left was all animal.

When he recognised me, he reached out with his right hand. I held it. He clasped my hand as if he wanted to crush it. I was probably the only one he knew there. Away from Charterston for so many years, he would be a total stranger to the township now.

'Please,' Zani said with a struggle. 'Take me home.'

'I will,' I said.

'Are you sure you want to take him there, Tee?' asked Buti with sudden concern.

I nodded firmly.

Since Zani clung to my hand, I tried to pull him up. Buti lifted him from under the shoulders to help him up. We eventually got him to his feet. I put his right arm over my shoulder and we began to stagger home. It was just then that Zani began to retch violently, and then vomited.

'Shit!' exclaimed Buti, as people scattered away to avoid getting splattered with vomit. 'I could see in there that this fellow could not handle his drinks.'

That was strange, I thought, considering the lecture Zani had given me that morning against smoking. He vomited again. The sour smell of beer which the

stomach had begun to grind steamed up to my nostrils.
I steadied him as he blew away whatever vomit dangled
in beads from his lips.

'Should we go now?' I asked him.

He nodded, wincing with pain. A few men followed
us as far as the charge office where the local constables
were sitting about nonchalantly. Not one of them had
come to investigate what had just taken place some
eighty yards away. By the time we reached the darkness of Thipe Street, no one was following us. Even
those we met going in the opposite direction barely
greeted us and passed on.

'What happened?' I ventured to ask.

'Please,' said Zani. 'Do not ask.'

As we got nearer his home, I began to realise the
significance of Buti's question. Was I really taking
Zani to his home? I had been acting impulsively and
had not considered the implications.

'You will have to go now,' I said when we reached
the gate of his home.

'Please, take me in,' he said.

'You know I can't,' I said.

But I knew he was in no condition to walk by himself. I looked at his home. There were tall reeds growing round the house along the fence. They rustled
slowly in the slight breeze and seemed to make the
space around the house darker than it actually was.
From the groggy chant of men's voices, I knew that
Zani's mother had customers.

'I think I'm bleeding again,' said Zani.

I steadied him. What if I threw a stone on the roof
and then left him at the gate. They would find him
there. But how could I afford the scandalous indignity
of such an act? Surely there was still some decency in
me. How could I face them in there: I who did not

even have the right to hate and be angry? A car turning
into Thipe Street and throwing our long shadows far
into the street decided for me. I eased Zani into the
yard and was glad to be out of the glare of headlamps.
I tried to knock on the front door, but my knock was
drowned by the singing drinkers.

'That is my room,' said Zani, 'but I did not take
the key when I left this afternoon. Please, let's go
round to the back.' We went. And I remembered that
the last time I was there, some years back, was to find
out why Mimi had not been coming to school. I came
round that morning to the back and found a row of
six men kneeling, each before a hole. They drank a
gallon of water into which Mimi's mother had put
some herbs. Then each man inserted his hand into his
mouth and vomited. MaButhelezi, Mimi's mother,
looked at them carefully from the door of the kitchen.

'Don't knock,' said Zani. 'Just open the door.'

I did as I was commanded and eased him in sideways. Three women had been laughing when I opened
the door. And then there was silence. Mimi stood up
slowly as our eyes met. But my eyes quickly went
from her to her mother, MaButhelezi, and to her
sister, Busi.

'What has happened?' said Mimi, her voice trembling
with emotion. But her sister screamed, and jumped
towards us, all the while saying: 'What have you done
to him?' She pulled Zani from me with such violence
that I lost my balance and staggered helplessly behind
them. It was the table that saved me from falling with
what would surely have been great indignity.

'Don't pull him like that,' Mimi shouted at her
sister. 'Don't you see you are hurting him more?'

'Don't shout at me like that,' said Busi sharply.

'Be careful,' said Mimi holding her brother's hand

and stroking it. Zani squeezed her hand. But it was a brief intimate squeeze, for Busi carried Zani out of sight into the dining room where men were drinking, and then further on into the bedroom. Mimi quickly yet steadily lowered a yellow basin that had been hanging from a big nail on the wall. She poured boiling water from the stove into it, cooled the boiling water by adding cold water, threw a glance in my direction, and disappeared with the basin after Zani and Busi.

Only their mother, MaButhelezi, remained unruff-led by what was happening.

Then two men appeared at the door between the kitchen and the dining room.

'What happened, Mother-in-law?' asked one of the men.

'Teacher,' said another who recognised me, 'are you the bringer of this trouble?'

I shrugged, then stepped away from the table so that I could find some security in leaning against the wall that adjoined the door through which I had just entered. From there I cast a nervous glance to-wards the third woman of the house, MaButhelezi. She continued with what she was doing without acknowledging my presence at all, or that of the two men at the door. The man in front turned round and pushed the other one back into the dining-room. It was rather like a stampede of cattle suddenly changing direction, with the front cows frantically pushing back those behind them.

MaButhelezi seemed completely unruffled. I became aware that she was humming. She was straining sorghum beer with such slow composure. Leaning against her thigh was a boy of about three or four years. He used MaButhelezi's thigh as a cushion for his head, and seemed to be struggling with sleep, for his knees kept on bending and straightening involuntarily. The contrast between the smallness of his frame and the hugeness of his grandmother spoke of the protection she completely gave him, and of his intuitive confidence that it would be freely given. I have spent long moments at the zoo, watching lion cubs playing with their mother. They were always so safe, inside a cordon of safety which was much more impenetrable than the cage bars.

'Teacher,' said MaButhelezi without raising her eyes from her work, 'may I request you to close the door.'

How foolish I had been! I could long ago and quietly have closed the door: from outside. Now I closed the door feeling as if I was sealing in the possibility of my condemnation. I leaned against the wall once more.

'There are chairs in here, Teacher,' she said again.

I sat down. She continued to work, and the boy's knees kept bending and straightening. I felt like going over to pick him up so that he could sleep on my lap, in my arms. Was that my child? I had never seen him. And at that moment, I knew that whatever retribution, whatever condemnation, whatever humiliation might await me, I felt deeply satisfied that I was there, and that whatever happened, I would know more about my child. Where was he? Was it this one?

MaButhelezi kept on scooping beer from one container and pouring it into another which had a white cloth spread over the rim, the cloth held firm by a wire that went the circumference of the rim. In the other hand, she held a wooden spoon with which she stirred the beer in the cloth strainer so that the liquid would seep through easily, leaving the brown grain residue behind. It was then that I became aware of the overpowering smell of fermented sorghum.

'What happened to my son, Teacher?' she asked.

'He was stabbed with a knife,' I said, glad to be asked. 'I was coming back from school. I had been working late. I was on my way home, and I saw this crowd of people just outside the beer hall. There had been a fight. So I went to investigate to see if I could help. It was your son, and he asked me to bring him home.'

'I am thankful to you, Teacher,' she said.

I wondered why she had not followed her daughters to go and inspect the damage to her son. She must have had some deep intuition that there was nothing too serious. Or was there something more? I thought I knew. I had lived long enough to know that there came a time in one's life when one let what had to happen, happen. No, it was far from fatalism. It was simply the result of the deepest understanding; that sometimes one could deal with the most harrowing of challenges with a calculated indifference. That way, one was assured of maximum vigilance without the indignity of anxiety.

'I met him only this morning,' I said. 'In the train from Springs.'

'I know,' she said. 'He told me.'

She finished what she was doing for I saw her remove the strainer from the rim of the big bucket and then wring out whatever beer still remained soaked in it. When she had finished she looked up at the ceiling as if she was listening intently. Then she called out.

'Busi!'

'Mama!' responded Busi from somewhere inside the house. MaButhelezi then turned to the child leaning against her thigh. She gently lifted him, and placed him on her lap in such a way that his head rested on the cushion of her huge breasts. The boy, finding comfort at last, curled up and was almost completely covered by MaButhelezi's big arms, like a blanket of flesh. Then she began to rock the child, so gently. And that was the first time since I had come in that she acknowledged my presence with a direct look at me. Those big eyes, she had given them to all her children. As she continued to look at me, I began to have a strong urge to explain myself. But I managed to resist actually saying anything. It would have been stupid, whatever I might have said. Busi appeared at the door.

'You called me?' she asked. But she was looking at me. And I saw in her face a bitterness and hate that had remained fresh over three years. I knew her well. As well as anybody in the township did. She was as tall as everyone else in her family, and as slim as Mimi and Zani. But she did not have their beauty. Nor was she ugly. No. Because of her full lips, which glowed perpetually red from a heavy application of lipstick, her thinned, darkened eyebrows so prominently arched over large black eyes, and her short hair, Busi exuded a whorish sensuousness which, for a man, was so frustratingly out of reach, if only because one had to contend first with an intimidating air of stern authority about her. Looking at her, you knew that you had to be much more than just a physically strong man to be able to eventually embrace her, and finally, to surrender to the joy of her gifts.

'There is an empty canned-fruit bottle up there. The one your father used,' said MaButhelezi. 'It's up there, on the uppermost shelf of the cupboard. It's behind the other bottles. The only one that's wrapped

up with paper. Bring it down, and pour the teacher
some beer.'

'Does he drink this kind of beer?' asked Busi with a
sneer. 'Or should I run to town now, and since the
shops are closed, break in, and bring the teacher some
whisky?'

'Busi!' called MaButhelezi. 'What kind of talk is
that?' She was not looking at Busi, she was gently
stroking the child's hair. She continued to rock him
gently.

I cleared my throat, and swallowed.

'Ma!' shouted Busi. 'How can you? In father's
bottle?'

'You heard what I said,' said MaButhelezi with
firmness in her voice.

'I will not let you insult my father in his grave,'
said Busi. 'And you, Mr Zamani. You are a teacher,
and you are many years older than I; but you are just
a dirty piece of cloth.'

'Girl! Girl!' shouted MaButhelezi with sudden
vehemence. 'This is my house. Do you hear? Until
you move into yours, and you seem determined to
avoid that, you will not be rude to people who come
in here. Do you hear?'

Busi glowered silently at me.

'Now,' continued MaButhelezi. 'The teacher comes
in here bringing home your wounded brother. Instead
of greeting him, thanking him, and offering him a
chair, you want to stir dust in my house!'

'Look!' screamed Busi. She was glaring at me, and
pointing at the child on her mother's lap. 'Look!
Look at your child. This is the first time you've ever
set your old eyes on him. And do you remember how
you made him?'

'Perhaps you should let me say something,' I said.

And at that moment I noticed that Mimi was standing behind her sister. There was alarm and anxiety in her face. I noticed, too, that there were some men behind Mimi.

'All I want to hear from you is your scream when I hit you with a red-hot poker!' said Busi, moving purposefully towards the stove. Mimi ran after her, and tried to pull her back.

'And you!' snapped Busi at her younger sister. 'You want to tear my blouse off and get me ready for your teacher?'

Mimi released her sister's blouse and turned away in shame.

I wanted to censure Busi for her cruelty. I felt I was helpless in a hornet's nest. All that I could do was wait for the inevitable stings.

Busi continued towards the stove. There was nothing she would not do to me. She had fought many men. That was what her fame in the township rested on.

'Girl!' shouted MaButhelezi. 'Are you full of dung?' Her massive frame rose to its full imposing height. She raised the child so that it rested its head on one of her shoulders. Then she passed her verdict.

'The man there,' said MaButhelezi, 'is a disgrace. When you look at him you see disgrace. But he is in your home. Now do what I told you.'

I followed her with my eyes. The men who had been peeping from the dining room door scampered away. The last thing I saw before I lowered my eyes, feeling the intense heat of my shame, was the top of my son's head as MaButhelezi disappeared with him into some inner room.

'You should go now,' said a voice that had been ringing in my ears for so many years.

I raised my head and looked at Mimi.

'You should go now,' she said again. How I loved her! The mother of my son. She bore the child I never had. How lovely she was!

Busi still stood where her mother had stopped her beside the stove. She could do whatever she liked now. But I suppose her final act of vengeance was her total refusal to do what her mother had asked her. I remembered her dark form in the street, an hour after Mimi had left my house crying. Busi had stood there, and dared me to come out. I didn't. And she smashed all the windows of my house.

'You should go now,' said Mimi for the third time. She must have felt that I wouldn't leave the house without someone's prompting. She must have known the heaviness of my shame. I felt old as I stood up slowly. I could feel my knee-caps moving. I went out. The dark night air was so refreshing. I went round to the front gate. I could have gone out through the back and walked home by another route. But even at that moment, I dreaded the possibility of stepping on children's faeces.

The front door opened as I passed, and I saw Zani silhouetted against the candlelight in the room. He did not give me any time to be surprised.

'I want to address your class next Monday,' he said. His arm was in a sling. And I could smell soured beer on his breath.

'Address my class?'

'That's what I said.'

'About what?'

'About life.'

'About life?'

'That's what I said.'

'Well, these are mere primary school children.'

'That's the point. They must be caught young.'

'Caught young?'

'That's what I said. There is so much to prepare them for.'

I walked away. It was better to walk away.

Everything is in silhouette. Everything to the west of me. Houses, trees, people, cars, horse-drawn carts, hats. It is the time of forms. For the sun finally set about an hour ago. And it is the time of forms. No wonder that this time of day has eternally been the time of stories; for it is the time of abstractions. It is the time when the mind is at rest; when it anticipates nothing else but itself, and fulfils itself in the infinitude of its creations.

I am sitting in the middle of the sofa, and I can feel the openness of space on either side of me. I choose not to fill it with the length of my body. I am sitting: in the middle of the sofa. I feel with my leg for the low table about two feet from the sofa. It is there. I am there. For I have felt it. I look across the room, at the opposite wall. And I can see the dull shine of the bookcase glass. I cannot see the books. But they are there. Old books that I have used for many years. I still take notes from them. And then Nosipho's books: old nursing textbooks, new nursing textbooks, hospital management, psychology. She reads so much. Has always read so much. As if she made a decision a long time ago that learning is what she would live for, Nosipho.

I will light no candle. I will light no lamp. I want no light in my house; for light is company. Only darkness is intimate solitude. Nosipho is not home. She will not be for some time. So I am alone, enjoying the lingering heat of mid-January, in the late evening.

It's been a long summer holiday. Since the beginning of December. I want to go back to school. I want
to teach again. I want to see the new children in my
class. Those new, eager faces full of reverence for me.
Agog with the achievement of moving to a new level
of learning. They are growing; for it is the time of life
when they become aware of change. The passage of
seasons, not the mere movement of the hands of a
clock. I want them. I have been too long away from
them. There has been enough profligacy; enough New
Year's Day picnics; enough visiting of shebeens in the
hot idleness of summer holidays. I want to teach.

Then there is a knock on the door. I listen. There is
a knock again. And this time, immediately after the
gentle knock, there is another sound. It is the sound
of a chicken croaking in discomfort. I get up, and,
instinctively, I move towards the kitchen to get a
match so I can light a candle. But I change my mind.
It will remain dark and warm; I will just go to the
door and see who is there, and we will talk in the
dark. Who is it there, I wonder. Probably someone
selling chickens. I shoot back the bolt and open the
door. I smell the perfume before I see the form of a
young woman, the smoothness of the outline of her
thick hair, the sturdy yet delicate line of her shoulders,
and the growing expanse of darkness behind her.

'Greetings, Teacher,' she says. And I know her
immediately, for her voice has always been sweetness
itself.

'Welcome!' I say.

'I was just about to think there was no one in,' she
says, and chuckles.

'And where have you been?' I say. 'Come in.' And
as she comes in, her arms move. She is moving the

chicken from one armpit to the other. The chicken squawks sharply. I shoot in the bolt.

'Sit down,' I say. 'There is a chair there close to the door.' I move over to the sofa.

'Well,' I say, 'I have not seen much of you in the last two years.'

'Yes,' she says.

'And then the next time I see you, I really don't see you. For it is dark, and I can only see your form. And then there is a chicken groaning under your armpit.'

We laugh.

'Ah!' she says. 'You know mothers. You know how they are.'

In the very brief silence that follows, I'm thinking: how wonderful! She has grown so much. The ease with which she speaks; sharing with me an adult dismissal of her mother's elderly fastidiousness. Mimi. She was so young. Now she is the very reward of a teacher: her growth. I feel a warmth in my mind.

'Well, as you know,' she says, 'since our local secondary school goes only up to Form Three, I have been travelling daily to Springs to do my Matric at the high school there.'

'Of course,' I say. 'Yes, of course. But you did not even visit us once! Only the other day Nosipho, my wife, was asking whatever happened to you.'

But I am curious. How come her mother sends a chicken? Is it for me? But I do not have long to wait to know.

'I'm bringing you good news,' she says.

Since she is good news herself, what else does she have to tell me?

'Mother asked me to bring you this chicken,' she says. 'She says she is thankful. She asked me to tell

you she is thankful. I am thankful too. I received my
Matriculation results today.'

She does not say more. I knew when she came into
my Standard Five class some seven years ago, that she
would do well at all times. I knew.

'Mother says,' continues Mimi, 'that if it were not
for you, I would not have loved education so much.'

The final, priceless gift of teaching! The gratitude
of parents! The final vindication, to children, of the
painful stress of learning. The final recognition of the
worth of the teacher.

Mimi chuckles.

Blessedness. Blessedness.

'Here is the chicken,' she says.

We stand up at the same time, and I see her move
towards me. I cannot see her eyes; I cannot see her
cheeks; I cannot see her lips; I cannot see the bulge of
her breasts beneath the dress; I cannot see the dress.
But I can see her shape. She is there. It has grown
darker now for it is finally night. I bump into the
head of the chicken with my tummy. She has proffered
it to me with both her hands. It squawks again. But I
feel no amusement now. Only a great, sad longing for
joy. My hands are not taking the chicken. They go
beyond the proffering hands to rest on two shoulders
that feel so small, so warm, in my hands. And in my
infinite gratitude, I squeeze the warm shoulders with
a deep, inner certitude that I would never let go.

I'm talking to her, but I do not understand my
words, for words have yielded more vividly to endless
years of seeing. There is no end to years. There is no
end to them. For they are as old as the world which is
ageless. And my years are nothing, for they are part
of the years of the world. Human years: so meaningless. They are a chain of visions to which the mind

can only give a transitory meaning. What is the meaning
of years and years of water? Vast expanses of water?
The beauty of steam hovering endlessly over the
water? And the fresh perfume of sorghum fields? See,
floating on the water, thousands of acorns, corn
seeds, wheat and barley, eyeballs winking endlessly
like the ever changing patterns on the surface of the
water, and the rain of sour milk pelting the water
with thick curds. I want to come into the water, but
I can't. I am trapped behind thin screens of ice. I
must break it down. I heave! And I heave! And there
is a deafening scream of squawking geese. The pain of
heaving! The frightening screams! And the ice cracks
with the tearing sound of mutilation. And I break
through with such a convulsion. And I'm in the water.
It is so richly viscous. So thick. Like the sweetness of
honey. And the acorns, and the corn seeds, wheat and
barley sprout into living things. And I swim through
eyes which look at me with enchantment and revulsion.

It is cold. It is cold. I know. Because I'm naked.
And the door is open. And the darkness inside the
house pours outside. And in the street is the fading
cry of a woman. I close the door and return to the
darkness of my house. I can feel a convulsion of
weeping gathering inside me, for I know the words
ringing in my mind: I'm a respectable man! I'm a
respectable man! I'm a respectable man! . . . And as
I grope in the dark towards the kitchen to look for a
match to chase the darkness away I stumble on
Mimi's chicken. It flutters and squawks like a voice of
atonement. I have to find it. And after a long time of
stumbling and falling and the breaking of glass and
the scattering of books, I find it. And with tremendous
force, I tear its head off, and release the chicken to
flutter to death freely in the dark. And as the fluttering

stops, I hear the screams of a woman outside.

'Come out! Come out, dog! Come out!'

There are many voices outside. Many voices. But I'm too fertile with shame to come out. And there is a shattering of windows, a festival cf falling glass, witnessing the coming of whatever sadness there will be.

Even though I did not see Zani for the next two days I never stopped wondering about him. There was something painfully immediate yet strangely liberating about him. It was as if he plunged me into experiencing the purest of sensations, the most uninhibited of impulses. That boy! He was pure fear, pure concern, pure indignation, pure conceit, pure profligacy, pure reason, pure irrationality. He seemed like a child who was trying everything because it was everything. Something like this new mathematics we were being forced to teach: the empty set that was contained in everything else. A concept which you retain only for as long as your mind is being exercised by it. And then it is gone, and you have to grapple with it again. Constant newness, constant mystery, constant frustration. Yes: every time I thought of him, those days, it was as if I was being given a new lease on life. And deep down in me, I was heinously grateful that it was he whose sister I had so horribly assaulted. And that was the pain of it all: I wanted to see him as much as I wanted to avoid him. And the joy of it was that I felt certain there was no such conflict in him.

Since that most terrible of mornings, when I ran after my wife and she ran away from me in full view of the location, Nosipho and I had not exchanged a word. It was on the evening of one Friday that I succeeded in making her open her mouth. I had been trying all along to act the contrite husband: coming home early; making a fire in the stove; peeling potatoes; dusting up. It did not work. And I knew it did not work because she was refusing my condescension; she was not allowing me to buy off painful moments with temporary acts of industriousness. No: it did not work. What worked was what came from genuine impulse: my preoccupation with Zani.

We were reading. That was the best way to fill the unbearable silence between us. Not that we did not read just as much at other times. Nosipho always had a book within reach, although she rarely read outside of her professional field. Yes, we always read: except that on that Friday evening I became conscious of the fact that the habit of reading had become the habit of avoidance. Nevertheless, we were reading. I was reading some book about civilisations. I don't know what Nosipho was reading. She was in the bedroom where she always preferred to read. I was sitting at the edge of the sofa in the living room where I always preferred to read. But if she was able to concentrate, I could not. The merry sounds of the location on Friday evenings filtered through the walls of the living room and settled in my mind. Where was Zani out there? How many people were drinking at his home?

I don't know how many times I stood up wanting to go to Nosipho in the bedroom to make a request. I would put the book down beside me, stand up, hesitate, sit down again, and pick up the book. Finally, I was not only standing but could actually feel the weight of my legs as I lifted them up to walk. Nosipho must have felt my presence at the door of the bedroom, for she lifted her head from the dressing

table where her book was lying, and looked at me.
Then she returned to her book once more.

'I have something to ask you,' I said, fully aware
that I had not said anything to her for two days. She
took her time before she said:

'What?'

'Well, you see,' I said, 'there is this young man
who got stabbed last Wednesday. A very clever young
student. I wonder if you could go over to look at his
wound. Or I could tell him to come over.'

'Who is he? What happened?' she asked with a
readiness that surprised me. But my surprise did not
last long for it was replaced by an indescribable flood
of gratefulness inside me. The readiness with which
Nosipho answered me, told me that she was ready for
conversation. Her answer, I felt, had nothing to do
with her professional concern for the injured, nor did
she really care who he was or what had happened; but
it had a lot to do with the filling of silence.

'Actually,' I said, 'he doesn't live far from here.
Just a young student.'

'Well,' said Nosipho, 'if it happened Wednesday
then it can't be that serious, for you did not say
anything to me about it that day, nor yesterday, nor
this morning.'

I shrugged my shoulders. Then she turned round
fully with her whole body for she had been sitting
with her back to the door, and had only turned her
head to look at me. Her turning round seemed to be
compensation for her rather accusatory logic. We
looked at each other. It was the first time in many
months that we had looked at each other for so long.
There it was: her firm-fleshed face. Dark eyes made
darker by thick eyebrows. Half-full lips, pinkish from
the natural colour of blood. Smooth skin. So richly

brown. Full firm arms. Living breasts. Full hips. Large firm legs. A beautiful woman in her forties. How did I look to her?

'What should I do?' I asked. 'Should I go and get him, or should we go to him?'

'Depends how far it is and how serious it is,' she said.

And then I tried to be as casual as possible.

'Oh,' I said. 'It's just the next street. At the Vuthela's. You know Zani: MaButhelezi's son. It's not far really. You'll judge for yourself the extent of the injury.'

She laughed with her lungs: the laugh of contempt in which there is a sharp ejection of air through the nose. No opening of the mouth.

'You know what, Duma?' she said. 'If there is one woman I'll never be, it is the one in the Bible who washed Jesus's feet and then wiped them dry with her hair. Nor, if I were a man, would I want to be Jesus either. The world is too big for me to claim to be carrying its sins. Jesus's is the greatest sin of self-righteousness the world has ever seen. No. I'm not capable of carrying your sins; nor would I carry them if I were capable. Take the boy to the doctor. Take him to some nurse. Carry your own sin, but do not use me as your holy water.'

'I thought we had long put that matter behind us,' I said.

'When we never even talked about it? The only language I recognised in you was your degeneration,' she said.

'What you do not realise is that I degenerated a long time ago. It was all inside. Then it came out,' I said.

'What do you mean?'

What meaning could I give her? She was doomed

never to know. I had cared enough for her all those
years never to let her know. The secret lay in the
breasts of a young woman; in the letter she wrote to
her brother, and in the restless mind of her brother.

I turned away to return to the sofa. But she pursued
me, and stood at the door where I had been standing.
This time I was sitting down and she was looking
down at me from the bedroom door.

'Let me tell you something,' she said. 'You are the
very picture of a man who has given in. All the self-
respect you had! Threw it away without a fight. All
the respect people had for you!'

I fingered the book of civilisations.

'And then the women. And then the drinking. And
then night after night of absences. And you know
what?' she said. 'To sympathise with you would be to
destroy you further. No. You should be given what
you have most desired: contempt. And then your
greatest salvation: the contempt of your woman.'

She retreated into the bedroom. It was not long
before I heard much sniffing from there. For I know
she loved me much. And much had she stung me with
her words. And the truth of them was the truth of
rain falling after a long drought. But the drought had
been too long; very little would grow again.

After a long time of staring at the book of civilisations, I put out the paraffin lamp next to me, and rose
to go and sleep. After undressing I sat naked at the
edge of my bed and looked at Nosipho breathing
regularly in her sleep. And I felt how worn my body
was. So unfit. Too unfit for any hard task. The sagging
breasts with wrinkles going across; useless strands of
hair around the nipples; a navel closed shut by flabs
of stomach; and from the depths of where a sagging
stomach met with tired thighs, peeped the point of a

circumcised penis, too tired now to be a release for
passion. Had it been consumed by the fire of its own
corruption? Perhaps that is why tears filled my eyes
as I stared at Nosipho in her sleep: once more, another
month would pass without my visiting her bed.

And as sleep slowly came to me in the dark, I realised
that I was massaging the upper part of my left arm, as
if I had a wound there.

Saturday. One of those rare Saturdays when I stayed
home the whole day. There was nothing really to
keep me home. Nosipho, as usual, was on duty at the
hospital. I suppose I had a strong desire not to see the
streets of the township. Most people, except those
who worked until one o'clock, were at home. I had
no wish to greet or be greeted. I had no wish to see
people dressed up to go to town for some shopping. I
had no wish to get the feeling that I was being watched from behind lace curtains. Nor did I have any wish
to be respected.

Yet it was a beautiful morning. The sky was clear
and blue in the bright light of the summer morning sun.
There was a languid freshness in its heat, resulting in a
mild narcotic feeling, which probably came from the
mixture of the heat with the smell of the trees, of the
vegetation in the garden plots of houses, and of the
thinning bluish haze of smoke from the coal stoves of
the township. Groups of township doves flew across
the sky. And there were swallows, seemingly in perpetual motion; and there were yellow weaver-birds;
and there were wild doves flying in pairs.

I took out my garden tools. I would turn the soil
and try to plant something. I had not seen those tools

for many years, for it's Nosipho who is the gardener.
Yet I remember when I bought them; how I wanted
to be the township's model gardener! It had not
worked. The dream was much easier than the work to
achieve it. I looked at the tools and tried to find some
fault in them, for I realised that I wanted a pretext to
go and see Zani. I would go to his home and say: 'My
spade is worn out, can I borrow yours?' Foolish. That
would be foolish.

I turned the soil in the back yard, raked up, and
prepared the little plots for planting. I sweated so
much. And the sun rose and became hotter and
hotter. And when I felt the sweat rolling down
my body inside my shirt and my trousers, I worked
even harder, wishing to sweat more and more. And
as I worked I felt an exhilarating unity of mind
and body, for my mind seemed to become clearer
and more alert; and I knew that for as long as
my mind felt that way I would work without
end.

It was only when I wanted seeds to sow that I
began to feel the fatigue. For I did not find any seeds
in the house. And then I thought of Zani again. Supposing I went to his home and said: 'I have run out of
seeds, can you give me some of your sorghum seeds?
Some maize, some wheat?' What would they think of
me? I would have to go to town to buy some seeds.
But I didn't go: I had no wish to venture out into the
world. The garden would have to wait. It was ready,
but it would have to wait.

Even after I had washed and was feeling new, I had
no wish to go out. So I slept on the sofa. As I lay
there, I could feel the occasional breeze of fresh air
coming in through the open windows. And it was
cool in my house, as if I were lying in the shade of a

gum tree in the middle of a wide open space. And I was glad that in summer we always kept the windows open. I slept for so long I did not even hear Nosipho come in. It was the splashing of water in the bedroom that woke me up. And I knew, my eyes still closed, that Nosipho was back and was washing herself in the bedroom. I could hear her going to throw the water out. I could hear her return to the bedroom to groom herself. And it was at that moment that I heard a slight, rather timid knock on the door. I opened my eyes and raised myself up to respond, and as I did so I noticed that Nosipho was standing at the bedroom door. She smiled at me.

'I'll open the door,' I said. And as I was about to turn the door knob I heard her speak.

'I've seen the garden,' she said. 'It's beautiful.'

We smiled at each other, and I wanted to tell her how beautiful she was. But I didn't. I could never bring myself to the frivolity of telling my wife such things. As I opened the door Nosipho went into the bedroom again.

At the door was Zani. We looked at each other, and the first thought that came to my mind was what, of all things, was he doing at my house? Yet there he was, full of the summer, for he was as handsome as the earth was alive. He wore a V-necked white T-shirt with long sleeves, well fitting grey slacks and sandals which had only one hole each for the big toe. His left arm was in a white sling. And against the lightness of his clothes, the blackness of his face came forth with a smooth, dull, sensuous sheen. And the sun was behind him, for it was about five-thirty.

Zani smiled respectfully at me before he greeted.

'I have come to greet you,' he said.

'That makes me happy,' I said. 'Please come in.'

'Well,' he said, 'I was just passing by.'

'And you wanted to greet me at my door?' I asked rhetorically. 'Surely, that is not being a person. I've never heard of a person who came to someone's door just to greet, and then turned away without entering the house.'

I could see he was embarrassed.

'Then I will come in,' he said.

I moved aside so that he could come in. He went straight to the sofa and sat there. This confused me somewhat because I always sat on the sofa, instinctively. I closed the door by leaning on it with my back, as I looked at Zani seated where I always sat. It was with some resentment that I took the chair next to the door. My resentment increased when he suddenly seemed oblivious of me and was looking over the living room with absorbed interest. He looked at the low table just in front of him. It had a glass top with three white crocheted mats placed diagonally under the glass. He looked at the shining tiles on the floor. But he spent more time on the bookcase and on the walls which were painted with many geometrical designs. When he finally looked at me it was as if I was part of the furniture, but his eyes soon cleared and I saw that he was fully aware of me.

'This house is beautiful,' he said. 'But . . . .' He did not continue. He shrugged his shoulders.

'But what?' I asked.

'You see,' he said, 'that is exactly what I came about.'

'About what?' I asked.

'I was going to say, you see, that the beauty in here does not come from you.'

We were silent as we looked at each other. Then he looked away.

'You see,' — he was looking at the books — 'that is what I've come about. I shouldn't speak this way to you. Sometimes I just blurt things out. I have not seen you since last Wednesday, and I've been feeling the pain of having done wrong. And I wanted to come to you to apologise.'

'So you were not just passing by?' I asked. He looked at me.

'Why didn't you let me get away with my lie?' he asked.

'I wanted to be inconsiderate towards you,' I said, laughing and trying to make my answer seem like a light joke.

Zani sighed deeply.

'I have come to apologise for all the terrible things I said to you. And then I want to thank you for what you did for me Wednesday night,' he said. 'You see, it's that sort of thing that led me to this.' He pointed with his head at his left arm.

'What sort of thing?' I asked.

'Since I came back here,' he continued, 'I've found out what loneliness is. And you're the only person I know. The only one I can talk to. It's a long time since I left this township to live with my uncle in Johannesburg. Everybody here is a stranger now. I'm a stranger too. I find there's very little that has changed, and if there is any change, it has been for the worse.

'But the real point of it all, Tee, is what should I do? . . . You see . . . . You see . . . . She is the heart of my heart.'

I was puzzled.

'Who?' I asked. 'The township?'

'She is the heart of my heart,' he repeated. And when he continued he looked either at the door or at the bookcase, never at me. He seemed to be struggling with something whose nature was vivid to him, yet whenever he reached out, it went away. Like walking in a tunnel when the light at the end keeps receding.

'For seventeen years,' said Zani. 'All my life so far . . . . For seventeen years, I wanted nothing to do with them. When you are a boy, six, seven, eight, nine, or even ten, and there is one of those silly games to be played, and all of them say: "I want Zani to be my husband! Zani will be my husband!" And the game would wait until the conflict was resolved. And you end up with three, sometimes four wives, and many daughters. And then the boys begin to mock you, for none of the girls will have them as husbands. And they mock you and say: "Maybe it's because you look like them." And then you begin to hate girls. And you hate them for so long, as a matter of habit, until you realise that you need them. And when you start after them, all those wives and daughters are no longer there. And you have to pursue them like a hunting dog.

'No. I had no patience for that. For there were other things I discovered that were much more worth pursuing: the vastness of the world. The universe, the earth, animals, plants, insects, the power of language and all the works of man.'

As I listened to him I felt like laughing. He suddenly seemed so old.

'And I spent hours and hours reading and thinking; reading and thinking. And all that work of preparation seems doomed to come to nothing. "If only. If only." That is the phrase that torments me. And all because of the only girl to mean so much to me from the very moment we first saw each other. It's not so much her beauty, she has stars of that; it's her intelligence! Her brilliance! The radiance of her mind! Why should she be the one to lead me into a ditch? What's going to happen now?'

'I'm not following you,' I said. But he ignored me.

'And it had to happen in a train. A swaying train. For the first time in my life. The indignity of it all. The sin of it all. In the swaying darkness of a moving train. Why didn't she refuse? Tell me. Yet she was so near to me. Never had I been so aware of another person. But how can I continue to love her? What will happen to all my dreams if they are to be lost in bringing up a child? And what will be the meaning of the matriculation exams I have just written? And then the meaninglessness of bringing up a child in all the meaningless life around you. My mother, my sisters, my uncle! What will their efforts have been for?

'And then I behaved like a fool at the station. Why didn't I wave back to her? Why did I just see in her the obstacle she might become? Will she forgive me? Yet how can I continue to love her? Aren't there higher things in life than marriage?'

How I envied him! He was new, so fascinatingly tormented by his first real joy! He seemed as helpless as he was the first time I saw him and the girl was waving to him. What could I tell him? What would he want me to tell him? I have spent so much of my life telling children what to do. Has it worked? Where are all those recipients of my wisdom? They have drifted into the oblivion of factories, prisons, and into a kind of indescribable, all-pervasive aimlessness. That has been the greatest lesson in their lives: not anything I have counselled, but the fact of what their whole lives have become. Besides, I didn't feel qualified any more to advise anyone about any serious problem. What social compulsion was there for a teacher to be exemplary? And the school: it was a place at which our children were groomed to give away the whole energy of their lives to something other than the dream of their history.

Zani was waiting for me to say something, and I did say something.

'What do you think I can tell you?' I asked him.

I saw a faint flicker of the old arrogance flit across his face as if he was saying: 'Indeed there is nothing in you.' Then I felt like laughing. Wasn't there something comically grotesque about the incongruity between his sharp perceptions, his intelligent and articulate arrogance on the one hand, and his pitiful immaturity on the other? But I prevented myself from bursting out. Yes, I had taught so many, but never had I come across such a bold type. Most of our young people had been so cowed by the impotent traditional authority of the elderly that talking to them was always a bore. They would say what they expected you wanted them to say. Was this the new breed? Zani? If so, I have had no lessons on how to deal with it. No preparation. Only an intuition of compassion might help: the impulsive feeling that they should do better than I.

'At least you love her,' I said at last. 'You should be grateful for that.' And you will learn, I said in my mind, that you cannot put aside everything in pursuit of dreams.

Just then, the bedroom door screeched a little on its hinges, and Nosipho emerged from the bedroom. She stood at the door and smiled at us. Zani looked at her, and there was a mortified expression on his face. He stood up slowly yet somewhat inevitably, as if a magnet was pulling him up.

'Nosipho,' I said, 'this is Zani Vuthela.' I thought

she would change her expression but she didn't.

'I thought so,' she said. 'It's the sling I saw. How is the arm?'

Zani did not answer. I don't think he even heard her. He gazed at Nosipho as if his eyes were for nothing else. It was as if he was seeing a vision. It was most intriguing. Nosipho advanced towards him, gently lifted his left arm, freed it from the sling, pumped it up and down, gently felt around the bandage, and then put the arm back in the sling.

'Who bandaged you?' she said.

'My sister,' said Zani with a distant voice.

'She did something for all eyes to see,' said Nosipho. 'You're on holiday from school?'

'Yes,' said Zani, nodding.

'How nice,' she said. 'One of these days you must come and tell us about it. I mean your school.'

Zani stretched his closed lips in a brief, confused smile.

'Now, let me bring you two some tea,' said Nosipho. 'Or do you want something to eat?' she asked looking at me.

'Whatever,' I said.

Nosipho went into the kitchen. And when she was gone Zani sat down as slowly as he had stood up. And then he shook his head, fixing his eyes on the floor. After a while he looked at me.

'Do you think?' he said. 'Do you think she heard everything?'

'Could be,' I said, shrugging my shoulders, and wondering why Nosipho had to come in just at that time.

'I should have known,' he said. 'The perfume; the smell of soap. What is she going to think of me?'

Zani stood up again; but this time more purposively.

He seemed in a trance as he walked to the door. He
opened it and walked out, closing it carefully after
him. He did not come back. Nor did I go after him.
His cup of tea would represent him. I just sat where I
was and waited for Nosipho to come back to overwhelm me with the self-assurance of her womanhood.

Monday the fifth was a very hot day. What a day to
begin examinations! The children were sweating, I
was sweating; they were yawning, I was yawning;
some just slept, but although I wanted to sleep too, I
couldn't. I had an examination to conduct and I had
to keep everybody awake. And that was a difficult
task, for it was the day of oral examinations. Someone would be reading or reciting a poem, or recollect-
ing some event in history, and others would be listening
and sweating, and yawning, and sleeping. Occasionally
a small, round paper missile, dripping wet with someone's saliva, would fly across the classroom. But I
would pretend to have seen nothing while the culprit
wore a straight face, convinced that no one had seen
him, and the victim would fume with frustration. In
the old days I would have whipped the whole class.
   It was while a boy was reciting from an epic poem
on a Zulu king that another boy entered the classroom. He had asked to go to the lavatory a few
minutes earlier. He seemed unnaturally upright when
he walked in and there was a mischievous look on his
face. I knew immediately that there was something he
carried under his armpit. The boy who was reciting
continued to jump up and down trying to recreate
the greatness of kings, while Daniel went to sit down.
It was not long before there were sniggers at the back

of the class, for Daniel had passed something under
the desk, and everyone who saw it laughed. I would
have let them be if their sniggers had not developed into
a low irritating rumble.

'Daniel,' I said without looking up from the table.
There was immediate silence. 'Come up here and
bring what you have just brought in from outside. I'm
sure everybody would like to enjoy it.'

I looked up and found that he was standing. He
might have been thinking up a lie, but he decided
against it. He brought out the paper from under the
desk and slowly walked up to my table. Everyone was
alert now. We all followed Daniel with our eyes as he
stepped up to my table on the wooden platform. He
stood facing me on my right and did not give me the
paper. I stretched out my hand.

'The paper,' I said.

But Daniel held on to the paper just long enough
to suggest his reluctance, and then accepted the calling
of fate. I looked at the paper and immediately recognised it. The township had woken up that morning
to find many handwritten posters placed all over.
Written with a black felt pen across standard type-
writing paper was: DAY OF THE COVENANT:
STAY HOME AND THINK. And on others: DIN-
GANE'S DAY: STAY HOME AND THINK. There
had been many of them in the morning, and schoolchildren and workers read them and talked about
them. It was certainly something new in the township.
There had never been anything like that before. All
we were used to were posters announcing coming
concerts.

'Where did you get this?' I asked Daniel.

'In the lavatory, sir,' he said.

So those in the lavatory survived, though the prin-

cipal had ordered that they all be torn down. Daniel's
poster had something more on it.

'Did you do this?' I asked him.

'No sir, I didn't, I didn't,' he said pleading. 'It was
not me!'

Of course he couldn't have done it. The drawing
was too elaborate. It was a drawing of a penis completely inside a vagina, such that even the testicles
seemed to be struggling to go in too. I had seen many
such drawings before, and what always struck me was
not so much the organs themselves, but that they
almost always had no people attached to them. They
were just organs locked into each other like discarded
nuts and bolts.

'Daniel,' I said, 'wouldn't it be nice if I showed this
to the whole class?'

Daniel looked down at his feet.

'No sir,' he mumbled.

'Why not, Daniel?' I asked.

'Just, sir,' he said.

Poor fellow! At his young age he already thought
sex was some disembodied obscenity.

'Sit down, Daniel,' I said. He shuffled away in
shame. And I looked at the reciter of epics a few feet
away. He still stood there where he had been torn
away from his recollection of history, and thrown
back into an obscene disembodied present which had
no vital connection with the recollected glories;
nothing in it to maintain the validity of the past. I
motioned him back to his seat and wrote down his
marks.

It was as I was recording the marks of the epic reciter
that there was a sudden shuffling of feet and a
shifting of desks as the children struggled to stand up
as they always did when another teacher or a visitor

entered the classroom. I looked at the door. Zani came in. I sat back in my chair and watched him come nearer. I think he was aware that he was intruding for his face carried a smile of appeasement.

'Good afternoon, sir!' chanted the children.

Zani was flustered. He gave me a sheepish look. I don't think he had ever been respected like that. I think that for the first time in his life he was confronted with the reality of growing up. The children had stood up for him. The full impact of his young adulthood shocked him and left him confused. And the children stood there looking at one who did not know as yet how to handle the demands of his age. Like a horse, they knew the new climber had no experience of controlling. I motioned them to sit down.

His left arm was still in a sling, and he carried a familiar leather briefcase in the other hand. He was cleanly dressed in a white, short-sleeved shirt, neat grey flannel trousers, white socks, and black shining moccasins. He was the very picture of coolness in that heat. His well combed hair seemed to have been brushed back by the breeze itself.

'I hope you're not surprised,' he said in a shy whisper.

'I must confess to be,' I said. I still sat back in my chair and felt I was looking at him rather lazily.

'But you knew I was coming?' he asked.

'Frankly, I did not,' I said. 'I did not think you were serious.'

'I'm a person who does what he says he's going to do,' he said. Then he seemed to relax somewhat, I think because he had made his first positive declaration since coming in. I wiped off sweat from my forehead with my hand and looked at the children. They were all eyeing Zani with interest.

And then he saw it; the poster on the table.

'What's this?' he asked. His voice was totally neutral. He picked up the poster.

'What?' I asked. 'The writing or the drawing?'

'Do you think this is a defilement of the poster or a defilement of the coming holiday?' he asked.

'It could be either, it could be neither,' I said.

'What is it doing on your table? Did you do this?' he asked.

I laughed.

'A schoolchild brought it in from the lavatory to show it off to his friends,' I said.

'What depravity!'

'Look,' I said. 'I think you have come at the wrong time. We are in the middle of an examination. In an hour's time school will be over. I have to finish.'

'But you're my only hope!' he pressured. 'The principal of the secondary school refused to let me speak. Your school is my only hope. Then I will pass on to the churches.'

'Exactly what do you want to talk about to these children?' I asked.

'What else can one talk about in this country?' he said. 'Look, every minute, every second should be an instance of struggle.' His voice was beginning to rise and with it the curiosity of the children.

'But they are so young,' I said.

'That's the important age,' he said. 'They may not understand what I have to say, but they'll remember the day.'

'Have you been to the principal?' I asked.

'No,' he said. 'He would refuse, wouldn't he?'

I decided I would probably finish the oral examinations later by keeping the children a little longer. I stood up.

'Children,' I said, 'listen. Do you see this person before you? He is a very important visitor. His name is Mr Zani Vuthela. Who?'

'Mr Vuthela!' came the chorus.

'Good! You may either know him or have heard of him. But this is one person who has read a lot of books. And when a person has read many books what does he have?'

'He has knowledge!' came the chorus.

'And when he has knowledge what does he also have?'

'The light of truth!'

'And when he has the light of truth what can he do?'

'He can lead his people!'

'Good! Good! Now, Mr Vuthela wants to talk to us. He wants to give us some of his light. He is Charterston's very own light. Soon he will be going to study where most knowledge is to be found: at a university. Where?'

'At a university!'

'Good! Good! And when someone has this much knowledge, he must be respected and listened to very carefully. Okay, Mr Vuthela, over to you.' I rose and went to the back of the class, where I sat next to Daniel. I looked at Zani from the back of the class. He went through all the motions of a speaker trying to gain confidence. He put his briefcase on the table, unstrapped it, peered into it as if he was looking for something very important, and eventually produced papers, which he straightened on the table. Then he looked at the class.

'Ladies and gentlemen,' he began, honouring all those ten-year olds. Then he lifted one of his papers and held it up lengthwise before the class. 'I want you to look at this paper and tell me what's written on it.'

A number of hands shot up.

'Everybody!' he said.

'DAY OF THE COVENANT: STAY HOME AND THINK!' went the chorus, while something dawned on me. Was Zani responsible for all those posters?

'Yes,' he said, as if answering me. 'I want to talk to you about the Day of the Covenant. They used to call it Dingane's Day. Why the change of name? I will tell you. You will know from your history that on the sixteenth of December, 1838, there was the Battle of Blood River when the Boers killed thousands of our people. Our people were ruled by King Dingane at the time. And from that time, the Boers called that day Dingane's Day. It was a day to commemorate death. And every year on that day, the Boers went out into the streets marching with guns and bugles, clearing the streets of any Africans. Death. The day of death and vengeance! The commemoration of death and blood.

'But even the Boers can undergo some refinement. With the passage of time, the ritual of physical cruelty becomes cumbersome; and it has to be dignified with something abstract. Now we have the Day of the Covenant. For the Boers tell us that on that day they prayed to their Christian God and said: "Lord of Lords! Father of David! If You can help us win this war, if You can help us finish off the savages, we will build You a Church; we will build You a country that will reflect Your glory, and live in solid fear of You." Yes, ladies and gentlemen, the Church of blood and death, a country of fear and oppression. When evil becomes a philosophy or a religion, it becomes rational or spiritual malice: the highest forms of depravity. Do you hear what I'm saying? Do you understand what I'm saying?'

That they heard, I was sure; but that they understood, was impossible. The children just stared back at him. I could sense his frustration. All the while he spoke, he kept the poster up and moved it from side to side as if the poster had the power to decode his words for their young minds. I didn't think the poster served more than for dramatic effect. And it struck me at that moment just how evenly serious Zani's language was. He had become his books, and when he moved out of them, he came out without a social language. He spoke to me in the same way he spoke to those children. Is that how he had spoken in the bar, and then got stabbed? I wondered if he was not another instance of disembodiment: the obscenity of high seriousness.

And then what I had dreaded occurred. The principal was passing my classroom. He looked in through the windows and then moved on to the open door, where he stopped to have a closer look. He saw Zani standing before the class, and he saw the poster Zani was moving from side to side.

'What, in the name of God, is happening here?' said the principal.

Zani looked at him and slowly lowered the poster.

'Who are you?' asked the principal. 'I'm not aware of having hired a new teacher. Where is Mr Zamani?'

'I'm here, *Meneer,*' I said, rising from my desk at the back of the classroom. I walked up to the front.

'What is going on?' asked the principal in Afrikaans. He used that language under the smallest pretext. He moved from the door and walked into the classroom.

'Nothing serious,' I said. 'Just a little talk about history from our guest.'

'It is a serious matter,' broke in Zani. 'I'm here to talk about the day on which we are cruelly made to celebrate our own defeat; and that is a serious matter.'

'*Meneer,*' said the principal glaring at me, 'I need a full explanation. Only this morning I ordered that all these posters be pulled down and destroyed. The next thing is I find them in one of my classrooms with a strange young man displaying them before these children . . . and . . . what in the name of God is this one on the table?' He seized the poster with the sexual organs drawn on it, tore it with much violence into very tiny pieces, and scattered them out of the window. Then he glared at me again.

'Mr Zamani,' he said, 'do you want to destroy me? Must you be my curse? I'm still waiting for an explanation.'

'Mr Lehamo,' said Zani with a composure I had not seen in him before, 'may I respectfully ask why you must raise your voice at your teacher in front of the children he teaches?'

'Young man,' replied the principal, 'I don't know who you are, and I don't wish to know who your parents are, for they would be shamed by all this. But of one thing I'm certain, I want you to leave the premises of my school right now. I will not have my educational institution turned into a nest of subversion.'

'But you have not even heard what was being said,' said Zani.

'I don't need to. Do you want me to call the police? I will not have my record with the government spoiled by an unknown upstart.'

Zani fixed his eyes steadily on the principal, and I could see that he was assessing him. Then Zani started laughing. He just started laughing. It was not the laughter of ridicule; it seemed to be the most appropriate way to express the sudden realisation of something one had merely heard about, and had then unexpectedly come across in a vivid example. It was the laughter of recognition.

'I think you should go,' I said to Zani. But I needn't have bothered. As he laughed, he put his papers into the briefcase. He fastened it, and prepared to go. And when he was ready, his briefcase hanging from his right hand, he turned to me.

'I thank you for your kindness,' said Zani, and walked out. Even when he had gone out, the principal and I continued to look at the door for what seemed like quite a long time. Then he turned to me.

'*Meneer,*' he said, 'I'm very disappointed. I'm afraid I'll have to make a report to the school board about this. Furthermore I seem to remember that this is the day for oral examinations; and so, the school programme was put aside for mindless subversion. That too, the board will have to note.

'Oh, *Meneer,* I'm not persecuting you. I'm not. It's just that . . . .' He shrugged his shoulders and threw his arms out. 'I'll see you later about this,' he said and walked out of the classroom.

I went to the table and sat on it, facing the children, and swept my blinking eyes over the whole class. They all stared at me as if expecting me to say something. How could they understand what I now realise I felt very deeply: contempt. Three months after they had fired me for rape, they sent a delegation to me in the dead of night. It was autumn, and the streets were full of fallen leaves. I heard footsteps crushing leaves right up to our front door. I opened the door for them: four heavily clad respectable men on a civic mission.

'Teacher, the events of the last few months have been hard on us all. But when the heavy rains have passed, and the clouds are gone, and the sun is out, and we see slanting trees, fences sagging, roofs blown away, and plants choked by what was meant to give them life, we have to look around to see where all the men are. As you know, Teacher, we are short of teachers. And we have to continue to produce good results. We are hoping to see a spade in your hand soon.' They had left it at that, at the compelling indefiniteness of metaphor.

'Let me tell you what my friend Mr Coetzee, the location superintendent, said to me in person when he learned you had been reinstated,' said the principal's letter to me a few days later. "You really are an immoral people, and that is as it should be." Think about that Mr Zamani. I hope the board was right, but I'm still not convinced.'

When people have very few choices, of what use is morality? Is it doing what has to be done? Perhaps it is not contempt I should be feeling, but the profoundest admiration.

'My children,' I said at last. 'You have just had your first real lesson since you came to school. And from today onwards, know that when you come in here to open your books you are like someone waiting at the railway crossing for the train to pass. But the train before you is a very long one: it is made of years, and years, and years. And while it is passing, know that the real school is outside there, and that today, that school was brought into this classroom for a very brief moment. And one day when that school out there is finally brought into this classroom forever, you will know that the train of years has finally passed, and it is time to go on with your journey.

'Now, let me look at my register here. Who is next? . . . .' The final bell rang. And immediately, there was the noise of fidgety children picking up books and banging them on the desk to straighten them. No, I would not keep them. Let them go home.

Friday the ninth: last day of school, last day of the year. Always on the last day of the school year, a teacher feels a terrible loneliness inside. It is then that he realises how much the children have become a part of his life; how much he has become dependent on them.

Two o'clock that afternoon found me alone in my classroom. It had been thoroughly scrubbed, the floor polished, the windows so cleaned that they seemed not to be there, and the desks and my table shining positively. The children were all gone. They had congregated just outside the school as they always did after they had been dismissed. I had told them not to close the windows, for the fresh air was part of the cleanliness and so was the smell of home-made polish, a mixture of candle wax and paraffin. I would close the windows when I left. I stood next to one of the windows overlooking Letsapa Street, and watched the children. Some were singing, others were playing and chasing one another, and there were the inevitable, immature courtships in which boys twisted girls' arms to submission. I felt so rejected. Not because I felt they did not like me, but because I would never again be young enough to be there with them.

It was not long before I heard the distinct chant that was so familiar to everyone in the township. It was coming from the direction of the beer hall. 'First Grade! First Grade! First Grade!' went the chant. I smiled in spite of myself. It was the familiar call of

Ndabeni, the township's popular meat hawker. He would go up and down the streets with his bicycle, selling meat. Children loved him; and so did their mothers who all called him their son-in-law. 'What have you got for me today, son-in-law,' they would say as they approached Ndabeni, holding in their hands enamel plates of all shapes and ages. And after a purchase, the children would follow after Ndabeni, all the while shouting 'First Grade! First Grade!' with him, while their mothers, enamel plates balanced on cupped fingers and raised just above their heads, went back into their houses with meat.

In a moment Ndabeni came into my view, and many schoolchildren in their black and white school uniforms milled around him. He pedalled slowly through the chanting children who jumped away just a fraction of a second before the front wheel of his bicycle could hit them. Occasionally, Ndabeni would thrust his fist into the air and the children would chant ever more wildly. And each time that fist went into the air I recognised the sleeve of Ndabeni's inevitable green jersey which he wore every day in every season. And I knew too that under his inevitable grey and white striped pinafore, he would be wearing his dark khaki trousers; and he would be pedalling with his big, aged boots, whose original colour it was hard to tell. Then I noticed, sitting on the metal frame over Ndabeni's rear wheel, someone whom I couldn't clearly identify from that distance. But they were slowly coming closer to the school, and the closer they got to the school, the denser the mass of chanting children they had to cut through. And when he was right in the middle of Letsapa and Twala Streets, Ndabeni stopped altogether. He was about twenty yards from the school now. He thrust his fist into the air

and the noise of chanting children rose into an insistent call and response rhythm, accelerating into a frenzy
of chanting and dancing: 'First-grade! First-grade!
First-grade! First-grade! First-grade! First-grade! . . .'
It was a dance of rain drops: little children in black
and white in the streets under the afternoon sun.

And then something else happened. The man behind
Ndabeni raised a big board and turned it this way and
that way. It had written on both sides in huge black
letters: DINGANE'S DAY: STAY HOME AND
THINK! THINK! THINK! It was held up by one
hand. I immediately knew that the other hand must
have been in its sling. And when Zani's free hand was
not turning the board this way and that, it was
thrusting it into the air rhythmically. And he was
shouting, though from the movement of his lips he
was not shouting what the children were chanting.
Then I saw Ndabeni pointing frantically to the board.
But his hawking call was no longer his; it belonged to
the children, and only they would stop it.

In another moment there was some commotion
further down in the direction from which Zani and
Ndabeni had come. A mass of children were scattering
away frantically. It soon became clear why. Three
local policemen were charging into the children with
bicycles. The chant faltered, picked up again, but
broke and scattered when more and more children
were blown away by the three-fold hurricane of
policemen. I recognised them in their tan uniforms
and shiny toney-red boots; their faces barely visible
under their over-sized helmets. By the time they
reached Zani and Ndabeni all the children had run
away from their idol. Constable Hlophe, who reached
the two men first, jumped from his bicycle while it
was still in motion. It moved on its own some ten feet

towards the school, until it fell to the ground from loss of momentum. Hlophe seized the poster and wrenched it from Zani's hand with such force that Zani's body followed it, though he did not lose his balance. Hlophe flung the poster away. And as he spoke to Zani he kept on pointing at where it lay, some distance down the street.

The second constable, Mbimbi, went after the poster, and when he got to it, stamped on it with his boots. He picked it up and tore it to pieces with wild violence. Then he scattered the pieces all over. Having surveyed the scene of his destruction with satisfaction, he walked towards Hlophe and Masikase, who was their sergeant. They stood on either side of Zani and Ndabeni. But it was Zani they were interested in. There was much gesticulation. Then Hlophe pushed Zani violently. But Zani sat up again without having lost his balance. Ndabeni shouted something, and Hlophe looked at him, said something, and then raised his index finger and placed it across his lips. Ndabeni looked away. Zani turned round to point at his destroyed poster, and then faced Masikase who waved him away with a gesture of dismissal. Masikase then pointed up the street, seeming to urge Zani and Ndabeni to proceed. But Zani turned round once more and pointed at his poster. Hlophe must have lost his temper, for he dragged Zani off the bicycle by the collar of his white shirt. Zani tottered backwards and fell on his back. And when he tried to crawl away, Hlophe kicked him in the pelvis, while Mbimbi kicked him in the ribs. Zani doubled over with pain. Sergeant Masikase raised his hands to stop them. Ndabeni laid his bicycle down and went to Zani's rescue. The three policemen walked away towards their bicycles. They pedalled away, more slowly this time, in the direction from which they had come.

Ndabeni raised Zani to his feet and helped him limp towards the bicycle. When he had lifted his bicycle from the ground he motioned Zani to sit. But Zani shook his head. Then Ndabeni pushed his bicycle forward, while Zani limped along beside him. They walked up towards Mbele's Store. A few children regrouped around them. Some children tried to revive the 'first-grade' chant, but there was no spirit for it any more. Zani seemed quiet, while Ndabeni seemed to be saying much to him. I watched them until they disappeared from view.

I withdrew from the window and went to sit at my table, and I looked at the empty classroom. The whole school, including my children, had just seen another first. Never in living memory had there been any public expression of political concern in the township. Charterston had always been a quiet, law-abiding community, no matter what upheavals took place in Johannesburg thirty-three miles away, or in any other major city in the country. Demonstrations had life only in newspapers. And then the first one came, and was put out like a candle flame. How many people had seen it before it was put out? How many mothers buying meat? When did Zani meet Ndabeni? How? Where?

But even though the township had just seen something new, I could feel no joy in me. In fact, I felt a deep disappointment. Something new has to come out of the unknown like ants coming out of the earth for their nuptial. And no matter how many swallows come in to devour the flying ants, no amount of destruction will overshadow the event of spring. Zani, with his poster flying in the air from his one hand, had seemed as powerless as the day he stood before my class and let his heavy words melt into the heat of the classroom. And who had put out the flame of his impulsive zeal? Hlophe, an unpopular township constable: tall, lean, and strong, notorious for his violent assaults on people and his lurid insults. He was the very epitome of brutality. It fed on nothing but pure hate, and was invariably directed at the powerless. And then, Mbimbi: as ugly as his name suggested. A short-tempered fellow with a long criminal record. And Sergeant Masikase, an old man who, in his early days as sergeant, used to wear brown pantaloons and ride his horse through the streets of the township in search of wrong-doers. His rolled up moustache, which was then bent forwards at the ends, so that the strands looked like the horns of a bull, made him look particularly fierce. And his dark face under the helmet, whose strap ran under the chin, made him the picture of a sergeant. They were all employed on the recommendation of the township's Advisory Board, most of whose members were also on various school boards. They were the destroyers of hope, for they knew nothing about hope; they were part of a world completely overcome by hopelessness. And it was this hopelessness that brought everything, including Zani, to the level of its own dreamless sleep.

When I finally came out of the classroom an hour later, the school was already completely deserted. I stopped at the school gate and saw, about fifty yards away, the deserted pieces of Zani's poster. Some had already been run over several times by cars. In time, they would just be part of the earth. They lay there silent, like the corpse of someone who had been alive a few minutes before. Over the silence hung a brooding sense of futility. The drama was over. It was over too quickly to have made any lasting impression on those who were part of it. The only lingering memory of it was a small group of schoolboys under the veranda of Twala's Butchery, who were loudly competing with each other in reliving their roles in the brief celebration of chanting and dancing.

I looked up the street. Zani and Ndabeni had long faded away. I wondered where they were. And only at that very moment did I realise that throughout the entire drama, not once had I felt the inclination to go and help him, nor had the thought ever occurred. And that made me feel desperately guilty. Although I carried a briefcase full of books, and more books under my armpit, I yielded to a vague command to go and look for them. I went up the street after them. When I reached Mbele's Store, at the corner of Letsapa and Bantu-Batho Streets, I searched for them with my eyes, but saw no trace of them. It had been foolish of me, of course, to have thought I would find them. But I continued to sweep my eyes in every direction, until a house in the open space behind Mbele's shop took my attention and held it. The house stood in the far distance close to the end of the open space. There was a cluster of small rocks that jutted out of the ground just in front of the house. It was the Stone-yard shebeen, one of the popular drinking houses in the township. I went there, for I would surely find company there, and I would celebrate the end of the year.

Well into the night, about eleven o'clock perhaps, I

staggered out of the Stoneyard. I had drunk until I felt
that one more gulp of beer would make me vomit. I
had drunk enough. So out I went, carrying books in
my briefcase, and books under my left armpit. Careful
now, I told myself as I stepped out of the gate, there
are rocks jutting out of the earth just outside here.
Tread softly, I told myself, for any unevenness in the
ground would be like stepping into a hole, and you
might dislocate your knees, because they will bend as
if to give in, only to straighten once more with a
painful jerk. And although you will not have fallen,
you will have hurt your knees. Tread softly. But what
would it matter? I'm drunk, am I not? And I'm alone
in the dark. So couldn't I do whatever I liked? Hurt
myself? No, there's something better. I could put
down my books flat on the street, unbutton my
fly, take out my penis, stand arms akimbo, and
urinate in full view of the night. I could move my
pelvis in circles, and draw unseen patterns on the
ground. Oh, the devil! Will I urinate on my books? If
I urinate on them, on the books, what will happen to
the knowledge in them? Baptism? Or corrosion by
acid? Urinochloric acid. What? Hho-o-o! Pull the reins
now. Walk slowly like a king. So peaceful in the dark.
So much freedom. The time of visions. The teacher
king is walking through the streets and no one to say
he is naked. Wake up, wake up all you citizens of the
township! Why did you sleep so early? Tomorrow is
Saturday. Wake up! See your teacher walking home
through your dark silent streets. And not even one
car to rape the darkness with its headlamps. Wake up!
Let's see, who have I not taught here? Tell me. They
are countable. Capable of being counted. 'As many as
your fingers?' Add my toes. 'Is that all? What more?'
Add my eyes. Add my nose. Add my nipples. Add

my navel. Add all the bones in my body. Have you
added everything? You see, it's finite. They are
countable. The rest have gone through the rigours of
my mind, and through the punishment of my hand. I
have always asked questions in class hoping the girls
would raise their hands, so that I could admire the
brown softness of their hands, and utter a prayer for
compassion from whoever read the wrong in my
eyes. Now, there is the Dutch Reformed Church
looming before me. Am I safe from the spirit of Piet
Retief? And I become conscious of walking along the
fringes of the township, for that was where the Church
of Dutch was built, so as not to be part of the con-
tamination of its creation, and the pain it sought to
propagate. Here is the Gospel according to Christian
Predation. And the Word of God, coming from the
sky said to them: 'Go unto the world and spread My
Truth. Tell them of the one true God. And bring
light to those in the dark.' See now, the missionary
maggots! For the land is infested with the glory of
their righteousness. Lift up! Lift up your hearts ye
backward ones, and come out of the long night of
darkness! See the light, and toil in chains for your
redemption. It is the will of God. Embezzlement!
How silly! The foolishness of young years. And now
Charterston creche! Why was it placed next to the
Church of Dutch? Was it to overwhelm our children
early with the message of its ominous history? I
belched. I had been belching so many times since I
left the Stoneyard. Now home is right there round
the corner. Tread softly. Nosipho, where are you?
Are you waiting for me? Here comes your husband.
I'm full of celebration. I can feel the books under my
left armpit changing into your soft right hand. And
we are marching in the street. Mendelssohn. What a

long, endless procession behind us! Finally, our true marriage! And there, at the gate to our house, stands Hlophe, tall, strong, and fearsome in his tan uniform, shining boots, and awesome helmet. Are we the animals on his safari? But your father is standing just next to him, my love. And what spiritual glee is on his face! Tee hee!

Knock! Knock! Knock! Knock! Knock!

Nosipho did not hear my knock. I knocked just as she broke into a long laugh. And then I heard a man laughing too, his male voice sending a tremor through my body and making me feel cold. Who was he? And as I asked myself the question, the cold sensation gave way to an intense heat as rage and jealousy tore through my body. But a hiccup brought me under control. I left the door, and tiptoed towards the open window of the living room. Nosipho and the man laughed again, and I let the books under my armpit fall to the lawn. They fell one after another with dull heavy thuds on the lawn like the wings of a big, heavy bird taking off.

'You make it sound too light,' said Nosipho, ending her laugh.

'But seriously,' said the man, 'sometimes I wish I was God in person. Be everything. Everything. So that with just a single act of mind and body, just one flash of lightning, I could remake our lives entirely. Just start afresh. A new world. I could even take a much shorter time than the making of the world by Christians.'

I smiled with relief! And I felt so grateful for that hiccup. There was nothing to fear. Not only was the voice youthful; not only was the sentiment familiar; it was also very definitely Zani's voice. So I had finally caught up with him. I prepared to go back to the

door to knock again. But the voice of Nosipho prevented me. The immediacy of listening to them
became more preferable to the delay of going in.

'Unfortunately,' said Nosipho, 'it's the old world
we have to deal with. All the same, I don't mean to
dampen your spirits, I understand you very well. I
too, wish you could go out there and remake the
world.'

'You really wish that?' asked Zani with some urgent
excitement.

'I'll tell you what,' said Nosipho. 'When an elderly
person like me listens to the dreams of such as you,
it's like . . . what? . . . how can I put it? . . . it's like,
perhaps, waiting for eggs to hatch, until you hear the
first cries of a chick. It's wonderful to have waited. I
suppose it's the most practical expression of faith.
Just as long as there is some sign of reassurance that
something important is being done.'

'You make it sound so wonderful,' said Zani.

'Young man,' said Nosipho with a chuckle, 'you
have echoed me so many times tonight.'

'Really?' exclaimed Zani. 'I've not been aware of
it. Forgive me.'

'Don't mind. It was just an idle remark,' said Nosipho.

There was some silence for a while. I wished I
could see what they were doing. I wondered what
time it was. I could not see my watch well in the
dark. The lamplight in the living room was not strong
enough to penetrate the curtains.

'You know what?' said Nosipho eventually. 'It
occurs to me just now that we have talked about so
many things already; but isn't it strange that you have
not told me anything about your school?'

Zani chuckled. It seemed a chuckle of shyness.

'How was Swaziland?' asked Nosipho.

'A very beautiful country, really. Flowing rivers, green mountains, miles and miles of pine forests; and what a heaven of fruit! All round our school grew wild guavas, mangoes and avocado trees. Plenty of pineapples and oranges. But beware of snakes! And don't you dare eat too many guavas!' said Zani laughing.

'And why?' asked Nosipho, sounding very interested.

'Well,' said Zani somewhat haltingly, 'they sort of . . . you know what I mean. They have a tendency, if I may say so, to block up the digestive system right at its end.'

They laughed.

'Oh, you do make me laugh, Zani,' said Nosipho. 'It's not what you've said, understand me. It's the way you've been speaking: so polite! But, tell me about the people there.'

'Oh, those?' responded Zani quickly. 'They would have been very friendly people if only they did not want to humiliate you first. They have to remind you at every turn, you know, that you're an oppressed foreigner, and therefore not the most deserving of people. You have to pay a high price for their friendship. Grovel before them and obliterate yourself, and only then are you welcome. But bear in mind, of course, that I'm talking about the educated, westernised lot that are being readied for power. The ordinary people are wonderful people.'

'How strange! But can you tell me why is that?'

'I'm not quite sure. There's probably some justification though. They may be hitting back.'

'Hitting back?'

'You should see our people walk through the streets of Manzini or Mbabane as if they owned the country, you know; as if they were some kind of missionaries bringing the light of South African civilisation to the Swazis. And then you ask yourself: how on earth can any intelligent person boast to someone else about the aridity of his land? It's probably a sign of our most debilitating, national, urban shallowness. You know: the Stetson up, Stetson down, Chev Impala outside if you please sir, kind of thing. Pathetic caricatures of Americans!'

'I hope this did not affect your school, though.'

'Probably not much. But then the Swazis in our school were too few for us to need to posture before them. We just overwhelmed them with our majority. But then, right there you have another problem. How could the Swazis ever be happy when most of their best schools were swarming with South Africans, and very few Swazis?

'So, as you can see, instead of showing off to Swazis, we had the usual foolish quarrels between the boys from Natal and those from the Transvaal. Utter foolishness if you ask me. I suppose that, out of temperament, I always sided with the Natal boys in spite of my own origins. You see, there is nothing so annoying as the clever emptiness of the Johannesburg types. I'm thinking of the whole paraphernalia of their stylish walk, street Afrikaans, jazz records under the armpit, Pringle cardigans, and Florsheim shoes. I always thought there wasn't much to them besides the illusion of their specialness.

'Anyway, I'm talking too much.'

'I'm listening. It's very interesting.'

'But it was the best school I could ever wish for,' said Zani, his voice suddenly settling into a pleasant tone of reminiscence. 'I will forever think of my two friends, Raymond and S'kwaya. S'kwaya is a Swazi. A wonderful chap. Two good friends of mine. We have been in the same class since Form One. And we have just written our matric exams. Somewhere along the way we developed a passion for science. We would hunt all over the school for textbooks on chemistry which had more experiments than our prescribed textbooks. And we would spend hours studying them. And we would steal into the school lab and conduct experiment after experiment. We particularly loved making gases. We were fascinated by our discovery that some army, I think it was the German army, used chlorine gas in the Second World War, I think it was. So we just made gas after gas. Our special achievements were methane, phosgene, and phosphine. Can you imagine? And with each gas we made, it was to us like the world had one big secret language and we were learning it more and more.

'The funny thing is everybody made fun of us. You know what we were called? They called us urine scientists.'

'What?' exclaimed Nosipho.

'That's right,' said Zani emphatically.

'I should have been there to twist their ears for them,' said Nosipho sympathetically. 'Have more of these.' There was some silence while Zani had more of whatever he was offered. Then I heard the sound of a plate being put back on the table.

'And the reason,' continued Zani, 'was that Raymond and S'kwaya worked at the school's rubbish dump. It was their duty to go and burn things and to clean up. And that's where we started our experiments. There were so many rotting things there. I suppose that was the source of our fascination with transformation. So we would be connecting rusted metal tubing, melting this and that, distilling bones and coal, and boiling hoofs and horns. So everybody said

we spent our time trying to find the chemical com-
position of our urine.'

Nosipho laughed. Zani took off time to laugh too.

'And S'kwaya,' said Zani laughing, 'used to say: "It
does not matter, even Noah was laughed at when he
built his ark." How funny it all sounds now. But our
esteem soon increased. When we were doing Form
Three we developed an interest in rockets and atomic
science. And we read everything available to us. It
was fascinating! We wanted to build a rocket.'

'You did?'

'Believe it or not, we wanted to.'

'And what happened?'

'There was, at that time, this group of big boys
who had formed a political party. They sent a delegation one day, inviting us to come to their meeting.
They met under the trees along the canal just below
the school. So we went there one night, feeling that
something very important was about to happen to us.
And when we got there, the gathering stood up. Yes,
they stood up for the urine scientists. So their leader,
a fellow called Styles, addressed the secret meeting
after everybody had sat down on the grass. He told us
that the revolution was around the corner. That there
was no doubt about that. And that their interest in
the revolution had made them very vigilant. And that
is how they had discovered that we were on to some
very important work. But the heaviest moment came
when he said: "Boys, the Central Committee has come
to the conclusion that the revolution needs you."
Something happened to me after that speech, which I
have not fully understood. I felt a great need to give
way to the release of laughter. Was it joy? I certainly
felt that; some kind of ultimate vindication. But then,
looking back, there certainly was some sort of humo-

rous strangeness about the whole thing, an amusing significance which lay, perhaps, in the imitation of adult ritual. Yet the serious impact of it was there. And so we became their scientists. The Party's scientists.

'But that was not all. Before we could be fully accepted, we had to "submit to Party discipline" by reading secret books which would make us committed scientists, so that we could appreciate even more who we were going to be working for. We started reading books about revolution. It was fascinating: Ghana, Russia, Cuba, China, Guinea, Algeria. And we ended up spending more and more time discussing politics and philosophy, and less and less science. I look back now and say what a pity. Deep down in me I still want to be a scientist.

'But I learnt one lesson out of all this. It is that we should have stuck to our science. You see, too much obsession with removing oppression in the political dimension, soon becomes in itself a form of oppression. Especially if everybody is expected to demonstrate his concern somehow. And then mostly all it calls for is that you thrust an angry fist into the air. Somewhere along the line, I feel, the varied richness of life is lost sight of and so is the fact that every aspect of life, if it can be creatively indulged in, is the weapon of life itself against the greatest tyranny.'

'Now I think I know why you want to be God,' said Nosipho.

'I wish I hadn't said that,' said Zani.

'Don't regret your words so early,' said Nosipho. 'You still have many years ahead of you to become anything you want to be.'

'You understand so much,' said Zani with some passion.

'It is my duty,' said Nosipho. Zani seemed to find some encouragement from this, for his next request came with the probing hesitance which had at last found an opening into something sacred.

'I wonder,' said Zani. 'Can I ask you something?'

'Ask me anything you like,' said Nosipho.

'I was just wondering what problems there were in your own profession,' said Zani.

'Forgive me,' said Nosipho after some silence, 'but now that you have asked, I find it so hard to talk about that. The thing is, it's not that I have not thought about my profession but that I have thought too much about it without articulating my thoughts. Mine is a very lonely life . . . .'

'That's what my sister Busi says,' said Zani interrupting.

'What does she say?' asked Nosipho.

'I'm sorry,' apologised Zani. 'I shouldn't have said that.'

'Didn't she also say I'm aloof?'

Zani did not say anything.

'They all say that,' said Nosipho. 'The whole township. But I'm not about to burden you with my problems, you're still too young for that. Besides, you're such a nice boy. Let me put it this way; every day I say to myself: just as your ears hear something new every day, your mind must know something new every day. So I do what is unusual for most women of the township: I read all the time. But there are the likes of your mother, whose books are people, and who have amassed a wealth of wisdom the proportions of which I can never even imagine. But you asked me a question, and I will answer you.

'You see, son, for a long time there were only two things an educated African girl could do. She could train to be a nurse, or train to be a teacher. So many girls go into these professions not because they are interested in them, but because it has become a terrible tradition. Very unfortunate, if you ask me. These two professions have become a railway line beyond which most women cannot think. In time, women become the railway line itself. Unfortunately, this fits in with the disposition of hospitals in this country.

'You see, I've always thought that white people run these hospitals as if it was in the military. Strict chain of command! Just like soldiers . . . .'

'But,' interrupted Zani, 'I would have thought that, just as long as patients get cured . . . .'

'No, child, it does not work that way. Perhaps, though. I still have to come across a study of that. But the thing is there are those of us who consider that healing people is not just a matter of X-rays, needles, and drips. No. It is also restoring that person to a complete human balance: to make him a father again, or a mother again, or an uncle again. To make a person continue to wonder about the world, and his place in it. Now, you see, the way healing takes place in hospitals, it's like marshalling an army against germs. The germs die, but so does part of the person.

'No, I think there has to be some kind of democracy in the hospital. And such a spirit will help to restore the natural democracy of the human body and the world around it. That's what I think.'

There followed a definitive silence.

'I have to go now,' said Zani tentatively.

'No, stay,' said Nosipho with a faint plea. 'You don't know how you have helped to fill for me the silence of many years of silent nights. I must thank you for that.'

I turned away. For some reason, whenever Nosipho

was about to speak, I had this fear that she might bring me in. Besides, I was really beginning to feel cold. And with increasing coldness I began to feel more and more sober. And the more I felt sober, the more I seemed to resent the peace that reigned in my house between my wife and a little boy. I was not part of it. And now I was losing my own inner warmth. For the first time that night, I heard a side of Nosipho I never knew existed. And it dawned on me that I did not know her. That all those years I thought I was hurting her and then repenting, she had fashioned a life of her own, that she had refused without any show of open defiance, to be thrown by me into some rubbish heap at some street corner. And as I began to feel a terrible loneliness, I could feel also, like an underlying melody, an indescribable anger rising in me. Rationally, it was directed at me, but a deep, irrational impulse to be unreasonable asserted itself, and I banged on the door. I had fleeting visions of the two inside my house, so happy, so peaceful, looking like vulnerable lovers, waiting to be preyed on by my evil. I wanted to see them run into each other's arms when I came in. And I would consume them with the terror of my wrath. What was a boy doing in my house with my wife past midnight?

'Open up! This very moment!' I shouted, banging on the door even harder, until I could feel the pain on the outer sides of my fists. The door opened.

Nosipho stood aside while holding the door, to let me go in. I kicked my briefcase aside and went in, smelling a fine perfume off Nosipho as I passed her. As I went further into the room, the perfume seemed to become more pervasive in that clean house that had maintained its freshness even past midnight. The perfume seemed to take over my mind as it lingered with a tingling sensation at the back of my neck. It was like walking through a grove of willows on a late evening in spring. The perfume threatened to shatter my anger, for it was not real anger; it was a desire to be angry, a need to be unreasonable, and each time I fought to be angry, I felt more and more debased. Nosipho closed the door behind me.

I stood with my back to the bookcase and watched Zani sitting with calm composure at one end of the sofa. He was chewing, and there was a half-eaten apple in his hand. I saw a dent on the other side of the sofa where Nosipho must have been sitting. And as she passed close by on her way back to her place, I resisted an impulse to slap her across the face with the back of my hand. The little table before them was laden with food: a grass-woven bowl full of fruit; newly made scones; peanuts; fresh tomatoes and lettuce, adorned with slices of boiled egg; and empty, used teacups. There had been much eating.

There was silence as they just sat there and looked at me with such peace in their faces, as if they were daring me to make a fool of myself. Nosipho! There was a freshness coming off her as if she had just bathed. She wore a light, blue, sleeveless cotton dress. And the brown sensuousness of her bare arms came off them like a perfume. The light glow of her eyes! The sternness of her beauty! If I could think of her this way, why couldn't I love her? All right, if they wanted me to make a fool of myself, I would, I told myself.

'So, you had to get a small boy!' I growled, showing the first flames of my unreasonableness through the smoke of my hostility. They looked at each other first. They were not appealing to each other, what went between them was an unspoken language of the profoundest understanding. When they looked at me again, almost simultaneously, I knew that I had to keep on my course, and punish myself further by seeming to punish them.

'Answer me! Or are you ashamed?' I shouted.

'Come,' said Nosipho standing up, 'let me help you to bed.'

'Just stay where you are and account for your sins,' I said, raising my hands in a gesture meant to stop her. She stopped but remained standing.

'So you had to get a small boy, I say!' I repeated.

'Duma,' she said quietly, 'how old was the girl you tore apart?'

'You are not good enough even to make any reference to her,' I said. And then added: 'Or are you jealous of the green fields in her?'

There was silence. She seemed suddenly drained of strength. When she sat down, so slowly, there was a vague look in her face.

'You're such an unhappy man,' said Zani. Our eyes met. 'Very unhappy,' he added. I looked away. I could not stand the peacefulness in his face. Nosipho stared vaguely at the floor.

'Do you see how much you have hurt her?' said Zani rising.

'No. He has not hurt me,' said Nosipho, looking up from the floor and turning her face to look at Zani. 'He is just lucky that you do not even hate him enough to want to look at him.' Then she looked towards me and said: 'Praise his graciousness.'

What had been the cause of all this? I asked myself. And because I could see no rational answer, I felt a deep surging of waves inside me, and I wanted to weep. But I did not. I had gone too far to retreat. But my next move contradicted my resolve. I began to walk towards Nosipho, my arms open, wanting to mend what could no longer be mended.

'Leave her alone, will you,' said Zani. 'Just don't touch her.'

I felt such a flood of gratitude to Zani. Suddenly, he had come out from nowhere to offer me the possibility of ending the whole sordid business without my seeming capitulation. I attacked him. I was so impatient to reach him, I had to go over the table. Perhaps, at the back of my mind, I had willed it: anyway, I missed the table and lost my balance. Then I fell over it. I heard the breaking of china and the smashing of glass. I heaved myself off the table and dropped to the floor, where I lay on my stomach; and then I knew that, finally, the end of my day had come. I would not get up. Not that I did not have enough strength to get up, or that I was too drunk to get up: no. It was just that I would stay there for as long as possible. It was most fitting that it be so. I belched, and then tried to vomit, at least to give them a reason for my not getting up. But nothing came out. So I just lay there on the floor, with the scattered food not far from my face. I heard Zani and Nosipho talking, but I did not understand anything they were saying. Then their legs came into view. They were walking towards the door. They went out together, and the door closed behind them.

This is it. It must be. One of the telegrams I have been waiting for for so long. I have always been one for terse messages. No letters. Just terse messages. Something to which no sentiment could be attached. Something to be read and then torn to pieces without regret, and then thrown away with the satisfaction that secrecy has been maintained. A small boy comes in with this telegram. The mail must have just been delivered. He says the principal said to bring it to me without delay. The boy walks out. His white shirt is so dirty; so are his black short trousers. Soiled by dust from too much playing in red sand. And he'll wear that uniform for the whole week. Probably his only uniform. And there are so many dirty ones in my class, too. And it's Tuesday, so early in the week. The week, before it ends, will be imprisoned in dirt.

They all look at me as I open the telegram. I feel like saying: take out your story-books and read, and mind your own business. But I don't. I open the telegram. I'm trying to control my excitement. Who is it from? Self-control is a wonderful thing. It offers one a calculated neutrality, such that one is ready to receive either good or bad news with apparent equanimity. But I'm dying from apprehensiveness. Finally, the telegram is open in my hands, and it says: ALL CLEAR. It is signed: YOU KNOW WHO. What joy! I will not be able to concentrate any more. I have been waiting for this telegram for the last three months. I look at the children in the class. They are so innocent. How long will it be before they master moral deception? I'm perfectly protected; I'm their teacher. They can expect nothing more from me than their socially determined belief in my exemplary truthfulness. But how could they ever know that there was no better feeling in the world than being accepted by a woman who was waiting for you? And once they got to know, would they forgive me? Whatever happens, there is no other way; I will go to her after school. But as I look at the children looking at me, I feel the excitement of my body transform

the alertness of my mind. And my mind seems to
become passion itself, as if the brain has been im-
mersed into a warm serum of sperm and sour milk. I
teach them. I teach them. And when the final bell
rings, I walk out as if I'm hypnotised. I walk straight
to the bus stop; and the bus, taking me to the station,
seems to be sailing through space in perfect motion. I
will get there. I will get there. I will get there. I'm on
my way to Payneville, Springs. I'm going to Candu.
ALL CLEAR.

Candu is a schoolmistress at a primary school in
Payneville. I met her last July at the school music
competitions in Wattville, Benoni. We just happened
to sit next to each other in the music hall. And as
choir after choir came on to the stage to sing, Candu
and I talked and listened, talked and listened; laughed
at the histrionics of some conductors; shared musical
opinions, and drew up a list of possible winners. And
she offered me tea from her flask, and sandwiches
too. I wanted to give her some of my sandwiches,
but after tasting hers, I was ashamed, because I had
bought mine from some roadside restaurant on the
way. How I wanted to hold her hand! But I would
have to wait. I told myself I would have to wait until
the winners of the competition were announced, and
then I would accidentally hold her hand during some
impulsive moment of applause. But when the time
came, I felt too conscious of having planned an
accident. Yet when I did come to hold her hand
at last, it happened naturally, when the competition was finally over late in the evening, and I held
Candu's hand to lead her out of the hall. The hand
was as soft as I had imagined. So moist. I led her
out of the hall and just kept on leading her until we
were far from the children, teachers and buses that

had brought them to the competitions from all over the Reef. And when we were far enough not to be seen, we gave way to what seemed to have been imprisoned in us the whole day. We kissed so wonderfully. And we stood there in the night, planning our next meeting; planning the telegram word for word, for there would be no letters; no messages.

Only when I finally arrive at Springs station, when the reality of seeing Candu again is closer than ever, do I begin to feel some kind of uneasiness. I begin to feel empty. Why did I come? I ask myself. Why such thoughtlessness? Why allow myself to be driven by impulses like a cock? But I have gone through this many times. The same feeling of debasement followed by rationalisation. I'll go. I'll continue. It's a duty. It's an agreement we had made, a pact. I must go. I must be true to my word. I must go.

She is waiting for me, for when I knock on the door of her small flat at Round 14, the door opens immediately. Had she been looking at me through the window? Here she is, just as she was; plump yet healthy; of medium height; light complexioned; large eyes. She is so young and beautiful. What could have attracted her to me? We hold hands; and that is all I want to do, for I have always remembered the softness and moistness of Candu's hands. We look into each other's eyes for a long time. What does she see in my eyes, for there is so much love in hers? We do not kiss, for I do not want to. I look away from her for a place to sit. There are no other chairs except the four around the table. And only then do I notice that the table has been well-laid. For two people, who are going to face each other when they eat. There is the smell of cooked food. And coming through the smell of food is the smell of moth balls. She lives in a small, one-roomed flat. Two-thirds into the room, a curtain runs across separating the kitchen and dining room from the resulting bedroom, which is made up only of the bed and a small wardrobe at the foot of the bed. I sit down.

'I have missed you so much,' says Candu.

'I have missed you too,' I say. 'Who is he?' I ask pointing at a picture of a man in military uniform.

'It's him,' says Candu.

I begin to feel anxious and deeply unwanted. She must love him so much not to say it's her husband. I curse myself, for I did not want any reference made to him. And yet I did, if only to prove to what extent I had succeeded in obliterating him. But I have to stay calm and seem casual.

'When was the picture taken?' I ask.

'He says it was in 1942, somewhere in North Africa, where a most important battle had taken place,' says Candu.

So she remembers all the details! No, I cannot obliterate him. Who can ever be more important than a soldier? Not even a teacher. I'm really nothing. Candu! I should have loved her enough not to have come here.

'Where is he now?' I ask.

'I told you it was all clear,' said Candu with a half-pleading, half-chiding voice with which she seemed to offer herself as the ultimate certainty.

'It's still good ▒▒▒▒▒▒▒▒▒▒▒▒▒▒▒▒ I insisted.

'Okay, then,' says Candu. He had to leave for Port

Elizabeth. A robber he is tracking down was reported seen there.'

A lucky man, I'm thinking. Was he a spy during the war to be rewarded with this kind of job? Others were simply given bicycles and then consigned to ignominious anonymity. Or was there any dignity in moving from the heroism of war, as a spy, to the undignified, nocturnal shadiness of being a detective? How well did he do his job? Was it routine to torture criminals? Or was he also sent after political offenders? But the more I'm conjuring the man's wickedness, the more I start to reflect on my own failures. Indeed, what honour was there in fighting my wars with undignified means? With ill-considered means? Yes, I was right to be trapped, and then be doomed to try and break out by dragging as many as I could into my own mire.

Candu puts a quart of Old Dutch beer before me. Why didn't I bring her something? Some gift? Wine? I feel like a parasite. I stand up, draw her towards me, and kiss her. I feel so much gratitude. It is not long before we are laughing and eating and drinking. She is such joy. Candu is such joy. And all the while I'm holding her hands over the table. We talk and drink and laugh well into the night, until the moistness and softness of her hands become so overpowering that I want to feel her whole body. And very soon I do. Her softness goes beyond her hands. It is her whole self. And I am conscious of nothing else but cheeks and breasts and thighs. I am here; oh, I am here.

But nothing happens. Try as I may, nothing happens. I'm trying. I'm trying. I'm concentrating; but my concentration yields only an awareness of tortured consciousness: strength without power; desire without fulfilment. So much corn to eat! So much harvest, and the fire of hunger in the stomach, and the hand lifting the produce to my mouth, but the mouth is sealed. Everything is ready but for the indifferent limpness of the penis, so much without sensation that it seems not there any more. Is this the thirst without end? Is this the thirst without end in a dry fire that burns without scorching? And the darkness is filled with the cries of a woman waiting; but there is to be no release. And if the soil is waiting, and the soil has been prepared, and is waiting: is there a killing pain at the centre of the earth, for the trees and plants, laden with seed, will not yield it to the earth no matter how strongly the wind blows? And will there be no more liberty for things to grow? There is no response to the wailing earth but the sense of annihilation.

I don't know whether I'm dreaming or not. But I can feel only the pure sensation of heat: the kind of heat that seems to be made of the darkness around, and seems to cling to the body like steam, destroying all sense of reality. It's as if I'm sleeping as well as waking at the same time. There is a rumble in my stomach. As the rumble grows, I can feel the sensation of my stomach filling up like a balloon filled with water to bursting point. I must rise and go to the communal toilet outside. I carry the warmth of the darkness with me. I am warm and moist. I squat and feel a great flow of relief pouring out of me. And then I'm trying to sleep again. But there will be no sleep, for I can register, gradually, a terrible, overpowering smell of something that seems to mingle with the darkness until they seem to have fused into becoming the very being of repulsiveness. I jump up because of increasing suffocation; and there, on a saucer on the table, and glowing incandescently in the dark, is a mound of faeces. Mine? I jump out of the bed with anger and hurl them outside through the window.

'Don't come back!' I shout. I close the window and jump back into bed. But the smell comes back, for what has brought it back has squelched back under the door, and is sitting on another saucer on the table.

'Didn't I tell you not to come back!' I yell.

They laugh.

'Get out, this very minute!'

They laugh. And the more they laugh the more incandescent they become.

'Silly fools!'

And they laugh, glowing more incandescently. And they laugh and laugh and laugh, until they laugh a song of laughter.

I have to go before Candu wakes. I don't know how long she cried before she finally slept. But I must go. I don't want her to see me. Not ever.

As I open the door, the cold early morning air hits me. I close the door quickly behind me. How can I face anybody now? But I'm glad it's still dark, for I yearn for perpetual darkness . . . .

I woke up where I had fallen. Dull light was filtering through the curtains, and there was a slight breeze blowing the curtains through the open window. The cool air seemed to refresh me. It must have been about five-thirty or so, for the light of the sun was there, but the sun itself had not yet come out. There was much singing of birds outside. And I remembered

that it was the first Saturday after the end of the
school year. I stirred, trying to get up, and only then
did I begin to wonder what had happened to me. I
remembered. Yet what had happened seemed so
distant, as if it took place some months ago. I looked
at the door. It was locked from the inside. So Nosipho was home. I concluded that since she was not up
yet, she probably was not going to work. I recalled
that my books were still outside and probably wet
with dew. What had I done? As I raised myself, trying
to get up, I noticed that under the table there was a
small wad of paper that had been folded in the manner
of a letter. I reached for it mechanically, slumped
back on my stomach, unfolded the papers. It was a
letter. I started reading;

> 161238 Emdeni South,
> P.O. Moroka,
> Soweto. Johannesburg.
> 6th December, 1966.

Darlingmine,

Just as you wrote to me not long after you got home,
I'm writing to you not long after I got your letter. I received it this morning. Now, tell me, why did you have
to kill yourself like that last Friday? Fancy, staying up
the whole night, writing me a letter! Well, I'm going to
do just that too, tonight. As I write, it is night, and I'm
lying on my stomach on top of the blankets, on my bed.
It's such an uncomfortable position; now I'm balancing
on the arm that's writing the letter, now I'm balancing
on the other elbow. There is a candle on my pillow. And
if the candle should accidentally topple over and ignite
everything, I will make no attempt, for a little while, to

call for help. I will want to be scorched a little, just as you were stabbed a little. (Joke).

My sister, on the other bed, has just ordered me to blow out my candle, for she will have no lover keeping her awake. She is a worker, and is tired, she said. She said you are not going to die, so I should write to you tomorrow. I told her to try and stop me. And mother shouted from her bedroom saying if we did not stop talking about love and death, and try and get some sleep, she will marry us off tomorrow. We laughed at her and said: "Get away! You're going to be crying here the day we leave this house." She said God help her, for it's our eyes that will be so full of tears that we won't see hers.

But you should see the one who said I should blow my candle out. She has her own candle! And she's lying on her back on top of her blankets, her knees raised so that her nightie has fallen into a heap on her stomach. She's so carefree. But I won't tell you more; you're not a woman. What I can tell you is that she is reading one of those love story picture books. I think she's jealous because with me it's the real thing, whereas with her, it's just a story she wishes would come true. I've just told her that, and she made faces at me. She keeps interrupting me so many times. I'll not tell you the things she says about you, although I threatened to, and she made a show of fear. I think deep down she'd like me to. I don't know why sisters are so crazy about their sisters' lovers. Mine is dying to see you, but I'm keeping a cloud of mystery over you.

Last Saturday afternoon I went to see your uncle, as you had asked me, and gave him your letter. He's such a wonderful man. Has a beautiful house too. He is so proud of his garden. Grows so many things there. Even watermelon. Can you believe it? Living in the townships, I tend to regard so many things as being impossibly out of reach, and then I realise that they can be done because someone else has done them and I'm so happy. I suppose because we do not have our lives in our hands, and endless prohibitions make the world so impenetrable, the achievements of others seem to lie beyond our understanding. And I am led to think that perhaps our ultimate liberty has much to do with our bringing as much of the world as possible into our active conscious-ness. Can you beat me for wisdom?

I'm sorry that I've not read a single book since I got home, as you had ordered me to. I live so much under your shadow. Sometimes I wonder whether I'll ever measure up to your exacting standards. But then, should I? The truth of the matter is that I've the worst time trying to understand you. Sometimes I think you don't understand yourself. Nor do you understand those you are seeking to change. I'm sorry to have to write to you this way. But how can I forget that after a most wonder-ful time with you in the train, you turned round to curse and insult me. I did not answer you then, for I was not riddled with your guilts; nor were great ideas swimming in my mind. I just wanted to continue the well-being of the moment. When I saw you pacing up and down that waiting room like a caged lion, I really wondered about you. Much more than I ever did before. I told myself that I would not have to love you at all costs, but that I would try, all the same, while the joy of having been with you still lasted.

You say you were stabbed as punishment for your cruelty toward me when you did not wave goodbye to me. Now that is foolishness. A far cry from the rationality you claim for yourself. The man stabbed you because you behaved foolishly towards him. You cannot convince people of your truth by telling them of their foolishness. Just like the Christian missionaries! They are so convinced of their truth that they have become foolish. So the man tempted you to drink, and I tempted you like Adam: where is your own responsibility?

Your teacher friend is really something. You seem much obsessed with him, though. Still, I can't imagine how the fellow could have been so brave as to walk into your home after what he did to Mimi. He reminds me of the man who lives alone about five houses away from us. The evil, whatever it was, that this man did in the past, has become legend. Some say he killed his mother, others say it was his wife he killed; some vow he raped his niece (Imagine! an uncle raping his niece!), but others say it was not his niece but his daughter. Whatever he did, it was real evil. But for as long as I can remember, he has been getting up very early in the morning, and going up and down our street three times, all the while shouting: "Forgive me! Forgive me! Forgive me! . . ." And he will be carrying a sharpened piece of wire, clearing our street of paper, which he stuffs into his pockets. And this walk for forgiveness is followed by a bonfire at the front of his yard. And he will keep lifting his arms over the flames as if burning his sins away. Nobody knows his real name; but we all call him, "Forgive me".

Now isn't that an example of someone for whom atonement has become the very condition of life? In fact, he no longer has any personality; for he has become atonement itself. The whole street has become so protective

of him. He's become our property. I remember when he
was ill a long time ago, my mother and other mothers in
the street took turns bringing him food.

Anyway, your teacher friend may not be like this. But
the way you described him: the drool in the waiting
room; his red, blinking eyes; his puffy cheeks, and rough
skin from careless shaving; faded clothes; and that sagging tummy you took so long to describe. The very picture
of decrepitude and lost glory. But, forgive me, the more
terrible things you say about him the more you seem
obsessed with him. Perhaps I'm wrong. Is he some kind
of lovable evil?

I don't know whether this has been a love letter or not.
But you asked me not to write you love letters. I don't
know what a love letter is, but to me, every letter I write
to you is a love letter, for whatever I say to you is said
with love. When I love you, I love everything. But I'm
boring you. Whatever you say, though, I love you. And I
want to hold those big ears in my hands, and aim lips at
your lips, and smack! Are you embarrassed?

> Ever and ever,
> Ntozakhe.

P.S. I've got a surprise for you on New Year's Day. Don't
go anywhere. Keep away from the teacher's wife. The
way you write about her! I can smell something. (Joke).

When I finished reading the letter, I rolled over and
lay on my back. I still clutched the letter in one of
my hands. I felt vacant; but not entirely so, for I felt
needled by something I could not fully understand. It
was something like when you know you are thinking,
but you do not know what you are thinking about.

But gradually, I began to focus on some aspects of the letter. I felt I had in my hand a letter from someone who had an uncanny understanding of me. I knew her well too, for I had seen all her quintessence during that brief moment when she was waving at Zani as her train was taking her away. She seemed to move with such ease between being lover and mother. It was this elusiveness about her that would keep Zani forever wavering between confidence and doubt in his relationship with her. The elusiveness must excite in him an inner ambiguity that was so obvious from his outer behaviour. She seemed so superior to him.

My mind went vacant again, and I closed my eyes for what seemed a long time. And when consciousness filtered back, the first thing I became conscious of was the letter in my hand. I felt it so deeply, as if its very texture had fused with my hand. I felt some kind of liberating oneness with the letter. But that feeling was not to last. It was replaced by guilt and a deep feeling of self-contempt. I had so irresponsibly, without even thinking about it, walked into an intimacy I had not been permitted to witness. But I had a strong urge to read the letter again so as to be let in, even if I was being resisted. I had a strong urge to read and to feel more fully condemned. And the events of last night and of the last few days crowded into my mind. Was my life a long night of atonement? I trembled. But it was a tremor that lasted only a few seconds. What gave her such an insight? Was it the vivid drawing of Zani's words, or Ntozakhe's own intuitive intelligence? Was that how I seemed to people? Of course, what I felt I was, must be what I appeared to be.

And then I thought about what should have occurred to me earlier: what was that letter doing there?

But I did not have time to pursue that question for at that moment I felt the presence of someone in the room. It was Nosipho. She leaned against the frame of the bedroom door, and looked at me. Instinctively, without really being conscious of my embarrassment, I calmly folded the letter. But, instead of putting it on the shattered table, I slipped it into the back pocket of my trousers.

'That,' said Nosipho, 'is not yours.'

'I know,' I said.

'Well?' she said.

I didn't say anything. I just shrugged my shoulders and looked up at the ceiling.

'It was not meant for you,' said Nosipho.

'I know,' I repeated.

She continued to look down at me; but I maintained my silence. It seemed best to do that. Then she leaned back into the bedroom, pulled out the chair we put our clothes on at night, and sat on it. She sat forward in such a way that her legs were spread somewhat sideways before her, and she rested her clasped hands on the sagging bridge her night-dress formed between her thighs. The bridge sagged a little under the pressure of her hands. I could not bear her eyes looking down at me on the floor, so I rose from the floor feeling very self-conscious, and dropped myself heavily on the sofa. We sat directly opposite each other. Only then did I feel the pain of a stiff neck. But I was glad of that, because it gave me something to do. I massaged it, and tried to avoid Nosipho's eyes. I was expecting her to start bringing up the events of last night. But she did not. I suppose it had become her habit to ignore my worst aberrations. A perfectly understandable thing. Eventually our eyes met, and the act of massaging my neck gave me the strength to face her eyes. Then she looked away and sighed.

'He told me,' she said steadily, looking at me again.

'Told you?' I asked, trying to avoid whatever was coming. 'Who told you what?'

'About his sister's letter to him,' she said.

I became aware of the lingering smell of Nosipho's perfume, and the events of the previous night came to me with more vividness than before. Everything seemed to come alive in my mind. I felt helpless before whatever Zani was doing to my life, and because I felt helpless, I could only respond with anger.

'So is that what he was here about? To betray me?' I shouted.

'Betrayal!' said Nosipho with a slight sneer. 'Can you of all people talk about betrayal? I don't think there is much in the actions of others that you can rightly condemn. You have left yourself so little room. But then, I wasn't looking for a confrontation. I'm tired of that. It is food that I have had too much of over the years. And then a chance suddenly came last night for us to try a new diet. I was not accusing you of something that exists only in the past in your mind. I only wanted to let you know that I know.'

'But that boy had no right to ... to ....' I really had nothing to accuse him of, so I just gave up and looked away.

'Why didn't you tell me?' she asked. 'All those years! I could have left.'

I have never been able to face crucial moments. I just kept quiet.

'I could have left,' said Nosipho again.

We were quiet for some time. Then Nosipho rose and went into the kitchen. She came back after a short while with two glasses of water. She gave me

one and went back to her chair where she sat down in
the same way as before. We sipped from our glasses
without saying anything, and I felt the coldness of
the water moving down inside my chest. It occurred
to me that this was the first act of kindness in years
that Nosipho had shown towards me which was not
done out of a sense of duty. It had been an effortless
act of considerateness. I did not even thank her for
it, because somehow the articulation of gratitude
would have diminished the serene genuineness of the
moment.

We continued to be quiet. I suppose there was too
much to be said. Then Nosipho spoke.

'But I will not leave now,' she said. 'I have invested
too many years of my life in what has all along been
the inexplicable discomfort of living with you. No,
I will not leave now.' She drank again from her glass.

Yes, I have never been able to face crucial moments.
Instead, I suddenly felt like laughing. I wanted to
laugh very deeply. Not because there was something
funny, but because laughter would express total
understanding. Crucial moments have always deprived
me of words, and I've always resorted to visions. At
that moment, as I looked at Nosipho, I felt as if I had
been swimming for a long time underwater. Each
time I tried to surface for air, I was pushed underwater again, until I found release, not in surfacing,
but in some huge underwater bubble. It had material-
ised from nowhere to lock itself on to my nose. And I
breathed with such ecstacy, while all the while knowing I still had to surface sooner or later.

And I laughed. I went into a great fit of laughter.
And tears started flowing from my eyes. And once,
when I wiped them off, I saw a smile on Nosipho's
face, and she was shaking her head. After a while I

heard her laugh too, but the quality of her laughter was not the same as mine. I think she was laughing rather at the way I was laughing, for there was a certain kind of loving condescension in the way she laughed and shook her head at the same time. But she did not laugh long, though there remained on her face a distant, yet warm, intimate look. I eventually stopped laughing and there was a long silence. Then Nosipho spoke again.

'He came here yesterday evening, about seven, looking for you. I had just finished washing myself. He just stayed on even after I told him you were not here. Eventually, I realised that he was very unhappy. Very sad. And I knew that he had something weighing down on him that he wanted to talk about. Apparently, something happened yesterday afternoon that depressed him a lot, something involving him and the police. He did not want to tell me what happened; but he just kept on blaming people who were too numb emotionally to react to anything meant to change their lives. And then he produced that letter, and seemed to light up with joy. He read it to me. I'm not quite sure what he wanted, but he wouldn't go.'

'He wanted you,' I said, smiling.

'Don't be ridiculous,' said Nosipho, trying to deny what her eyes affirmed. 'I think he wanted some kind of reassurance. And what a night of honesty it became. Until you came. But then, in a sense, you displayed some form of honesty too. There is something in you that he admires and pities all at once.'

'Like what?' I asked.

'You'd have to ask him,' said Nosipho.

'And you baked cakes, laid the table with fruit and . . . .'

'Yes, and everything I would have done for my

husband.'

I looked at her in silence for a while. But I turned away from her unblinking eyes and looked at the table and its shattered glass top. I leaned over and tried to pick up some fallen food from the floor. In a moment, Nosipho knelt on the floor and was picking up food and putting it into her empty glass. Soon we were busy clearing up my mess of yesterday.

I did not see Zani until 16 December. Not that I did not try to see him before then. It was just that every plan I devised seemed stupid at the point of execution. Nor did Zani ever come to see us. I began to wonder if his 'disappearance' did not have something to do with his letter. He must have known that he had forgotten to take it with him on the night of my 'scene.' In which case, his embarrassment was perfectly understandable. That is why every plan I made to see him revolved around returning the letter. That letter even seemed to have become some sort of obsession with me. I carried it all the time, and on many occasions when I was walking, it would suddenly filter into my consciousness. And I would feel it against my buttock when I walked. It seemed to become heavier and heavier each day. But I never had the inclination to read it again.

I woke up early on Friday 16 December. It was the first time, in our twenty years or so of marriage, that I walked Nosipho to the bus stop on her way to work. But the bus did not come, as was always the case on holidays. Nosipho eventually took a taxi. As the taxi took her away, I stood alone at the bus stop, and looked after it until it disappeared. I had never felt so vulnerable before when Nosipho left me to go to work. And, as if I did not want to face the quietness of our house, I took a long walk around the township. It was such an exhilarating walk. There was something new about the houses, the streets, the shops, the churches, the community hall, and the schools; they seemed to breathe in the early morning air and the first rays of the sun. It was one of those rare days in one's life, when everything seems unaccountably beautiful.

At the end of Moshoeshoe Street was the Presbyterian church. Beyond, about two hundred yards away, were the Indian and Coloured sections of Charterston. In the distance, still rather hazy under a thin veil of mist, was one of the ancient landmarks of the township: two yew trees at the apex of a high hill. They were known as the 'eternal twins', and had been there for as long as anybody in township history could remember. I wanted to go out to them, but I felt unprepared. Taking on that distance needed the kind of resolve which, like going on a pilgrimage, has to be preceded by spiritual and mental preparation. So I was content to stop at the fence that went round Charterston, keeping the Indians and the Coloureds out, and to take a rest while I looked at the 'eternal twins', high on their hill.

The 'eternal twins' were the subject of countless sermons in the various churches of the location. They were a perpetual illustration of the necessity for human unity. They stood together in eternal companionship through days and nights and weeks and months and years. Like the Sphinx, they seemed to gaze continuously at the township with a strangely reassuring indifference. And the question was always asked: what did they see? And the answer was in-

variable: they saw division. They saw a township
dominated by two buildings: a community hall, and a
beer hall. The rest of the buildings, houses, were a flat
mass of sameness. And there was the drab Coloured
section just outside the township. There was no out-
standing building there, only a mass of wooden or
corrugated iron shacks. Here and there the brick
houses of teachers or businessmen. The whole depress-
ing sight accentuated the tragic illusion of people
conditioned to draw their greatest inspiration from
the little white blood in them. They lived in the
perpetual uncertainty of not knowing whether they
were loved or hated. The trees also saw the Indian
section: surely the most enviable in the area, with big
houses that were the fruits of commerce. It maintained
an aloofness that had less to do with achievement,
than with compliant indifference. That's what the
trees saw.

Yet how obvious the analysis ascribed to them.
Zani was right. The obviousness of analysis! A mind
given completely to a preoccupation with an unyield-
ingly powerful, unabating negation, is soon debased
by the repeated sameness of its findings. And in the
absence of any other engaging mental challenges, its
perceptions of viable alternatives become hopelessly
constricted. But the trees would remain there gazing,
until a new day gave them a new voice.

The sun was rising higher, and was becoming un-
bearably hot. I decided to walk towards home. People
were beginning to come out of their houses, and I had
the urge to run back home so that I could stay with
my thoughts unchallenged. Without willing it, I realised
that I would go home, stay there and think. That
made me feel a certain link with Zani which would
compensate for my not having seen him. By the time

I got home, I was sweating. I was not sure whether it was from the heat of the sun, or from the easy exertion of walking. I walked into the house, and leaving the door opened, slumped on to the sofa to rest, and perhaps to think.

I was awakened, late in the afternoon, by a light knock on the door. I slowly awoke from a long uncertainty about whether I had been awake or asleep. Since I had told myself it was the day for thinking, I had willed myself to think; but my mind had been unable to focus on any specific thing. I had willed without any direction. And I had become aware that I did not really know how to think; how to induce the mind to work; that it was really possible to be dedicated without any real aims to be conscious of; that it was possible to have smoke without fire, only if you think of smoke. That is the ultimate ignorance. Ignorance is not not knowing something, it is wanting to know something without knowing what to know. It finally breaks into revolution. It must . . . . Thinking about thinking, I *had* been thinking. I had smiled and then closed my eyes and tried to think about something concrete. Nothing came but colours: red, white, blue, green, and black flashing across the screen of my closed eyes. For such a long time. Was I thinking or not? Was I asleep or awake? It was the light knock on the door that brought me to full consciousness.

There was a little boy at the door. He must have been about seven years old, and wore only a short, dirty pair of black trousers. His black skin was all grey and dusty as if he had been swimming in a river, and had then come out and walked away without .

drying himself off, and had then walked into a reddish brown dust storm. There were many dry trails of water all over his body. His short uncombed hair was like soil that had just been turned. He kept on sniffing back mucus. As I looked at him, it struck me suddenly that he was the thing I should have been thinking of. As he stood at the door, he seemed such a large part of the world just behind him, for he was bigger than it, and had blotted out most of it with his body. His presence there seemed to be the beginning of questions. Even though he saw that I was looking at him, he knocked again.

'Come in, my child,' I said.

As he walked in rather timidly, I noticed that in one of his hands was a white envelope. He knelt on the floor a few feet from the door.

'What is your cry today, son?' I said.

'Some brother in the street said I should bring this letter to teacher Zamani,' he said.

'Who was that brother?'

'I don't know,' said the boy. 'He just found me playing in the street and sent me to give this letter to teacher Zamani.'

I looked at him, and thought of my son. But not for long.

'Bring me the letter then,' I said.

He stood up and came to me at the sofa, his arm outstretched towards me. I took the letter, and he walked back to where he had been kneeling, and knelt again, facing me. I looked at the envelope and found countless, brown, tiny fingerprints on it. They were so clear. I opened the envelope and took out the letter in it. It was a short note written on a page torn out of an exercise book.

'Teacher,' went the salutation. 'Just got word that

there is a picnic in the wood at Rand Nigel. Please come and help me; I'm going to break it up. You'll find me there. Yours for the future, Zani.'

I lay back on the sofa, looking up at the ceiling, while I absentmindedly folded the letter and put it back in the envelope. Once more, I felt something without being quite sure what it was that I was feeling.

'Shall I go now?' said the boy.

I looked at him, and our eyes met. He drew his mucus back three times. I heaved myself off the sofa, dipped into my pockets and fished out a handkerchief. I went to the boy and cupped the handkerchief over his nose. And he blew and blew and blew until there was nothing more. And when I removed the handkerchief, the boy's nose and the place just above the upper lip stood out strikingly in their cleanliness from the rest of the body. Such a healthy black shine!

'Who are your parents?' I asked.

'My grandmother,' he said.

'I mean your parents,' I pressed.

'Grandmother,' he said, sniffing again. But the nose was dry.

'Where's your mother?'

'Somewhere,' he said.

I stared down at him for a while and then left him and went to the kitchen, from which I returned with an orange.

'Here, take this,' I said. 'And thank you for bringing me the letter.'

The boy scuttled to his feet, cupped both hands, and curtsied when I placed the orange in his hands.

'Stay well,' he said as he walked out.

I followed him to the door and watched him walk out of the gate into the street, where he started running. I wondered why he had started running just as soon as he was out of the gate. Had he been afraid of me? Did he feel free out there? What was it like to bring up children? Was that the whole purpose of living; or was it breaking up picnics?

It was only at that moment that I realised my real attitude towards Zani's little call to action: it was irksome. I had a compelling desire to continue to lie on the sofa, hover somewhere between sleep and wakefulness, and be left alone. How little I had learnt about living all these years! What would I be taking to my grave? Simply the experience of being left alone to run all over but where I should have been running to: Nosipho? But even the freedom I had permitted myself to run unrestrained seemed to have resolved itself into the impotence of a fortnight ago. Had it taken me so long to come round to the truth of learning to do what I did not want to do? That was surely the utmost responsibility.

But I couldn't help also feeling that I was rationalising the feeling of being once more in Zani's clutches. Or was that another instance of what his lover called atonement? But what I felt pulling me towards him was not responsibility; rather I had a strange feeling that I was going to see something whose significance to my life I could not as yet fathom.

Since I had already followed Zani's little messenger to the door, I merely pulled the door behind me and walked away towards Rand Nigel.

It was about four-thirty when I finally arrived at the entrance to the picnic grounds. The gate was about fifty yards from the road. I was getting rather tired from having walked in the hot sun for almost two miles. As I approached, I noticed that there was a group of people at the gate, and there seemed to be some disagreement, for there was much shouting. People were still arriving, for behind me was a group of picnickers who carried picnic baskets, and who were playing music from a tape recorder as they walked along. Most were dressed in tight knee-length trousers and colourful floral shirts. They looked like the American tourists I've seen in films, visiting some small island in the Caribbean. They had stopped quite a few times along the way to dance to some particularly nice song.

As I got nearer the gate I could hear clearly what was being said.

'This is exploitation!' shouted one voice.

'Exploitation!' exclaimed another. 'Boy, do you know what you're saying?'

'Very much,' replied the other. 'My subject is exploitation. Why should people pay the full amount at this time of the day?'

I felt a chill run through my body, for I recognised both voices. What on earth was Principal Lehamo doing there, selling tickets to a picnic? I saw that next to him was Buti, Mr Charterston, who stood in the intimidating posture of a bouncer, and seemed ready to pounce on Zani whenever the principal gave word.

'Boy,' said the principal, 'do you know who you are talking to?'

'You know very well that I do,' said Zani. 'Didn't you chase me out of your school?'

Just then, two car loads of Boers screeched to a stop just opposite the gate fifty yards away. They seemed to be talking to the group that was behind me. We all looked towards the road in silence.

It was not long before shouting started between

the Boers and the township picnickers. The two
groups started waving fists at each other. And then
the Boers made as if to open the doors of their cars.
The picnickers scampered away towards the gate to
the picnic grounds whereupon the Boers banged the
car doors shut, and drove away laughing and waving
their fists in derision. They honked their car for
some hundred yards and disappeared. There was an
uneasy silence at the gate as we watched the newly
arriving picnickers coming towards us.

'Boers are crazy!' they kept shouting, more out of
embarrassment than real anger. Most people at the
gate agreed with them.

'But I told you!' shouted a woman to her husband.
'We should have stayed home. You know how Boers
are today.'

'Okay, sweetie-wife,' said the man. 'We are here
now, so we might just as well go in and enjoy ourselves.' There was some general laughter.

At that moment, the picnickers' disc jockey switch-
ed on his tape recorder, and soon the crowd at the
gate was dancing to some fast soul beat. Dust rose
into the air from stomping feet and from revellers
who, scooping soil with their hands as they did
monkey jive moves, knelt on the ground.

In the confusion I looked for Zani; our eyes found
each other accidentally. He seemed in despair. He
quickly looked away from me. I really did not know
what to do. Just then the principal saw me and his
face lit up. I smiled involuntarily. He raised both
hands into the air like someone who wanted to call a
meeting to order.

'Please! Please!' he shouted. 'Please, people of
Charterston. Let's control ourselves.' Buti left the
principal's side and wriggled his way through the

dancers towards the disc jockey. When he got to him, Buti shouted into the disc jockey's ear. The music stopped as abruptly as it had started. Buti walked back to his post.

'It is much, much better,' announced the principal, 'to enjoy ourselves inside instead of outside the picnic grounds. I'm sure you'll all agree with that.'

'Sure! Sure Tee!' went the general agreement.

'Then get your five rands ready,' said the principal. 'There is free booze and free music in there waiting for you.'

I was about to walk towards Zani when he started talking again, and I stopped where I was.

'Wait!' he shouted. 'Wait a minute. Before you take out your money, consider that we have some rights to fight for. Listen to me carefully. There are two rights to fight for. The first is the right to lead full lives. You all know what the meaning of this day is, and instead of coming here to dance away our lives, we should be at home trying to figure out how to win our rights back. You have just seen for yourselves a few minutes ago what kind of people the Boers are. Can you defeat them with picnics?'

'Now listen here, young man,' said the principal. But Zani ignored him. I began to wonder what my role really was.

'The second right,' continued Zani, 'may not be that important. But why should you pay the full five rands for an hour and a half before the picnic is due to end? Is that not exploitation? But there may be no need to assert your right not to be exploited if you appreciate the need for the first right, for you will just turn back and walk away, thus saving five rands to buy some milk and bread for your children, brothers and sisters.'

'*Meneer!*' called the principal to me. 'Please, talk to this boy. I do not want to injure him.'

Many picnickers turned to look at me. I shrugged my shoulders and involuntarily walked towards the principal.

'What's the problem?' I said when I got to him.

'You have just seen and heard for yourself,' he said. 'That boy has been a nuisance for the whole of this afternoon. And we are not going to tolerate him any more. Give him some good advice. We have spent much time and money promoting this picnic from house to house, and we have a dance band in there from Brakpan.'

And indeed, only then did I hear the strains of a foxtrot floating from the trees in the distance, towards us.

'So Pita's Band is really here?' exclaimed a picnicker.

'Of course,' said Buti, 'how can we deceive you?'

'Well then, don't waste our time, we want to go in there. That's what we have come for.' There was general agreement. But the principal seized his opportunity.

'Young man,' he said to Zani. 'What has education done to you?'

'What is the relevance of that question?' responded Zani.

'Do you want to answer an elder's question with a question?'

'A question is a question. An answer is an answer.'

'Do you see,' said the principal, desperately sweeping his hand towards the people. 'Ordinary people have no problems. They don't make a nuisance of themselves. They, these honest people, just want to pay and enjoy what they have paid for. But you, you have to display your education. In fact, I don't have to take this any more.'

'I told you,' said Buti, 'I could have dealt with him a long time ago.'

'*Meneer,*' said the principal, turning to me. 'I told you to advise this boy, but you have ignored me. I don't know what connection there is between you. Maybe you are conspirators. But I'm dealing with this boy now. Boy, who do you think you are?' I could see that the principal had made up his mind to deal personally with the problem before him. To give it to someone else might have undermined his own esteem.

'*Meneer,*' I appealed to the principal. 'I think this matter can be resolved with some understanding. You are a respected man, you know.'

'*Meneer,*' responded the principal, 'you had this boy in my class the other day inciting my students to subversion. He is continuing that here, and is threatening to destroy my picnic. There is nothing to understand.'

'Don't disgrace yourself,' I said. But he ignored me, and started advancing menacingly towards Zani. Buti followed him.

'Wait a minute,' I said desperately, trying to hold Buti's arm. But he pushed me away.

'That night,' said Buti, 'you saved this boy and took him home. There is no chance of that happening here.'

Zani backed away. This seemed to encourage the principal who now increased his pace. Zani also increased his backward pace. The principal broke into a run. Zani turned and fled. There was a roar of laughter. Zani ran towards the road with the two men in hot pursuit behind him. I could hear coins, possibly from the gate takings, ringing heavily in the principal's pockets. At that moment, quite a large number of the picnickers at the gate, realising that the gate was unguarded, poured into the picnic grounds and ran towards the trees from which I could hear a crash of cymbals. A few remained at the gate, I was not sure whether out of honesty or out of curiosity to see how this drama was going to end.

I looked at the three men running down towards the road and was just in time to see the principal pick up a stone and hurl it at Zani. It missed. They were close to the road now. The principal picked up another stone. This too missed, but found another moving, unintended target. It was an old, black, 1957 Ford driven by a white man. The stone hit its roof resoundingly.

Immediately, the principal clasped his hands at the back of his head like a woman mourning. Buti stopped in his tracks, and seemed undecided whether to remain where he was or to retreat. But the principal turned and walked back towards the gate, his face a mask of agony.

'Oh, my God, what have I done?' he cried. 'What have I done?'

The white man stopped his car some thirty yards away, and slowly reversed, carefully backing on to the side of the road, and stopping not far from Buti. He heaved himself out of his car, for he was huge, though he was short. There was grease all over his clothes and on his face, and so much hair on his exposed arms that he would have had to blow it away if he wanted to have a look at his wrist-watch. Calmly, he looked at all of us, and then walked towards the boot of his car and opened it. He took out a whip.

'Hey, you,' he called out to the principal, who was all the while asking what he had done. He stopped, lowered his hands and began to walk towards the Boer. We went nearer.

'I must apologise,' said the principal. 'I must.'

'Should I call the police?' said the Boer when the principal was close enough, 'or should I deal with you myself?'

'Please, my *baas*,' pleaded the principal, 'try to understand.' But the Boer ignored him.

'Either way,' said the Boer, 'you will get a thorough beating. But at least with me you'll get home to your wife sooner.'

He seemed so confident, so much like someone who wielded absolute power and did not even doubt that things would always remain so. The possibility of resistance to his power seemed as unthinkable to him as the revolt of chickens. At the moment I felt a loathing such as I had never felt for anyone before; the Boer seemed to have become the very essence of contemptuousness, by which he completely deprived us of any human quality. And indeed, the more the principal pleaded for forgiveness, the more he so piteously annihilated himself to become the ultimate justification for contempt.

'Please, my great king, please,' pleaded the principal, 'I was only trying to discipline that young man over there. It was all a mistake.'

Zani had stopped some twenty yards away to witness the sudden turn of events.

'A mistake!' growled the Boer. 'When has it been a mistake to discipline a young man? I would soon discipline you for thinking that a mistake. But listen here, I warn you, I have had that car for as long as I can remember; and people who go to the toilet should aim well. So never throw stones unless you can hit accurately.' Then he turned towards Zani.

'Hey, you black arse,' he yelled, 'come here!'

'*Voetsek!*' Zani yelled back with an insult. Some people laughed, but realising they shouldn't have, they turned and fled into the picnic grounds.

'Hey, you,' shouted the principal, 'you cannot go in there without paying.' But the picnickers ignored him and continued to run towards the trees from which the beat of a tango now came.

Just then, the Boer charged at Zani wielding the whip in the air. Zani turned and fled in the direction of the town, up the hill. The whip cracked, but missed.

'Come on,' said the principal to Buti, 'let's go and help catch that boy.' And he started running after the Boer. Buti seemed unenthusiastic, preferring to man his post at the gate.

In spite of his size, the Boer ran remarkably well. But Zani was much faster, and soon outran the Boer by a wide margin, despite his arm that was still in a sling. The Boer had cracked his whip so many times without success that his frustration was clear from the fury with which he ran, aimlessly lashing his whip at the elusive target. He eventually gave up and stopped. Then he looked back and saw the principal coming on behind him, and without warning, lashed his whip at the principal who doubled over with pain. A second blow landed on his back, and he jerked up and seemed to have the presence of mind not to wait for more. He turned back and fled with the Boer fast behind him. Everyone at the gate ran into the picnic grounds, followed by Buti and the principal. But the Boer stopped at the gate, and decided to return to his car.

And then he saw me, for I had not moved through all this. He was going to have to pass very close to me on his way back to his car.

'And you,' he sneered, 'why are you not running?'

I fixed my eyes on him, stared at him, challenging him to a contest of wills. He cracked his whip; I knew then that his whip was all there was to him. He had cracked it to help him look back at me. And then he appealed to his voice.

'Answer me, blinking eyes!' he shouted.

I merely stared back at him.

'What are you doing here? Why don't you run into those trees where you belong? Or are you deaf? Should I do you the favour of opening your ears for you?'

I continued to look at him, and came to the decision that if he lashed at me with his whip, I would have to fight back. But then he would be sure to beat me, for he was infinitely stronger than I. But he would have to beat me. It was not until he actually started lashing at me repeatedly, that I knew I would not give him the kind of victory he wanted. I felt sure that no amount of violence against me would give him any self-respect. He was of the same substance as his whip. I offered no resistance as he lashed at me. I just stared at him. I struggled hard to absorb the searing pain, trying to subject my body to the total control of my mind. I wanted to scream. It was as if my skin was peeling off and boiling water was being thrown over the exposed, lacerated inner flesh. But my silence was my salvation; the silence of years of trying to say something without much understanding; the silence of desperate action. This would be the first silence that would carry meaning.

The Boer came at me again and again, his face so red that it seemed to have become the very blood he wanted to draw out of me. He did not look at me any more; he knew where I was. He looked only at the ground, at his feet, beating down the grass around

him, to leave a small patch of clearing as a sign of the
futility of his battleground. He seemed to grow smaller
and smaller the more he came at me. Then I felt
totally numb. My mind had shut out all the pain.
And, for the third time in about two weeks, I felt in
the depths of me, the beginning of the kind of laughter
that seemed to explain everything. And when the
sound of laughter came out, it filled my ears, shutting
out the pain even further. It seemed to fill out the
sky like a pounding drum. And that is when the Boer
started weeping. And he seemed to weep louder, the
fainter the power of his lashing became.

The blows stopped; and I knew I had crushed him.
I had crushed him with the sheer force of my presence.
I was there, and would be there to the end of time: a
perpetual symbol of his failure to have a world without me. And he walked away to his car, a man without a shadow. The sun couldn't see him. And the
sound of his car when he drove away seemed so
irrelevant. There he went: a member of a people
whose sole gift to the world has been the perfection
of hate. And because there was nothing much more in
them, they will forever destroy, consuming us and
themselves in a great fire. But the people of the north
will come down and settle the land again, as they
have done for thousands of years.

Slowly, I walked up in the direction Zani had
taken, trying to find him. I looked up at the hill: he
was not there. I had to go up and find him. I lumbered
up the hill, and the last thing I heard from the picnic
grounds, as I reached the summit of the hill, was a
crash of cymbals signalling the end of a tune, and
the beginning of a waltz.

From the top of the hill I could see, there in the
distance about three miles away, the town where the

whites live. On the left of me was a huge field of corn that ran along the road to town. On the right was an empty space. I could not see Zani there, nor did I see him walking along the side of the road. I concluded he must have gone into the corn field. Indeed, I saw a spot where he had parted the corn stalks, leaving behind him a trail of slightly bent stalks.

I found Zani in a small clearing somewhere deep in the corn fields. He was sitting down, clutching his raised knees with his right hand, and resting his forehead on his knees. He looked up at me when I came, and then looked away. I had expected to see pain in his eyes, but I found instead, a pensive look. I did not sit down; I just stood silently next to him.

'So,' said Zani eventually in a voice with a faint suggestion of resignation, 'I suppose they are still dancing, drinking, singing, and fornicating in the trees.'

I shrugged my shoulders.

'And that's the point of it all,' he continued. 'We're just drifting. All without the liberating formality of ritual. Isn't that what we have lost: the dignified and demanding formality of civilisation?'

I shrugged again. He sounded so adult. Whenever he spoke that way, it seemed as if there was something, some disembodied essence, speaking through him. He was grasping out to be part of it, but his arms were not long enough. What did he really mean by what he had just said? I was not quite sure.

'I'm not sure what I have found. I'm not sure what I have found in you,' he said. 'When I first saw you at Springs Station that Wednesday morning, I knew you immediately. I hated you, as I had been hating you all these years, for the shattered dreams of my sister, and the shame you brought on us. But I struggled to contain my hate, for I had taught myself to give everyone a chance. I wanted to see if there was anything of value in you. But I'm not sure what I've found.

'What have I found anywhere? Everything seems so small. Am I that small too? Tell me. Have there been many years in which this smallness has turned into a tradition; many years of this crushing sleep of smallness? What is there to be done? It is so easy to make plans, and then everything comes crashing down because the proper act seems so rare. So many acts get done, and so few of them are proper. For example, you did not help me. Everybody. They preferred to sleep in their safety. But I ran too. And the wind that blew against my face as I ran sounded like the very sound of shame. The sound of victims laughing at victims. Feeding on their victimness, until it becomes an obscene virtue. Is there ever an excuse for ignorance? And when victims spit upon victims, should they not be called fools? Fools of darkness? Should they not be trampled upon?'

There were tears in his eyes. They dripped out of his eyes like the disjointedness of his thoughts, measuring the very essence of his age. Once more, I shrugged. He was his own meaning, and there was nothing to be said. I unbuttoned the back pocket of my trousers, and dropped his letter on the grass beside him.

'That is yours,' I said. He looked at the letter and then up at me. He picked it up and put it in his sling. Then he looked up at me again, and, as I looked down at him, I suddenly felt a great love for him. He seemed all I could have become if I were to start afresh.

'Listen,' I said, 'I have to leave you now and go home. I'm not sure why I really followed you here. But I know I had to. I have grown up to this point in

my life, and there is not a single piece of the world in
my hands. And you; you are too young to have it in
your hands no matter how much you can claim to
know it. That will come with time. You have your
whole life to learn from.' I turned away to go.

'Tee!' he called, to startle me once more. 'Your
wife . . . your wife . . . she's so wonderful . . . she is so
wonderful. I wish I could hold her hands forever.'

But my surprise did not last long. I looked at him
for a long time, and finally shrugged, smiling briefly
before I turned to go. He seemed suddenly so young;
too young even to be my son.

As I passed by the entrance to the picnic grounds on
my way home, I noticed that some revellers were on
their way home already. But I also noticed, coming
towards me, two young women, some sixty yards
away. They stopped briefly to talk to some of the
revellers, and then proceeded towards the picnic
grounds. And as we got closer to each other, I realised
with slight trepidation that I knew them. It was Mimi
with her sister-in-law, Ntozakhe. There she was,
Ntozakhe, beautiful, tall, and upright like the secretary
bird. I noticed her more because I still could not look
Mimi in the eyes. I knew, too, that as soon as Mimi
had recognised me, she quickly relayed some information about me.

'I know who you are looking for,' I said, taking the
initiative.

'Is it true what we have heard from those people?'
asked Mimi without observing any preliminary
formalities.

'Where is he?' asked Ntozakhe.

'He is up there somewhere, in the corn field,' I said, 'I can take you there.'

'No,' said Ntozakhe, 'we will find him.' There was a note of concerned determination in her voice, the quality of which I felt I had always known. I would not challenge it.

I stood aside, and they passed on without saying anything. I could feel that I was being dismissed; certainly a result of what they had been saying about me when they saw me. I watched them go to find their brother, lover, and son, in a corn field. Then I began to feel tired; very tired. And it was then that I began to feel the searing pain from the weals of the whip all over my body. It held me like pincers. For a moment I though I was going to collapse, but I tensed my body and tried to squeeze the pain out. I had to go home, but it was going to be a long, painful walk. Nosipho was surely back home from work. She was home. I had to get to her.

ANN ARBOR. MICH. PUBLIC LIBRARY